Love Is Dead(ly)

by Gene Kendall

Burning Chair Limited, Trading As Burning Chair Publishing
61 Bridge Street, Kington, HR5 3DJ

www.burningchairpublishing.com

By Gene Kendall
Edited by Simon Finnie and Peter Oxley
Cover by Burning Chair Publishing

First published by Burning Chair Publishing, 2020
Copyright © Gene Kendall, 2020
All rights reserved.

ISBN: 978-1-912946-10-5

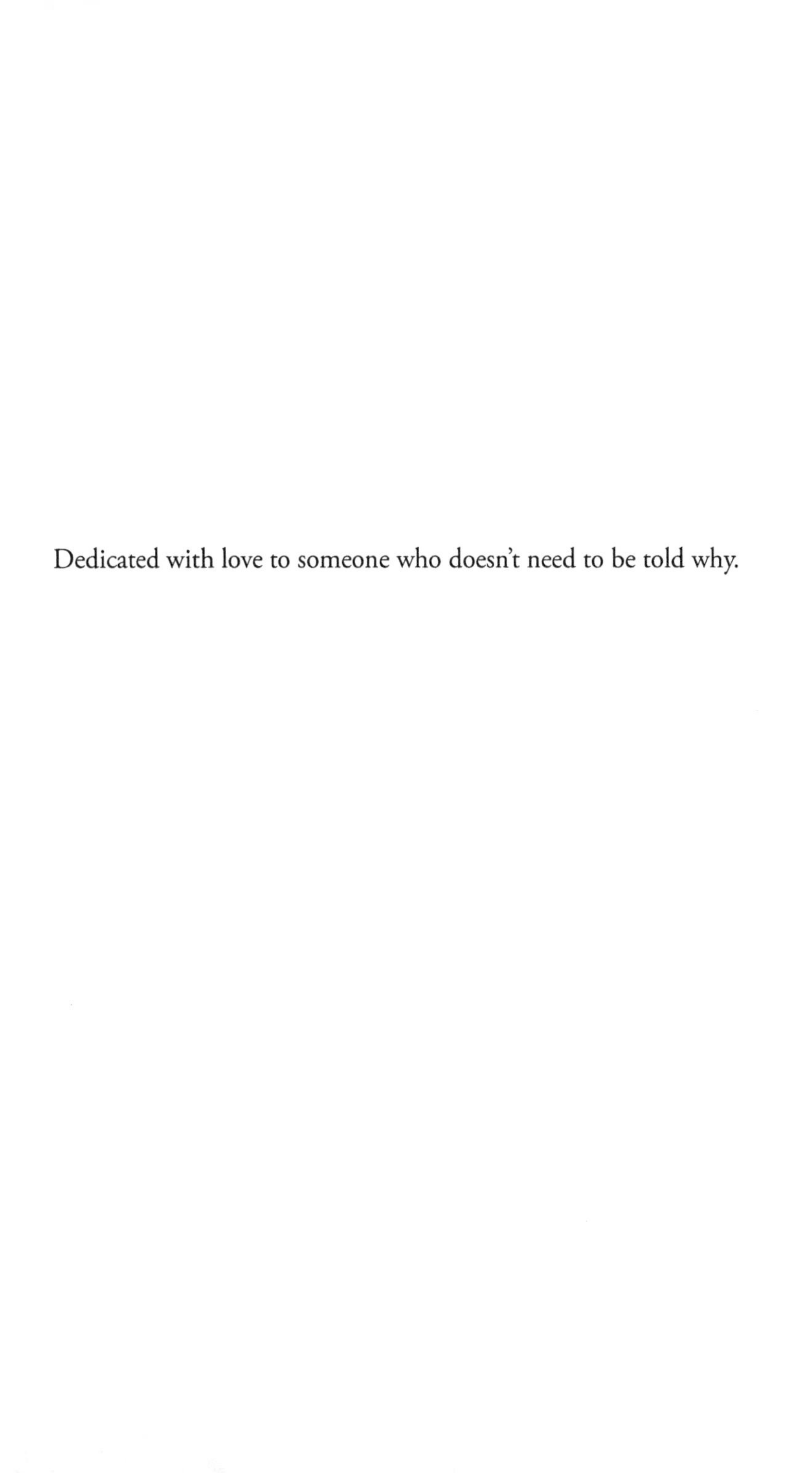

Dedicated with love to someone who doesn't need to be told why.

CHAPTER ONE

Bradley Burns

Ghosts are assholes.

I didn't come to this conclusion lightly. My initial encounter perhaps prejudiced me against our departed brethren, but the years of paranormal experiences that followed saw only more confirmation of this hypothesis.

They're pissant punks, the lot of them.

Imagine floating. Floating, with no direction, no purpose. No job to make it to by 9am. No Friday hangouts with the gang. No weekend barbeques or soccer games or drunken hookups to distract from your aimlessness.

They just *exist*. And that lack of purpose, that disconnect, makes them bitter. The nastiness, it's often expressed in rather antisocial ways. Poltergeists, phantasms, apparitions, what have you. They're pissed at the world, and they take it out on us.

My theory, at least.

Some of us lowly mortals have the pleasure of hearing their moans of discontent. I don't know why I was chosen to receive this talent, and I'll freely admit most in my profession are coldhearted scam artists, but here I am—seated at a kitchen table in some tits-cold farmhouse, chasing the supernatural breadcrumbs left by young Alexandria Abernathy.

Alex, as she was known to her friends, was the sweetest little girl in her graduating class of *New Beginnings Christian Academy*. I've been perusing her yearbook: cheerleading, volunteer nights at the homeless shelter, missionary trips to Venezuela. Sugar wouldn't melt in the kid's mouth, I'm sure.

A different white powder would later dominate Alex's life. Poor, dear thing moved out to my town and found herself living the kind of debauched lifestyle that awaits most arriving at the corner of 6th Street and La Brea.

I guess, to Alex's credit, she made it to twenty-five before the cocaine and bulimia took a toll on her precious heart. Most small-town free spirits loose in the big city never hit that quarter-century mark.

"I still don't understand. How do you know so much about our Alex?"

I resist the impulse to expose every trite detail surrounding their darling's loss of innocence… and life. "It's my gift, ma'am. Though, in all honesty, it is often more a curse. But I made a pledge—a sacred *vow*, ma'am—that I would use these abilities to help others. And that's why I came here today, Mrs. Abernathy. I know that I can help Alex find peace, but I can't do it without your help."

I call this my '*Man in Tights*' pitch. Usually, I don't have to lay it on so thick, but the father's been giving me nothing but hesitancy and nasty looks since I walked through the door.

"And by 'help', you mean our money."

Not that I blame the fellow. If I received a call from a total stranger, promising to reconnect me with the lost soul of my only daughter, I'd be more than a little skeptical.

And that's where I excel over my competition.

I'm not tossing out vague generalities, or cryptically hinting at personal details anyone could've gleaned from social media. I really *am* attuned with this ditz, so the accuracy of the reading I've provided her parents is not in doubt.

There's another nagging issue, though…

"Sir, I'm not going to lie. This is an expensive proposition. But it's not as if I'm living high on the hog here. I have expenses, and you must realize that what I do… It's a *calling*, sir. I have no other means of income. Some cases can drag on for months at a time. And, as nice as things are out here in Newnan, life in Los Angeles is, well, different. It's not cheap."

"Ten thousand dollars."

"Ten thousand dollars. To bring your daughter into the light. To finally grant this lost soul the peace she deserves."

"And you think, Mr. Burns… You truly believe Alex is in distress?" the mother asks, eyes moist.

"She's caught between two worlds, ma'am. All she wants is to be set free so that she can finally find eternal glory. I know that's what I would want for *my* daughter."

My phone buzzes, third time since I entered their home. There's enough of a lull in the conversation to justify checking the message, provided I give the nice folks an index-finger-in-the-air apology.

Ah. Donna. Well, patience, darling. Out of town. Lovely photos, though.

"Ten thousand dollars."

"Paul, stop," the missus scolds as I pocket the phone and wipe the grin off my face. "We're talking about our daughter here. And if he can bring her peace, if he could stop those dreams—"

Pops does *not* like this. "Darlene! We talked about this. He doesn't—"

"Oh, my word. Mrs. Abernathy. She isn't… Alex, she… You're not telling me she's communicating with you in your *dreams*, is she?"

The mother looks to her husband twice before finally saying anything. He gives up on the second look, throwing up his hand at her and turning away.

"Mr. Burns, we didn't want to tell you this—you have to understand how skeptical we were—but I think this is something you need to know. Yes, I see Alex in my dreams. Sometimes weeks will go by without a vision, other times she's there every night."

"And Mrs. Abernathy—I know this might make you uncomfortable, but I need to know this—does Alex seem desperate?

Like, perhaps, she's lost somewhere and can't find her way?"

"I… I think that's one way to describe it. She's there, I can feel my Alex, but it's as if she can't find the words. You're right… It's like she's lost, and maybe she's looking to me for help. Oh, Paul…"

"Dear, let's not get ahead of ourselves."

"Mr. Abernathy, you're skeptical, and I can respect that." He's smart enough to know he's outnumbered two-to-one on this, but that doesn't mean I can take his acquiescence for granted. "Isn't Minnesota the '*Show Me*' state? No? Well, regardless, I know how crazy all of this sounds. But dream visits… I didn't realize the situation was so dire."

"Dire?!"

Pause for dramatic effect… Okay, long enough… "Yes, and I don't use that term loosely. Your daughter needs help." I inhale, close my eyes. "She's crying out in pain and her scream is reverberating throughout the astral plane, invading your wife's dreams. Alex needs help, and she needs it now. For an additional three thousand dollars, I can make this a top priority case."

"*Three thousand dollars?!*"

"With the additional funds I'll be able to devote our resources solely to this case, make sure we don't lose her trail… I realize it's not small change; but with that money I think your daughter will find peace much faster. I feel confident, in fact."

"Paul, we can't let this go on. This is our *daughter*."

"Darlene, why don't you wait in the living room while we talk?" The missus exits the kitchen, all color drained from her cheeks. He waits until she's out the room then rounds on me. "Okay, son, let's get into this. I need to know, and don't hand me a line—are you running a con?"

"This is no scam, sir. Do you think some con artist would be able to know the things I know? Could some scumbag off the streets be able to deliver you messages from your lost daughter?"

He can't deny this. Truly, it was a damned fine reading. When I caught that memory of Daddy walking her door-to-door, Alex's first Halloween (in their matching Bert and Ernie costumes), even the old man began to well up. The father shifts in his chair, looks away.

"Yeah… And you're asking for *thirteen thousand dollars.*"

"I get your reluctance but, truthfully, would any amount be too much?"

"Oh, I think we reached the 'too much' figure a while back, Mr. Burns."

"Can you put a figure on your departed daughter's eternal peace? On the assurance that she's no longer left in this limbo, but is in fact finally reunited with her creator?" Am I going there? Yeah, I think I am. "Mr. Abernathy, sir… Can you put a dollar amount on a good night's sleep for your wife?"

He runs those calloused fingers through his hair and shakes his head. "I can't believe she told you about the dreams."

"I know how much she loved Alex. How much you loved her, too. The two of you had issues, but she was always Daddy's Little Girl, wasn't she?" He takes a breath, fights back what I know he wants to do. "Mr. Abernathy, you have to understand this isn't a sales pitch. She's lost, and I'm the only person who can guide the girl home. I'm asking for the last time—don't you want your poor daughter to find peace?"

As stated earlier, I'm no con man. I truly can deliver on what I'm selling. And I don't need any second sight to know these poor people are going through absolute hell right now. Experience tells me it's not going to get any better for these folks, either.

Shame, really. They seem like decent people. Did what they could to keep that girl's soul from going rotten. And maybe it's an irrational burst of nostalgia, but this place… I grew up in a home not so different from this one. Knew all kind of girls like this Alex, if I'm being honest, in those not-quite-halcyon days before I relocated to the big city.

I've seen what these hauntings can do. Have a subtle chill creeping up my spine at this moment, imagining what's ahead for this couple. Thinking of that girl in their photos, and what's likely got its hooks into her now. So, yes, I'll offer my aid. I'd be a monster not to help, wouldn't I?

And, nope, this help is not coming cheap. This astute mystic warrior possesses a unique set of skills, in addition to an obscene amount of credit card debt.

CHAPTER TWO

Sandra Jones

"He went to *thirteen*? How'd you manage that?"

There's that smirk. "Just used those superior salesman skills your old man taught me out on the lot."

I'm balancing the laptop against my knees while shuffling through the case files. A muted *Seinfeld* rerun plays in the background. Alexandria Abernathy… Wasn't expecting this case to become a priority so quickly. The venture capitalist who lost his fiancée during that sailing expedition was our hottest lead, up until thirty seconds before this teleconference.

"Yeah, right. Dad told me you couldn't sell rubbers outside a Thai whorehouse."

"Your daddy is in need of cultural sensitivity courses," Brad answers, still smirking. My less-than-couth father wasn't exaggerating by much; Brad might've been blessed with a paranormal ability to converse with the dead and provide them guidance into the hereafter, but he couldn't move a Lincoln Continental if his life depended on it.

"Uh-huh. I'm guessing this girl's father is suffering some nasty guilt over whatever happened between him and his darling angel," I say while minimizing the chat window, replacing Brad's cocoa-brown hair and amiable blue eyes with a list of my digital files. I pull up the social media page maintained by Ms. Abernathy during her final days on this earthly plane.

"I picked up a bit of that. But we can't forget the subject of our hunt; *she's* the one who sealed the deal."

"Really? What did this Alex do for us?" I'm browsing through her photos as I ask the question. Body shots, bong rips, little pills in magical colors, perfectly segregated lines of white powder… and these are the photos she chose to make 'public'. I'm not under the impression our party gal was much of an altruist.

"Princess Alex is a dream-walker; the heartless ghoul is actually haunting this poor old lady's thoughts at night. I swear, if my wallet didn't have a literal moth flying out of it, I would've taken this one *pro bono*, just to give that pitiable woman a good night's rest."

"Oh, right. That's not the most outrageous lie you've ever told me, no sir…"

"I mean it, Sandra. If I didn't have this nasty, money-obsessed business partner, always on my back about mileage records and expense reports, I'd be free to share my gifts with the world."

"Sure."

"I'd wander the plains, with only the clothes on my back, touching hearts with the dearly departed and providing them a roadmap on their journey… Their journey all the way up to that glorious mansion in the sky."

His window is still minimized. I don't need to see his face when he's launched into full sarcasm mode. I know it far too well. "Yeah, that business partner of yours. Sounds like she's just ruined your life. Still, you got them to *thirteen*. With five thousand upfront? Maybe when you get back, this horrid business partner of yours can take you out for a night on the town."

"You mean *Pizza Hut*, don't you?"

"*Little Caesar's*, actually. Our Hut coupons expired last week."

Unlike Brad, I'm not conversing in sarcasm. The IRS was not particularly kind to our itemized list of expenses from previous tax seasons, a fact made known in a series of increasingly pointed letters. If we have any shot of getting out from under this, then

Brad had better get off his butt and escort this coked-out bimbo into the sweet hereafter, *tout suite.*

Thirteen thousand? Proud of my boy. Dad was right—divorcing him remains the smartest thing I ever did—but I always try to give Brad some credit whenever he manages not to totally screw something up.

CHAPTER THREE

John Horton

Rumor is, Peterson was named Executive Producer because he's having an affair with one of the network heads. Don't buy it.

I'm sure he's still cheating on his wife, yeah, but I doubt his sexual prowess landed him this job.

"This is crap. Where's that footage of her crying in the bathroom? That was a snot-dripping 'my life is over!' classic. I practically wet myself when we got it."

Peterson is E.P. because he's a merciless bastard who doesn't hold human beings in any higher regard than the fish sandwich he had for lunch. An ideal quality for a reality television producer.

"Beth wanted it cut, remember? Said it killed the mood of the episode," I tell him as he leans over my shoulder in the editing bay. He reeks of Scotch and body odor.

"Beth's too soft on these psychopaths. That was fine footage, and we're gonna use it. Make that crying scene the Second Act break."

"You sure about that? Because the start of Act Three is Caitlynn and her friends giggling and shopping for prom outfits."

"So what? That'll be a nice reprieve after the drama of… whatever-the-hell reason why this girl was bawling her eyes out."

"I believe it's because her baby's father sent her those texts, claiming the kid wasn't his and he'd never speak to her again."

Peterson doesn't bother to look in my direction as he heads for the door. "See? Classic *Prom Mom* drama. We need those hints of sadness to offset the conclusion, when the kids dance to whatever rap song we can afford to license and everyone has a perfect prom." He makes sure I'm staring directly at him before unleashing his parting shot: "And if I *ever* hear of you cutting a crying scene again, I'll make sure you're back doing local commercials. You clear on that, John?"

I could take a stand for creative integrity. For the dignity of this girl who's allowed us to capture this intimate moment. But I find myself lacking the courage. And, shamefully, this is no surprise.

"Crystal. I'll have the new edit ready for you in an hour, sir."

*

It's Friday, it's 7pm and, if I had any real friends, maybe we'd be unwinding after a long week, exchanging acerbic-yet-affectionate barbs and inside jokes at a local bar or coffee shop.

Truthfully, I've always found friends to be overrated. I'm waiting on a different appointment, anyway.

I can't say she keeps a strict schedule, but she always seems to know when to make her entrance. Days I'm forced to edit together footage of a pregnant teenage girl sobbing her eyes out, as my piggish boss chortles with delight—before he screams at me for using the wrong cheaply-licensed Goo Goo Dolls song as the score—tend to rate right up there on the Suck Meter. And that's when I can count on her company.

The first hint she's arrived is when the television flickers. I shouldn't even have the thing on, considering what it now reminds me of. The lights go out, then back on, three times in a row. I call out to her. I hear a faint titter.

I look to my left and there she is, straightening her miniskirt while taking a seat on the couch. I inch closer. Like two kids in the basement, debating whether to hold hands while waiting for Mom to come down the steps with snacks. Yes it's a tad awkward, but that's not her fault.

"Bad day, I assume?" she asks, genuine concern in those hazel eyes.

"A pretty typical one, of late. Unfortunately."

She nods sympathetically, then plays with one of the countless bracelets on her arm. "I had a feeling you were down. How is it I always know?"

"Because there's a connection, isn't there?" I attempt to smile, just not too wide.

"I'm not trying to be a bother, but I wanted you to know I'm thinking about you."

"Hey, I'm always thinking of you. It's what gets me through the day."

She shyly turns away. "Awww…"

"And you're no bother at all. I love your little visits, girl. You know that."

She reaches out and, even though we've replayed this scene a dozen times, the same futile motions repeat. Our fingers will meet, hers will pass through mine, then we'll chuckle uneasily about the whole crazy scenario.

This time, though, there's a bombshell. The result is the same—her hand turns to smoke as soon as we make contact, and doesn't regenerate until she pulls away—but tonight, there's just a whisper of resistance as our fingers meet. This sounds batty but, for a brief moment there, I think I actually felt her, felt her physical presence, the milky texture of her skin, as our hands joined.

Alex puts her hand to her chest, and—Good Lord!—she gives me the cutest 'surprised girl' expression I think I've ever seen.

"Oh!" she gasps. "That's never…"

"I-I know. I didn't think…" I wish I could say something clever. Or, at the very least, comforting. I'm not too fast on my feet, sadly, and can tell as the pristine image begins to evaporate that our date is at its end.

"Sweetie, sorry I have to go like this," she tells me with a pout. As if those lips needed to be any plumper.

"I totally understand. Don't feel bad about things. We'll talk later, right?"

As she disappears, she gives me a goofy smile while making a 'thumbs up' gesture. Too damned adorable for words.

Her name is Alex and, regardless of her current state of being, she's a sweetheart.

CHAPTER FOUR

Bradley Burns

I don't say anything as I enter the door, but apparently I have 'That Look'.

"C'mon… you don't appreciate the irony in flying *Spirit Airlines*?" she snorts while setting the table. That strawberry blonde hair is longer than I can remember her wearing it. Should I tell her I've noticed? Is she consciously growing it out, or just avoiding another bill?

"I'd like to one day again experience the luxury of a reclining seat." I drop my bags in the hallway and kick off my vintage Chuck Taylors. "Perhaps an aisle seat. And flights that don't depart at four in the morning. You really think one night at a hotel would bring us to insolvency?"

"Aw, is the big baby too delicate to nap at the airport?" She gifts me a half-ironic pat on the shoulder. I used to get a hug 'hello'. Even in the bleakest days, during the worst fighting, I could at least get a 'welcome back' hug.

"After the second delayed flight? Yeah, he is. I brought home a five thousand dollar check, Sandy. I could've had quite the night out in Duluth, let me tell you. But I'm a good boy, aren't I?"

"Yes, the goodest. That five grand is what's going to keep the two of us away from a respectable white-collar prison for maybe another six months."

"Well, perhaps one day the government will recognize the ethereal investigative arts as a legitimate profession, with legitimate business expenses and whatnot," I tell her, cracking open a soda. "By the way, are you *sure* the divorce doesn't protect at least one of us? And by one of us, I mean the cutest? As in, me?"

The *Pizza! Pizza!* has gotten *Cold! Cold!*—which wouldn't be much of an issue, had we not pawned the microwave two weeks prior.

"Nope." Pale green eyes flash as she adds, "We were 'married filing jointly' those years, and your signature is on that return right above mine."

"Darn. So, what did your research turn up?"

"Looking at those social media pages, I see Ms. Abernathy spent many a wild night of girl-on-girl kisses and vodka shots at the Cold Slither nightclub. Also, she was often tagged at a dive bar called Flannigan's out on Simmons Drive. Shockingly, she didn't seem to spend too much time volunteering at the library."

I swallow a mouthful of mediocre pizza. "Okay, I'll go by the club tonight. See if I can pick up any resonances. Assuming I can get in. It's not surrounded by those autograph hounds and *TMZ* jagoffs, is it?"

"Oh, geez. Not since the days of trucker hats and the Britney-Christina feud. If anything, you'll be overdressed." Sandra gives me a look. "Can you really do that?"

"Do what?"

"Collect specific psychic... whatevers in a crowded nightclub?"

"Once I know what, or who, I'm looking for, absolutely. Just a matter of tuning out the extraneous noise and focusing on that one specific voice. Also helps when I have a talisman from the deceased to connect me with their spirit." I fish through my jacket pocket. "Look at what the fine Abernathy folks have bequeathed unto me."

I hand Sandy the porcelain ballerina music box: a vintage piece that's been in the family for three generations. Alex was supposed to take it to L.A. with her, yet her parents found it in her bedroom the day they finally mustered the strength to pack up her belongings. As a child, Alex used to stare at the delicate, narrow-faced danseuse for hours and hum along with the modest tune. I dismissed the story as nostalgic fancy until I did the consult and discovered, straight from the spectral source, the story was in fact true.

"Huh. Nice piece."

"Yeah, I think they honestly loved their little girl. The precious angel. The evil succubus we're hunting this week. Seriously, this wicked beast is haunting her own mother's dreams at night. Aside from the cash, that's reason enough to make sure sweet Alex is dealt with. Now, I'm assuming you're on Sap Patrol?"

"I'll stop by her apartment building and see if anyone's gotten a visit from an ethereal cutie." Sandra wipes off her fingers with a leftover *Taco Bell* napkin and stretches across the table to open Alex's case file. After flipping for a second, she proudly produces a glossy of a stunning beauty with windswept auburn hair, dimples, and shockingly full lips. One of Alex's modeling pics. "Think any guy's gonna turn this down, dead or alive?"

"The females are truly the nastier of the species."

"Bull. The Lotharios do their damage, too. We don't call them *'Widow Hunters'* for nothing. Do you have any idea what *Ghost* did to my kind?" This conversation: we've had a time or two. "Hell, lonely or not, the old Patrick Swayze fantasy is hard to shake. Talk about dangerous propaganda—that stupid movie made even the best of us susceptible to the occasional bout of spectrophilia. They ought to know what they're doing, every time they rerun it on cable."

I toss my paper plate in the trash. "Yeah, but the ladies seem to make more of a game out of it. And I think they go out of their way to pick the more pathetic marks. I know, both usually target the lonesome, but those male victims are so friggin' *sad*."

Sandra's incredulous. "Think baby-faced Alex needs to target another Asperger's-afflicted systems analyst or computer programmer who's afraid of girls? Look at that face. I think *I* have a boner right now. And her friends weren't any slouches, either."

"Heavens, San. I didn't even notice," I respond after she hands me the folder. Yeah, the photos prove her right: Alex was apparently Queen Hot Pants in a cabal of unbelievable, gouge-your-eyes-out exquisite young femmes.

"I'm sure you wouldn't mind interviewing a few of the gals, just to find out more about our target, right? I mean, for strictly professional reasons, of course."

And why does Sandra feel the need to bring this to my attention? It's her daily reminder of my failures as a husband; another opportunity to break balls and keep some dirty laundry in a perpetual state of exposure. I used to think she did this to incite a fight, but the habit stopped provoking any (noticeable) reactions from me weeks ago.

It's just a thought always lingering in the background of our relationship. Regardless of the jokes, in spite of our efforts to keep this crazy business afloat, even as we continue to live within this awkward truce.

Bradley Burns: You're a degenerate pantychaser who violated your partner's trust and ruined our marriage. And you will not ever forget this. I'll make sure of it.

CHAPTER FIVE

INTERLUDE I

You deign to enter the prison chambers yourself, refusing to send an aide for the task. The stench always hits you, always makes you regret this act of self-assertion, if only momentarily.

You select the man, the emaciated shell of what used to be a man, personally. He should thank you for the honor. Perhaps he would, if he possessed the ability to speak.

Upstairs, the blade is pressed against his neck. You watch the crimson syrup drip from his veins into the cauldron. Watch it blend with the water, the crimson diluted into a shade of cerise.

Always a sacrifice must be made. This man, this Marshall Nalley, was once a good provider. One of a multitude whose essence was drained to provide the energy demanded by your home. But all livestock reaches the age where it can no longer contribute, where the justification to preserve its existence grows thin.

Reaching across the void is no easy task. You know this. And you desire to see the one who birthed you. The one wrongly cast into exile.

You cup the water, drink deep. Your body shivers as the liquid passes through. The convulsions have you on the floor soon enough.

She is not with you, yet you see her. See her lovely face again.

Her features are not unlike your own, but you recognize her

beauty will always surpass yours. The envy is present, but dwarfed by the unfeigned joy in your dark heart.

This is your mother. Your sister. Your reason for being.

She laughs good naturedly at the sight of you. She asks how goes the domain; you give an honest answer. A diviner is snooping about again, interrupting affairs in the birthrealm. You'll deal with him, should circumstances arise.

She reminds you that a diviner's blood is precious. That it might even hold the key to her return.

You ask if Lilu is not living up to his bargain. What are his servants accomplishing in the birthrealm? Why have his incubi failed to produce a female diviner to aid our cause? A female diviner's blood is much stronger, we were always told.

Her tone chastises you for overstepping bounds, yet she provides an honest reply. Lilu and his ill-disciplined boys have swapped loyalties yet again. They've returned to Lucifer's side, sister, please respond accordingly.

No, not with war. We'll build our army in the birthrealm first. But that can't be done while your loving kin is floating in the ether, now can it?

CHAPTER SIX

Bradley Burns

For a club that had its 'Tres Chic' card revoked years ago, Cold Slither can still pack them in on a Wednesday night. I asked around; seems the club has a loyal clientele, based on the owners' stubborn refusal to ever water down a drink, and a prime location on Sunset Boulevard. The establishment also participates in the shockingly outdated practice known as 'Ladies' Night', in spite of threats from the city council to pass an ordinance.

Cheap drinks to draw in pretty girls and the delusional men who pursue them? How *do* these monsters sleep at night?

No shortage of working stiffs and gorgeous-yet-anonymous wannabes denied access to whatever trendy club the paps are stalking tonight. I wasn't lying to Sandra earlier—I really can open a dialogue in the midst of this chaos—but perhaps it's not as easy as I implied.

I scour the tables, looking for one I recognize from Alex's photos. She seemed to have a favorite, and it's right… here.

There's a lady sitting alone, nursing a whisky sour. Made-up for the evening; perhaps too much cover for the sins of aging, but no warm-blooded male would deny her allure. Sadly, that's an insufficient standard of beauty for this town. The odds of a casting agent discovering her at this late date are pretty slim; unless she can clean up enough to play a few flummoxed moms or IBS-afflicted schoolteachers, I doubt her lovely face will ever grace the small screen.

Oh, listen to me. Trying to conceptualize a life story for this stranger. Who's to say she ever aspired for stardom in the first place? Why can't she be a nice lady having a few drinks after a hectic day at the office?

Hey, there could be a million reasons for moving here. I certainly didn't come to have my heart crushed under the unfeeling boot of Hollywood... I moved here to exploit the lingering spirits of those hearts crushed under the unfeeling boot of Hollywood. That's totally different.

"Excuse me, mind if I have a seat?"

The woman looks up from her drink and wipes a strand of implausibly blonde hair from her left eye. "Sure you can't find another table?"

"Sorry, but I think the place is filling up. I'd hang out at the bar, but I don't have a great history with that bartender."

Before taking my seat, I gesture towards the comely redhead pouring drinks twenty feet away.

"Yeah? Bad service?" she asks, before realizing I've officially joined her as a guest.

"Bad breakup." I'm praying the firetop isn't this lady's niece or best friend or part-time aerobics instructor. "But, y'know, I love this place too, and it's not like she has a right to dictate where a man takes a drink. So... Have I seen you in here before?"

She's at least momentarily stunned into silence. I hesitate to declare I'm 'in luck', since ideally this table would've been free in the first place. Yet, I am fortunate to immediately divine a presence lingering near. It's a man in his early fifties, sporting a crew cut, mechanic's overalls, and about eighty extra pounds. I'd be a laughably horrific medium if I didn't recognize who the fella is.

After she swallows down her annoyance, my new friend formulates a polite variation of *'Piss off, weirdo'*. It goes, "I'll be honest with you, I'm not here alone."

The shadow lording over her bats those pathetic eyes at me. *Let her know I'm still watching over her… Don't tell her how much it hurt at the end… Let Lizella know everything will be okay…*

Like I'm going to fall for the innocent act? Who does he think he's fooling with?

Sorry, bud, but you've stumbled across the wrong 'gifted'. But, hey, thanks for subconsciously radiating the horrifying details of your death. Just the mental image I needed for the evening: a vivid flash of your flabby body as it's crushed by the 1987 Buick Grand National your drunk assistant failed to properly secure atop the hydraulic lift.

I shake off the images and offer Liz a smile. "That's fair. Listen, would you mind terribly if I snatched the table from you guys? I could maybe make it worth your while…"

I once felt so smooth doing this, tossing out hundred-dollar bills to pesky civilians impeding my search for paranormal truths. Now, I'm reduced to sheepishly offering them twenties. After registering the foul expression on her lovely face, I notice I've pulled a mere *five* dollars from my wallet. And, because I'm a dope and didn't think to ask Sandra for any petty cash earlier, I'm also faced with the knowledge it's the only bill in my possession.

She ogles me. "You… I think you just tried to bribe me with a five dollar bill?"

"Yeah. That could've gone better, I admit. Listen, can I be frank? I need this table for a reason, and while I might eventually stumble across the proper lie and convince you to give it up, I'd rather cut to the chase." I hand her my card. She makes the predictable face.

"*Bradley Burns - Paranormal Desperado.* What's that supposed to mean?"

Sandy has a card, too. It has whatever official title she lists on our tax forms, but I like mine better. "Short answer: I actually do see dead people. Now, what you said earlier about not being here alone? I gathered as much… As soon as I spotted a certain someone lingering over your shoulder, grease stains splattered across those denim overalls."

Liz gasps, can't bring herself to say the word. "You… You

see…?"

"Yeah, dear old Dad. And he has so many things he'd love to tell you, Lizella." She wheezes, mouth agape, after I speak her name. "But now isn't the time to get into that. Would you mind taking that card and calling to set up an appointment for later?"

She doesn't speak, but Liz does bob her head while staring at the card, and I'm reminded of our unpaid Office Depot bill.

"And in exchange for a complimentary reading, could I maybe have this table for the evening?"

Again, no words. But I trust we've reached an agreement: as she stands, grabs her purse, and carelessly steps out of view. Nice lady. I'll likely omit a few factoids during our next conversation. Like how dearest daddy has been seducing an isolated spinster, a beloved neighbor from her childhood, for the past eighteen months.

She probably doesn't need to know such things. But if she'd like to see sainted father escorted into the bright light, to have some assurance of his eternal rest, and happens to have an extra ten grand gathering dust in a bank account… we can make small talk.

Secure in a place Alex will surely recognize, I remove the music box from my jacket pocket and place it in the center of the table. Top opened, the porcelain dancer's song chimes indistinctly under the blaring rhythms of the talentless house band. I suppose it would be asking too much for Elton John's 'Tiny Dancer' to be playing at the moment.

Assuming anyone's sober enough to notice, I must look quite the fool: sitting alone at a table, eyes closed, while a diminutive ballet figurine twirls for my amusement. I call out to Alex and, as my concentration deepens, the soundtrack of weekday drunks and slumming hipsters melts away. Finally, a voice emerges.

"You… I don't want you touching that."

It's the sound of barbed wire dipped in honey. A lost soul, a young one, consumed with the nastiness that escorts all beings who delay their release from this mortal coil. Her form materializes across the table, that flawless face giving me death stares.

"Ah, there we are," I say to her. "Lots of unforgettable nights out here, huh? Want me to call Becky and Trina? See if we can reunite the old crew?"

Her eyes won't leave that music box. "I don't know what you think you're doing, but I'm sick of you hovering around."

I lean forward. "Buy a clue, sweetie. You're the ghost; *you're* the one who hovers around now." She needs to understand that I'm not someone to be trifled with. That I'm not one of her playthings.

"Who do you think you are? Why were you talking to my parents?"

"Why are you stalking your poor mother's dreams at night? You think that's going to help the woman find any peace?"

"That's my *mother*; you don't get to tell me when I can see her. You don't have the right."

"When you're a detached spirit, preying on the innocent and overstaying your welcome on this plane? Yeah, I do have the right. Here's the thing, Alex. Hate to break it to you, but you're a succubus. A fancy way of saying 'ghost whore', basically. And when you're not busy exploiting the lonely and sucking the life out of sad mama's boys, you have a nasty tendency to disturb the dreams of the woman who selflessly gave birth to you. Even by wraith standards, that's low, girl."

Intentionally provocative? Yes. But dominance must be asserted in these interactions. She needs to know that I can't be charmed. That her ethereal draw holds no appeal for this mortal. That I'm not gazing into that immaculate face. That I haven't noticed just how round those hazel eyes are.

"I'm not trying to upset anyone. But I need to see her. I have things, things I wish she could hear," she says, with what almost sounds like sincerity sneaking into her voice. Eyes go back to that music box before returning to meet mine. "Why am I telling you this? Why were you at our house, calling out to me?"

Oh, and those lips. I have *not* been staring at those delectable crimson pillows during the entire conversation.

She notices I haven't answered the question. I clear my throat. "Because your parents needed proof, Alex. To know you haven't gone into the light yet. Now, don't worry, I didn't let them in on the whole 'ghost skank' bit—that one's going to stay between us—but you need to realize what you're doing is wrong. You're *hurting* people."

She snorts. "And you're gallantly swooping in to save the day? To set things right?"

"Oh, hell no. I have bills to pay." Goodness, I think I might've made her smile just a tad. "I'm untangling you from this mess because your parents loved you enough to dip into their retirement and rent my expertise. But, from your perspective, what difference does it make? I'm the only person who can lead you out of the murky nonexistence you're currently stuck in. That should make me your hero, regardless of my personal motivations."

"What makes you think I want to enter your precious 'light,' buddy?" She leans forward, resting her head against her arm. "Why wouldn't I be happy the way I am?"

"Because I know ghosts, and I know you're all miserable. To a person, you're all pricks. Some of you can put on a sweet act when it suits you, but the real experts see through that nonsense. Face it: you wouldn't have that streak of pure spite in you if you were happy, sweetie."

She closes her eyes. Buries her face into folded arms. "Shut up. I don't want to hear this."

I caught a glimpse of that face before she concealed it. Like a girl who doesn't want to hear one of daddy's lectures. And the way those lips puckered before her face went down… Gaah, I need to concentrate. "Of course you don't. Your kind never does."

"You need to leave me alone." Her face pops up. An eyebrow arches. "I don't think She is going to be happy if she knows you're snooping about." Suddenly, Alex flashes a devil's grin.

The girl's no dummy. Been waiting for just the moment to drop that reference, I'm sure. "Yes… the mysterious 'She.' I'd love for one of you spooks to someday elaborate on that one. By-the-by," I continue, "you're hissing a bit on your 'S's. 'Ssssshe knowsss you're ssssnooping about…' Another sign pure malevolence has rotted your soul."

An even wider smile, covering her annoyance. No Midwest farmer's daughter wants to be compared to a serpentine she-beast. "You're wasting your time. And I think we both know what happens if these chats run a little too long, don't we?"

Alex rises—as a human would do—and walks past. I feel her presence on my shoulders. That arctic touch is unmistakable. She squeezes. Hard.

"For your own sake, you'd better go find some other soul to save." She leans forward to whisper in my ear. "And, if you know what's good for you, stay the hell away from my family."

With that, she's gone. I collect myself, take a few breaths, and try to think this through. I think about how this farm / party girl turned out to be tougher than I anticipated. I question why so many succubae toss around this phantom 'She' as an intimidation ploy.

But, most of all, I'm fixated on whether or not saline lip injections can last into the afterlife. Is it possible those things are actually real?

CHAPTER SEVEN

Sandra Jones

An online search revealed his name. John Horton, age 45, the current inhabitant of Alex's former apartment. No record of a marriage license and no paper trail connecting him to any children. Sounds like a prime target for one of these harpies.

Who knows? Could be he's an absurdly attractive bachelor who's refused to ever settle down. Maybe when he opens the door, I'll have a Season One-era Dr. Doug Ross staring back at me.

Embarrassingly, I examine the shapeless jumpsuit I've adopted for the task. Not the best showcase of my feminine wiles, I have to say. Maybe I should've gone full sex kitten for this guise? If the man behind the door is a perfect physical specimen or just the dud from the *Mystery Date* game, he'd likely respond to a flash of cleavage more than he'd react to this potato sack.

I knock on the door, tell myself that it doesn't matter. I also grouse that this really shouldn't be my job in the first place: I handle the business side of things and Brad does his mystic voodoo. That was the deal. How'd I get roped into the tedious but necessary chores he doesn't want to touch?

Okay, door has opened and we have our potential target. And, yeah, I'm getting more of a sad trombone vibe than 'Hearts and Flowers'. John doesn't quite look his age, but there's a decent amount of gray mixed in with that blond hair, and it's likely his black horn-rimmed glasses are mere fashion ignorance and not an ironic statement. Truthfully, I doubt his sickly, anemic frame is attracting too much attention from the fairer sex.

Our undead cousins, however, would consider poor John a fine meal.

"Yes? Can I help you?" he asks, clearly not expecting company. I gleaned from my research that he works in the entertainment industry in some capacity. I'm not sure if he's made friends with anyone in the wardrobe department: factoring in the plaid sweater vest, Dockers, and dark-beige Nunn Bush loafers.

"Hiiii, I'm Sandra, and I'm working with Carmine Plumbing Solutions?" I answer in my best Valley Girl. "I hate to disturb you this morning, but there's a drainage issue that needs to be worked out?"

He isn't fully opening the door. Surely he doesn't find my five-foot-three frame *that* intimidating? Should I have dragged the sexy soccer mom ensemble out of retirement? Am I deluding myself into thinking I can still pull it off?

"I'm sorry? What kind of issue?"

"Other residents have reported a blockage in their drains. Mind if I check out your sinks and make sure everything's okay?"

I catch him looking me over. The only verification I have for my identity is this jumpsuit and the *'Sandra'* patch that's sewn above the breast pocket. It's usually enough.

"I don't think there's been a problem…" he says, thinking. "But if you want to take a look, I guess that'd be all right. I leave for work soon, though."

I smile reassuringly as he opens the door, giving him an apologetic head bob as I enter the apartment. He points me towards his kitchen sink. "So, you lived here for long?"

"Moved in around a year ago. Thought it'd be nice to be closer to work, and was pretty lucky the place became available," he replies, still in the living room.

I play around with the faucet handles and make meaningless marks on my clipboard. "Yeah? What do you do?"

"That." He points to his television. I pop my head out of the kitchen to see what's on the screen. A girl, still in braces, is holding a fussy baby to her chest. She's wearing a champagne-pink gown, speckled with lime-green vomit. The television is muted, but it's obvious both of these children are upset.

"Dude… You work on *Prom Mom*? That show is amazing!" There's not a lot of acting here. The show's a guilty pleasure. Anytime I think about my precarious financial situation or moribund love life, I can always reassure myself with the knowledge I'm not Rhonda with the opiate-addicted baby-daddy, or the already-divorced-by-graduation, currently pregnant with twins, sad sack known as Janae.

"Yes, I think this is probably my finest moment," John says sarcastically, as the girl on the screen frantically wipes away the vomit with wet paper towels, her baby boy pitching a fit on the edge of the girls' room sink. "Oh, don't worry about this cliffhanger. Gemma catches the baby before he falls to the floor."

I write more gibberish on my clipboard. "So, what's it like working on such a popular TV show? That's got to be a thrill, man. What do you do on it, exactly?"

He shrugs. "I'm the story editor. And it's nothing glamorous. Usually, we're getting back hours of footage of kids scrolling through text messages. And, regardless of what I edit, it never seems to please my boss, who expects at least one nervous breakdown per act."

"I guess it's a turbulent time in a young lady's life: getting your driver's license, finding the right date for prom, the burdens of gestational diabetes…" I examine my surroundings, pretending to be impressed. No family photos, no decorations. Barely any furniture. "Anyway, it certainly seems like a nice place you have here. How'd you manage to pick it up?"

"I think the previous tenant vacated suddenly, so I guess I lucked out." John leads me to his hall bathroom, eager to change the subject. Has Alex already made contact with this mope?

"Uh-huh. Left in a hurry, did she? She leave anything behind?"

I ask as I open the cabinet beneath the sink and tap the pipes with my pen. "You'd be amazed at what you can find when a motivated tenant flies off in the night."

"Nope." His voice cracks. "It's… It's like she was never here."

"Uh-huh. Okay, this looks fine." I turn off the faucet. "Got a bedroom bath, I'm assuming?"

"Yeah, I wasn't expecting company…" he says as an apology while opening his bedroom door. The bed's unmade, with only one side occupied the previous evening—but hey, I'm in no position to judge. I discreetly have a look around as he leads me to the final bathroom; sometimes the marks get into all kinds of freaky rituals with their ghostly lovers. Candles, ropes, ceremonial knives… Fun stuff. It's no casual fling; it's usually a lifestyle commitment.

Up until the moment the victim's lost all interest in food and water.

If Alex is skulking around the place, she likely hasn't reached that special stage of the relationship with ol' John. He's skinny, yeah, but not outright gaunt. The only object on his bedroom floor is a PlayStation and its wireless controller, which I nearly trip over while stepping into his bathroom. "Okay, that's the last sink," he says.

I continue the nonsense inspection, tapping on pipes and playing with the faucets as he lingers awkwardly in the background. I guess it's possible he's had no contact with our subject, and there's no law keeping her from selecting someone else in the building as her target, but John here is such easy prey.

I honestly hate doing this.

Closing the cabinet doors under his sink, I make my gambit. "So, John, I know this sounds crazy…" I begin, evoking those six weeks of acting courses from so long ago, "…but I think I remember…"

"I'm sorry?"

"Yup. Didn't occur to me until just now, but this place is eerily familiar," I say while moseying over to his toilet. The errant pubes, glued to the seat with aged urine, provide more evidence

I'm dealing with a heterosexual male, one who likely hasn't had a lady over in ages. "Back in my wild grad school days, I could've sworn I ended up at a party, right at this place. Dollars to donuts I once hurled my cookies in this toilet right there," I tell him while flushing the commode.

"Wow. Small world."

"Yeah, I got dragged here by an old girlfriend of mine. A real party girl." Here's the bit that makes me queasy. "But she was nothing compared to the skeez who was renting this place."

He pauses. "I'm sorry?"

"I'm guessing she was the tenant you snatched this place from. Bet her daddy was paying the bills, not knowing what his innocent angel was up to. Oh, man… Did this chick have a reputation."

"Huh. I, um, wouldn't know anything about that." I was hoping, for John's sake, he'd have no reaction, but I can tell he's becoming agitated. I'm getting the confirmation I need, even as I'm increasingly disgusted with myself.

"Oh, yes. Every guy in our clique knew about the girl. Said all you'd need to have a shot with her is an ATM card and half a tank of gas." I try to smile, to keep this light. "They'd act like charming schoolboys around her, then snicker and high-five one another behind her back."

"Really?"

"Sure. One guy I knew used to call her 'snow dog', because if you had enough white stuff in your palm, she'd follow you around like a smitten puppy. You catchin' my drift?"

"I think she sounds like a girl who just had some problems," he says, clearly annoyed, while I open the door to his shower.

"Ha! Yeah, but it's the kind of problem a trip to Planned Parenthood would fix right quick."

Subtlety is, perhaps, not my strong suit; a realization reinforced as I turn the shower's knobs. Instead of the same faint stream you'd experience in any mid-priced L.A. apartment, a powerful rush of water roars from the showerhead, knocking my arm back with conspicuous force.

"Your shower do that often?"

But John's too stunned to answer. The flickering lights kick in, as I suspected they would. I know, as well as John likely does, that we're not alone here. And, while he might be shocked by his sweetie's tantrum, this is classic psychokinetic, poltergeist behavior: obviously inspired by one tasteless joke too many.

Water pressure ramps up as the pipes vibrate, a rumble behind the walls making its way to the floor. The showerhead can only take a few seconds of this pressure before it shatters.

A deafening blast. Water shooting in every direction. Luckily for John, I take the bulk of this liquid explosion.

On our left, we hear the unmistakable crunchy racket of exploding glass. As perfectly timed as a Christmas lightshow, every bulb installed above John's vanity detonates in order.

I'm questioning how bad this tantrum will get when that toilet starts making grinding noises. "What is going on here? What did you do?" John asks: asks *me*, not the psychopathic spirit causing this mess, expressing no gratitude for the countless gallons of water I've just absorbed for him.

The impulse to shove this geek in the path of the imminently-erupting toilet rises, but there's no time. The anchor bolts are the first to go, lifting the toilet as they shoot into the ceiling. A geyser appears where it used to be, rocketing the toilet directly overhead.

I duck with only a fraction-of-a-second to spare, and don't have the time (or presence of thought) to warn John of the approaching toilet-rocket. He's nicked in the shoulder and falls to the floor in shock.

The toilet's momentum isn't slowed as it hurls into his vanity mirror, spraying the left side of the room with glass shards, a matching set for the exploding pipes decorating the right side of the room.

A firehose spray of toilet water is assaulting my back as I shout at John to leave the room. He freezes instead. I shove him out of the way; shattered glass and light bulb *crunch-crunch* beneath our feet as I slam the door behind us. Truth is, Alex can easily continue this fit, regardless of which room we're in. But at least there isn't a negligently-scrubbed toilet in this room for her to keep hurling at my pretty head.

"John! Ask her to stop!"

He stares. "W-what? Who are you talking about?"

"John! Don't play dumb: we both know this is Alex. Tell her to stop this!" He looks away. More pipes detonate in the bathroom. Something—I'm guessing his sink—crashes against the wall. "Tell her I'll go away if she'll just stop this nonsense *right now*!"

He inhales, shuts those wounded eyes. I have no idea what he whispers, but the look on his face seems open and sincere. A few seconds into their chat, the rumbling in the next room stops, the lights are back, and we're left alone.

We collect our breath. It takes time.

An awkward situation remains. Neither of us knows what to say to the other. I give him half of a wave goodbye and make a wordless exit.

CHAPTER EIGHT

Bradley Burns

"I told you I don't need any—*owaaWWaah!*—alcohol, Brad." I tell her to be still as I squeeze her arm and go back for another dab at the cut. The scratch is just above her left cheek, shining against her pale skin. Her soft, porcelain, truly flawless skin, I should say. My fingers haven't been this close to her face in months. "Better safe than sorry. Just let me finish cleaning this."

I'm tempted to make a joke about her being a good girl and getting a lollipop later, but I have a feeling she'd hit me. Geez, she actually got cut. It's not deep, but just the thought…

I get one more dab in, one more chance to brush against that downy, pink cheek before she pulls away. She stretches across the table and grabs the hand mirror. "The *Band-Aid* was more than enough. It's not that deep a cut: only a few grazes from the shattered glass."

Sandy's fumbling with another *Band-Aid*. I take the bandage from her and rip open the paper packaging with the edges of my fingernails.

We're trying to keep this light. Trying not to acknowledge that the glass shards were millimeters away from blinding her. "You realize you're only supposed to prod them a bit, Sandy. See if you can get them to poke their head out. I didn't think you'd go full-on abortion joke there."

"Okay, I took things too far," she says, leaning over the hand mirror and applying the new bandage. I'd have done this for her, if she hadn't snatched the thing from my hands. "Dirty mind. Me. We know this." She looks up. "But I'm serious, Brad: I never want to be caught in something like that again."

"Eh, you've probably seen worse. The walls didn't start bleeding, did they?" God, why did I say that?

"Going out there alone isn't a lot of fun in the first place, and to have to deal with weird crap like… Brad, I'm not the psychic voodoo guy. That's your deal. It's not fair to force me into doing your grunt work."

"Okay, honestly, I wasn't expecting all of that." What happened to the tacit agreement to downplay the recent unpleasantness? "I would've gone had I known… Well, anyway, I was still recovering from the, ah, lingering effects of my spectral dialogue with the target."

"Uh-huh," she says, returning the box of *Band-Aids* to the cabinet. "And not in bed, maintaining your kid-on-summer-vacation hours. Nope."

I guess I have to be the adult this morning. "Now, John… How did he handle this?"

"I'd describe his response as a mix of shock and horror. Do you think Alex is moving on to another victim?"

"Oh, no. I'm certain she'll be able to worm her way back into John's lonesome heart. He's sure to be blaming you for upsetting the poor dead dear, anyway."

"Think this guy is so hard-up he'll welcome back the unholy manifestation who violently trashed his bathroom?"

"As you were so eager to point out yesterday, *she shoor is purty*."

"Ah, men. Typical. Of course he's going to risk his life in order to chase the hottest skirt he's ever seen, live or dead. God forbid he talk to the sweet, plain girl who works at the coffee shop. Your species would be better off if you were all born blind."

I take the shredded wrapper to the kitchen trash. "Misandry is real, Sandra." I squeeze her shoulders on the way there. "It's real and it *hurts*."

The doorbell chimes.

"Who's that?"

"Oh! It's after ten, right?" I check my watch. "I bet I know. That's probably Trina."

"Who?" Sandra asks with just a note of venom, moving towards the door.

I follow. "Trina. One of Alex's friends. The hot, dark-haired girl of unknown ethnicity in those photos?"

She snorts. "Which one?"

Fair point. Alex's collection of friends was a living *Benetton* ad, each insanely-attractive girl sporting eyes, hair, and a skin tone that would confound the average racist uncle.

I acknowledge Sandra's joke—or was it just a pissy comment?— and smile. "She's the one Alex seemed closest to, so I wanted to talk to her. I called her last night after you went to bed."

Sandra takes her hand off the door knob. Gestures towards the back. "So you want me to go hide in my room?"

"Huh? Why?"

"Just asking. Don't want to be in the way of... y'know... your *thing*." Her fingers dance during that last bit, her usual mocking reference to my abilities. "Since this is your guest, why don't you open the door?"

What's up with her today? Still reacting to what happened a few hours ago, or did I do something else to summon the beast? As she backs away from the door, I try to keep that grin going; avoid any unnecessary escalation. The bell rings again as I'm opening the door. On the other side, lit perfectly by the midmorning glow, is Trina. She's taller than me, even without those heels, and I suspect a stiff wind might knock the girl over.

This doesn't distract from her beauty. Clearly a model, Trina's honey-brown skin is impeccable, aided only with a hint of makeup, those dark eyes and curvy lashes of hers perfectly complementing her lengthy black tresses. I could be a pig and describe the way her tank top is clinging to her chest, or provide a detailed accounting of every fringe that lines her Daisy Dukes, but we're not going there, okay?

"Yes, I'm supposed to meet a Brad Burns?" she asks, looking me over.

"Right place. Hi, I'm Brad. And this lovely lady is my associate, Sandra Jones." Once, I accidentally referred to her as my 'assistant'. Give me credit for not kick-starting that four-hour argument today.

Trina shakes hands with both of us. "I recognized your voice immediately." She turns to Sandra. "Isn't it so smooth? Like a Top 40 radio D.J. from back in the day. I'll be honest, I was ready to dismiss the guy as a creep, but that voice on the other line was just so intriguing, don't you think?"

"He has his charms, yes. Would you like a drink?" she asks, motioning for Trina to come inside. Trina responds that water's fine. A nice, humble, simple girl… who happens to resemble an Ancient Egyptian goddess.

I take a seat on the couch next to our guest while Sandra heads for the kitchen. She looks back at me, catches my attention, and then rolls her eyes. She returns ten seconds later with a bottled water from the fridge. It's the store brand of the independent grocer we've been going to lately; Trina gives the label a curious examination while twisting the cap.

Before Sandra makes any comments about our poor-people-water being safe to drink, I try to keep this moving. "Well, Trina, I hate to jump into business, but, as you know, we do have something of a serious mission today." I give Sandra a look to indicate that all of this is important, and not merely an excuse to have a blistering-hot model keep our couch cushions warm. Honest.

"Yes, it's… ah, very serious," Sandra says, taking a seat across from us, a token effort to play along.

"Sure. And if this video we're making for Alex's parents can help them grieve, that'd be wonderful."

"Yes, absolutely. They're good people, and we appreciate you doing this for us…" Sandra can't think of the girl's name. She looks to me for help and I mouth the two syllables. "…Trina. Thanks so much."

"Whenever you're ready, we'll take a video on Sandra's phone, and we'll intercut your story with the other testimonials we're collecting. We just need you to tell us some fond memories of Alex." Fond memories of the malicious beast who, just this morning, attacked the woman I once pledged my life to.

Trina nods and smiles. "Okay, just let me have a moment to prepare myself," she says, her hand now gripping my knee. I'm not looking over for Sandra's reaction. Not gonna do it.

It's less than a minute before Trina says she's ready to talk. And talk she does, telling us the story of Hermes, a homeless man Alex's clique encountered during a night out. Hermes would charm the ladies exiting the clubs, offering decaying flowers he'd pilfered from the neighborhood florist's dumpster, a special price of $1.99. Initially, the girls brushed the vagrant away but, per Trina, Alex couldn't forget the look on Hermes's face that night. She tracked him down the next day and offered to buy him lunch as an apology.

I'm going to assume his response was something akin to "Coconut! Baseball! Valvoline!" but Alex interpreted it as a friendly "Thank you". And, from that day forward, Alex could often be found in West Hollywood, stalking this hobo and enticing him out of the alleys with a bag of *In-N-Out* burgers. Her clique initially made fun, ridiculing the small-town girl for adopting like a pet the first homeless bum she'd ever encountered. They soon realized that this was just Alex.

And now Trina's all weepy. If she only knew what her special friend had been up to lately.

"You know, when you talk, Trina, I really feel that connection you have with your friend." I look over to Sandra, who remains stone-faced. "It's obvious—obvious to both of us, right?—how much you miss her."

"She was a special person. I just wish she knew how much we all cared for her. And I wish we could've helped her, but we didn't... We didn't know..." Trina says, now sobbing. I give her a reassuring pat on the back before I make my move. Not *that* move. The move where I reveal the true reason why I invited this Cleopatrian beauty over.

"Trina, I realize this might sound, well, odd, but you know what I do for a living right? You've seen mediums on TV, haven't you?" She wipes a tear. "Okay. The reason I know Alex's parents in the first place is because they trusted me to get back in touch with their girl."

"And did you?"

"We had a reading and, yes, Alex came through. It was just a… A beautiful experience. Not to be too forward, Trina, but would you like a reading?"

"You mean… to talk to Alex again?"

I notice I still have my hand on her shoulder. "I can't guarantee anything but, considering how close you were, I have a feeling that Alex would want to reconnect. I don't want to push anything on you, and if you have any spiritual beliefs that might make you uncomfortable…"

"No, no. I mean, this sounds like it could be something nice, doesn't it?" She squeezes her hands and thinks for a second. "Okay, I honestly wasn't expecting anything like this, but I… I think I'm going to take you up on the offer, Brad."

Suddenly, I hear the sound of Sandra walking past, not acknowledging our presence as she's digging through her purse. "Don't mind me," she says, not looking up. "Just gonna go run some errands."

"Is she mad or something?" Trina asks, one second after the door slams.

CHAPTER NINE

John Horton

I can hire a service to clean the mess. That's not the issue.

But whatever *that* was… That can't happen again. And I'll tell her this, the next time she decides to pop in here. I'll be firm, but I won't be a dick about it.

What was that about, anyway? Who did that woman think she was, bluffing her way into my home and spreading those lies about Alex? Why was she trying so hard to make Alex upset?

Maybe Alex knows something about the lady. I'd ask, but this isn't your typical relationship. It's not like I can just shoot her a text and invite her over. And when she does appear, it's rare that I get more than a few words in before she fades away.

The practical complications of dating a ghost. Someone should write a how-to guide.

They shut off the water to the building—that'll make me very popular with my neighbors—an hour ago. I've already called in to work, told them the partial truth that I had some pipes explode, but now I'm questioning if I should just come in anyway. Anything beats kicking around this place, reliving that horror show all day. Maybe work will give me some kind of distraction: even if it's editing together another gnarly montage of sloppy, pink babies being extracted from underage wombs.

But could anything distract from what I saw? That's probably going to require months of repairs, and who knows how much of this damage I'm going to be liable for. More disturbing is the horrible, repetitive thought that someone could've gotten killed. Will something like this happen again? Is this what my life is going to turn into?

The severity of the situation now dawning, I flop onto the couch, close my eyes, and attempt a breathing exercise. A therapist taught me this method years ago, when those panic attacks first surfaced. I try to think of something relaxing. I think of Alex. The way *I* know her. The delightful, impish girl who only wanted to make me smile after a bad day. Such a sweet nature, she'd never harm a fly. A kindhearted filly totally incapable of…

Give me a second I… I need to get my story straight…

Huh? What was *that*?

I never meant to cause you any sorrow… I never meant to cause you any pain…

I know I didn't turn that radio on.

Why can't we talk it over… Oh it seems to me… That sorry seems to be the hardest word…

And, nope, I'm not sitting on the remote, either. And I have my *Sirius* menu memorized; these channels are nowhere near each other, anyway.

Go build yourself another home, this choice isn't mine… I'm sorry, I'm sorry, I'm sorry…

"Okay, girl… You never told me you were into classic R.E.M." The lights shut off and on, three times in a row. I sit up, look to my left, and there she is. Pouting.

"Was I too subtle? You got the message, right?" she asks, gently regarding me with Bambi eyes.

I mute the radio. "Yeah, obviously. But, seriously: what happened this morning? Why'd you flip out like that?"

"Johnny, I wish I could explain it to you. I'm not sure if it's something that you could understand, living here on the other side."

"Can't you try? I mean, I don't want to come down too hard on you, but that was pretty intense."

She turns her body fully in my direction. Tears are forming in her eyes, the poor thing. "And I totally understand that." She's barely able to speak the next sentence; she's trying so hard to fight those waterworks. "Johnny, you must hate me."

"No, no. I didn't say that."

"I wouldn't blame you if you did. I mean, you've been so good to me." She wipes her eyes, composes herself. "*So* good. Keeping me company, keeping me connected to this world, and then I had to go and pull that stunt."

"Well, Alex, I'm assuming you did this because—I don't know—because you were triggered? Because you felt you had to?"

"See? That's such a good way to describe it. I knew you'd understand, John, understand in a way others wouldn't. Here I was, nervous to talk to you about it…"

"So, it was that woman? I've got to assume hearing those lies did something to you."

"It did, yeah," she answers, eyes shut, nodding. "And, this is hard to explain, but since I'm in this new form, my emotions don't quite work the way they did in the past. Feelings kind of… radiate out of me. So when I heard those things, those awful, awful things about me, I guess I just…"

"Exploded?"

She comes to life. Okay, not literally. But she perks up and playfully points at me. "*There's* the word. Wow, John. Why couldn't I have met you… y'know, before I ended up like this?"

"Hey, I ask that question a lot. Every night, in fact."

She giggles, takes a good natured swing at my arm. "Silly."

Her adorable love tap surprises both of us when it actually connects.

"Alex, did you feel that? Your hand… It happened again!"

"I… I guess it did." Wheels are turning. Her next question is out of a dream. "Want to give it another try?"

She offers her hand, and we touch, palm to palm. I can feel the texture of her skin and, while there is an iciness there, I ecstatically sense some humanity mixed in with the chill. No, it's more than a hint. She's here, with me, and I now know the touch of her skin. My index finger and thumb run across her smooth, alabaster fingers, then graze against the edges of her manicured nails.

'*Cold*' never felt so warm. I give her hands a squeeze and she squeezes back.

Alex studies our hands then, in a near-whisper, she says, "Johnny, I know this might sound a little forward, but if you're willing to dare a kiss, I am too."

I oblige the girl. Yeah, yeah. I know…

"Alex, that was so… It felt so…"

I think she's blushing. "Magical? No, too strong?"

"*Exactly* the word I was going to use. Alex, I can't even believe—"

"Oh, are you freakin' *kidding* me?" In a heartbeat, her face changes. Still lovely, but that nervous smile is missing. In its place is a dreadful scowl. "What do you think you're doing?!"

"Alex?"

"You're pulling this shit on me *now*? Do you have any idea how much of a *pest* you are?"

"Honey, are you feeling—"

She's stomping her feet on the floor. The lights flicker again, the television set zaps on and off, and I think I hear the microwave shorting out.

"*Piss off! Piss off! Piss off!* And, in case you didn't hear me the first three times, *PISS OFF*, you irritating mother—"

And, just like that, she's gone.

CHAPTER TEN

Bradley Burns

"I just want you to relax, Trina." She's seated across the kitchen table. Our hands are joined and I'm trying not to fixate on the lingering scent of her perfume. "I want you to center yourself, take a deep breath, and think of your friend."

It's *Miu Miu's L'eau Bleue*, by the way. The scent she's wearing.

"Okay." She pulls her hand away and rubs the back of her neck.

I'm also trying to keep Sandra off my mind. If this séance has any shot of working, I have to remain focused, open to whatever force enables me to commune with the departed. Any distraction could cause the entire ceremony to go haywire.

Plus, whatever way I might've hurt Sandra this time, history reveals her as a forgiving gal. Not forgiving enough to withdraw that divorce petition, even after our night in Reno, but sufficiently high-minded in the friendship department, which I do appreciate. Not that I tell her this often enough.

"But what do we do if she appears?" Trina asks. I catch myself: for a second I thought she was referring to Sandra. Focus, man. Focus.

Trina's eyes are growing even larger. "I gotta admit this is making me a little nervous. I'd love to speak to Alex again, but the thought of talking to a ghost is… *freaky.*"

"You don't have anything to fear. There's love here, right? That's what she'll respond to. She'll be drawn to that loving spirit."

Not entirely a lie. Spirits are naturally curious about souls they've made connections with. Much easier to draw one out with an old friend or lover than with a total stranger. 'Love', though? That's a tricky concept for a spirit.

Trina again offers those soft hands. "And we can just... talk? Like she's sitting right here and we're just having a conversation?"

"If we're lucky, I think that's possible. Alex is going to sense you reaching out to her and, through that void, she's going to respond to your calling. When she comes, and sees who's here to greet her, I bet she's going to be *ecstatic*."

Our eyes are closed. I shut out all extraneous thought and, in my mind's eye, stare into the void. In that white emptiness I have a vision of our target. She's seated on some poor sap's couch, putting on a show for him.

I whisper her name. She has a predictably caustic reaction but, in the end, she can't resist the soothing lure of my voice.

Hey, I have that effect on women. The dead ones.

Alex materializes, mid-rant, in the empty chair closest to Trina. Our 'special angel' has the voice of a circular saw blade cutting through rusted sheet metal. "—er! Who do you think you are?! Do you know who the hell you're dealing with, you little maggot?"

Trina nearly jumps out of her seat. I reach back for her hands, try to calm her down. "No, Trina, it's okay. Sometimes the spirits are disoriented. Sometimes they say things they don't mean, just like anyone else."

"I... don't like this. I think I can feel her, and she's... She's definitely not happy."

Alex turns to her friend. "'Not *happy*?' What was your first clue, you retarded skank? Got a hole in your brain to match the one in your septum, Trina?"

I grip her hands even harder, and watch as her mouth drops ajar and her bronzed skin hastily fades to white.

I have to get control of this situation before she breaks free and leaves a Trina-sized hole in the wall. "Okay, Alex. I don't think that was particularly nice."

"*Nice?* You want to talk to me about *nice?* How many times do I have to tell you to stop stalking me?"

"Brad, why is she saying these things? I don't like this. I-I think I need to go."

"No! Ah, Trina, maybe I wasn't clear: Alex isn't quite herself at the moment." Realizing how hard I'm grasping her hands, I ease up a bit. "It's like, I suppose you could say, what it's like to be awakened from a deep sleep. Some people react better than others, right? As for *spirits*, well… Being jerked out of the void can be traumatic. What Alex needs right now is some understanding." I pull her arms closer, get her attention. "Can you do that for us, Trina?"

Her lips—sumptuous, but not as impressive as her undead gal-pal's—quake a few times before she gets the answer out. "I think I can. But if this isn't helping Alex, then we need to stop."

Alex leans forward. "So, you dragged *her* into this, too? Why are you so *obsesssssed* with me?"

Too many *S*'s in one of those words. Naughty Alex is coming out to play. "I only want to help, Alex. And that's why Trina's here, as well. Trina, maybe you could share something comforting with Alex?"

She looks to me for reassurance and I nod. She turns her attention back to her friend. "Hi, Alex. I just wanted you to know that I miss you. I think about you every day."

Alex snorts. "Uh-huh. You also think about that guy you 'accidentally' took home from the bar? The one I'd been dating for three weeks?"

It only takes Trina half a second to form a reply. "That's *extremely* unfair. I apologized for that a thousand times, Alex. Is this what being on the other side does to you? Just turn you nasty?"

"Aww, po' widdle Twina. Why don't you call Daddy and cry on his shoulders? He still paying your bills, sweetie? You still hiding away the pills and baggies you don't want him to find every time he comes over?"

As entertaining as all this is, it devolves into background noise as my breathing steadies and my consciousness enters that peculiar, blurry state. Can't always pull this off, but maybe the fates are benevolent today…

"I think that was more *your* deal, Alex. *I'm* not the one hung up on what my father thinks of *me*."

"Is that so?"

"Yeah, and another thing… Considering that any club promoter, D.J., or photographer in the entire city was your 'boyfriend' at some point, one of them had to eventually land at someone else's place."

"And the truth comes out, I guess. So that's how you always viewed me, huh?"

"I viewed you as a friend: a friend with some issues, maybe, but still a friend. All of those times you were sweet to my face, was *this* what you were really thinking about me?"

"I… Trina… Listen, I'm not sure why I reacted like this. You can't possibly understand—"

I tap the angel on her shoulder. The contact breaks against my finger like sped-up static electricity. "She can't understand. You're right. But maybe give me a try?"

CHAPTER ELEVEN

Bradley Burns. Again.

The expression on Alex's face is simply priceless. Most likely, the girl didn't expect a tippity-tap on the shoulder from an astral projection of my consciousness. She does a double-take, confirms that my corporeal form is still seated on the other side of the table.

Ol' corporeal me has that look I get on my face whenever Sandra's dad gives his sermon on the simple wrongness of interleague play in Major League Baseball. I gaze at the meatsack that previously housed my being and pray I don't start drooling this time… Not with Trina still attached to that form.

Trina has many gifts, I'm sure, but she isn't 'attuned', so my astral self remains invisible to her eyes. I figure she'll eventually notice she's holding hands with a dead fish, though. Not all models are slow on the uptake, so let's not give in to stereotypes. I've heard of psychics who could exit their body and maintain a dual consciousness: physical form and the floaty-spirit thing. Not so lucky, this guy.

Even if Trina gives in to the most rational response to this madness—that aforementioned Trina-sized hole in the wall—I'm confident Alex's pretty well ensnared. With both of us in spirit form, she can't just disappear on me now. I'm here with her, my hand on her shoulder, and I'm not going to let the perp escape the long-arm-of-the-paranormal-law this time.

"Okay, sweet pea. We both know it's past your bedtime. Why don't you let poppa escort you off to bed? And by 'bed', I'm speaking of that incandescent white tunnel that awaits us all someday."

Alex is so stunned she can barely speak. "How could you do that? You're not one of us; you shouldn't be floating around like this."

"You a stickler for the rules, now?" I grit my teeth, trying to concentrate as my consciousness blurs. I can't fully describe the sensation of entering this bizarre in-between realm: the one that allows a man to drift as a spirit, yet doesn't grant me the sweet release that accompanies death. What I do know is the path to the light is clear in this form, and my history with these spirits has shown that, once I've brought them near the tunnel, they act like good little boys and girls. Float where they're *supposed* to float.

I'm dragging Alex through the void, which now co-exists simultaneously with the aerial view of my kitchen, when she wraps her left leg around my right.

"Don't you realize what you're giving up?" she hisses. "Haven't you thought about what I could offer you... especially on *this* side?"

"I think I've made it clear I'm not one of your marks," I answer, although my resolve might be weakening on that front. Earlier, I made some crack about the girl having lip injections. Simply immature and thoughtless on my part.

Up close, it's clear Alex is an untouched beauty. That's no duckbill, post-op plump job. Her body pressed against mine, I realize how natural the girl is, all around. Even if she is dead.

I untangle our bodies, while a gnawing urge declares me an idiot. "Hey, I'm flattered, but I'm merely a guy with a pecuniary interest in escorting you to your heavenly home and, guess what, I think I hear those angels calling out to you right now. C'mon."

See? That sounded convincing, right? Just a guy doin' his job. Nothin' personal. Don't look at me with those cartoon eyes, girl. Don't stick those lips out. Don't... morph your face into that misshapen, demonic form, sweetie. Not flattering.

"And I told *you* earlier the lassst thing you wanted to do wasss make Her angry," she hisses, literally.

Can Trina see her old bestie right now? I still have a glimpse of her at the table, although it's growing hazier by the second. Alex's intimidation ploy hasn't worked out like she planned; if anything, it's reminded me that time is of the essence.

"These threats are pathetic, Alex." I stare the girl down, as her face morphs back into that angelic loveliness. "You can't charm me and I don't scare easy, so stop this dithering around and get to the climax. The type of climax you're not used to, that is."

A miniscule anxiety appears; I've never pushed my powers this hard. Never had to drag a subject so deep into the light. I steel myself. Turn back towards our destination.

I'm greeted by a woman, twice my height, wearing nothing but the expression the good Lord gave her. Long, raven locks fall past her perfect, tiny navel.

She says nothing at first, just allows me to bask in her presence. Can't blame her: an eleven foot-tall nude woman, posed like a fine art sculpture, ought to make an impression.

"Oh. I get it. You gave me a cue to turn around twenty seconds ago, didn't you?"

Somehow, deep in my gut, lodged somewhere in my soul I've never examined, I recognize the olive-skinned female. And yet, I can't place her name. The necromantic beauty smiles, almost, as she offers this greeting: "Hullo, mortal. Do you realize you're involved with affairs you can't begin to comprehend?"

"I think that's how my ninth-grade Geometry teacher introduced the class. Nice accent, by the way." I can't help myself. I go full smartass whenever I'm nervous. Should've seen me the day I proposed to Sandra.

"I have no tolerance for your antics," she continues, in that peculiar Mediterranean / Egyptian / Israeli / Who-Knows accent. "And you've interfered with one of my children for the last time, Bradley Burns. I think it's time you became more than a simple dilettante in this field."

A wind picks up behind her. *Never* felt wind in this odd plane before. "If you're so enchanted by life beyond the mortal coil, I suspect we can provide quite the education."

I grip Alex's arm tighter as this mystery female approaches. Scared out of my damn mind or not, no way is she taking my bounty: that's what I tell myself. I'm giving this broad a glare that'd make Eastwood proud, but she just barely smirks as she approaches.

I study her narrow, perfectly-straight nose, those indifferent, condescending eyes. Her brows are shaped just enough to indicate she's, perhaps, slightly irritated at the moment. This realm is eerily quiet as always and yet, as the wind continues to build, faint echoes of some creepy-ass Wagnerian composition are growing louder with each footstep.

I curse, scream at her to back away. The smirk grows wider as she grasps my right shoulder. A pain beyond words.

If the forty million incisions into my nervous system weren't enough, there's the sickening sound of a steak on the grill as our astral flesh connects. I jerk backwards, but that grip doesn't lessen. In the corner of my eye, I see Alex escape my side and run behind her mistress.

Those hands move across my shoulder, up my neck, finally caressing my face. The smoke that's sizzling off my skin obscures my view, or perhaps the pain is causing me to black out, but I do catch one good look at this hideous goddess as she pulls my face to hers.

Gray eyes smile. "Enjoying your lesson, Bradley?"

"No! Let go of me!" I shout, in tears. Maybe I could've given her a pithy rejoinder, but whatever remains of my consciousness at the moment is devoted to *getting the hell out of here right now because holy shit this is no joke this crazy bitch is for real going to KILL ME.*

Seconds pass before I realize this collection of petrified screams is not my own.

I'm back home. Trina's here, covering her face in horror.

"You… You-you… I thought you were dead! And your skin…

What happened?"

Yes, what about my skin? I'd likely reply, if my brain were capable of transmitting any coherent response. I look over at my shoulders. See a bubbling, blood-red mess where the top of my shirt used to be. I try to turn my body around, get a view of the nearby wall mirror, but find myself greeted by the floor instead.

"Brad! Oh, my God. Brad?!"

When I regain consciousness, that lovely face is again hovering above me. I think my charming way of thanking her for her concern comes out as: "Hey, nice to see you didn't...make that hole...ow... hey, Cleopatra...forgot your name...mind taking me to that white building?...the one where George Clooney worked before he got... ungh!...real famous?"

The next thing I know, I'm lying in the backseat of a silver Ford Fiesta hatchback, because when Cleopatra tried to buckle me into the front seat I kept slumping over and banging my head against the dash. With only a view of the roof, I think about Clooney. Probably a better Batman than he got credit for. Sandra and I used to watch those *ER* reruns every night before bed. Remember the one with the blizzard? That was something.

It'd be nice to feel something that cold right now. Not ice-cold, literally, because ice can burn your skin and *sweet mother of holy God am I burning right now why am I babbling about canceled TV shows when my skin is melting off?!*

CHAPTER TWELVE

Sandra Jones

He acts like he's never been to Glendale before. Like he's never seen a half-dressed Armenian in his life. "Oh, Trina... Tell us about yourself... How did Alex manage to find a friend even prettier than her? Let us hear your story, Trina, just let the *healing* begin..."

Ugh. And that skank fell for it. I mean, if this helps us clear the case and cash that next check, great. At least she did one useful thing in her life.

"I recognized your voice immediately. Isn't it just so *smooooth?*" I think that's what gets to me, her falling for the alleged 'charm'. I'd love to know what he told her on the phone last night to get her over. And doesn't a girl who looks like *that* have better options than my ex? Fine, yes, she *is* physically perfect. He's, what, fifteen years older than her? Not like that's ever stopped a man's libido before, but I've got to question what exactly he thinks they're going to be talking about.

Yeah, okay. They're not going to be 'talking'.

I shouldn't care, for around a hundred thousand reasons. And I shouldn't be shocked, given Brad's past. But, seriously, I would *never* do that to him. Never flagrantly invite some young piece of ass over and giggle and flirt and try to charm my way into his good graces while the person I used to sleep next to every night, the man

I thought I was building a life with, sits right there next to me.

And I certainly wouldn't pull that crap on the *same freaking day* I'd sent my ex out on what was promised to be a trivial errand that ended up nearly costing him his eye. I'm considerate like that.

"The Federal Reserve." That's what he told me once, when I asked him what he talks to these bims about. *"I ask them their opinions on the Federal Reserve, and we debate the merits of a central banking system versus a purely free market monetary structure."*

I did laugh, as I kicked him in the shin, the first time he told me this.

It's been around five hours since I left the house and, having exhausted any plausible errand I could possibly run, there really aren't any obvious excuses for not being here. He's likely not thrilled with me skipping out like that, but I figure I can match him quip-for-quip without things escalating too terribly bad before we order out for Chinese.

No. Forgot. Last check to Family Garden bounced, so we are not at this time held in high regard by that fine establishment. Sandwiches tonight, assuming we have enough bread. Hey, one errand I actually did forget to run today. Could be a nice excuse to bolt again if he decides to get too snotty… Or if a certain pneumatic car show model is still on my couch.

As I open the door, I see no one's on the couch. Or in my kitchen, although there's a chair on the floor, one no one bothered to return to the table.

Oh, great. Now I have a mental picture of Brad and Trina reenacting certain scenes from *9½ Weeks* and not particularly giving a damn if they knocked that chair over while clawing at each other's clothes, all a tease for the moment when he lifts her petite-yet-curvaceous body over his shoulder and escorts her into his bedroom, the room where the two of us once shared our… Nope. I don't do that anymore.

I'm not obsessing over this. I'm putting the chair back where it belongs and I'm not going to nose into his business. If I see him again before I go to bed, that's fine. I'll ask Brad how the case is going, and give him whatever encouragement he needs—carrot, stick, abject humiliation—to get us that second check from the Abernathies.

Another four hours pass and Brad remains a no-show. I pop in my earbuds and allow the distant yet warm voice of the esteemed Mr. Hansen to escort me to sleep, abandoning irony as he sings of loss, bitterness, and despair. Maybe I'll feel like pulling out *Odelay* on some other night but after today the acoustic, meditative later-releases are better company.

*

Next morning, and I'm checking each room of the house. Empty. Given my personal experience with the man, I'm certain no passionate act of love-making with Brad is going to last *this* long. Also checking my texts and emails: still nothing. He's officially missing, and I'm going to drop the pose and just admit the boy has me nervous now.

I leave a note on the fridge for him to call if he returns while I'm out. I consider peppering it with choice language, but behave myself like a lady: holding on to the hope that this is merely another instance of Brad's insensitivity, even while a gnawing in my gut says something's off here. That gnawing is confirmed when I make another inspection of his bedroom and realize he's left his wallet and phone on the nightstand.

*

Thirty minutes later, I'm standing at the door of John Horton's apartment, the only lead I'm currently willing to acknowledge in Brad's disappearance.

He answers after the third round of agitated pounding. His expression betrays he's not excited to see me. Understood, but irrelevant right now.

"Yes?"

"I get I'm probably the last person you want to see, John, but we need to talk. Have you seen Brad?"

"And Brad is…?"

I place my foot in the door, fearing he won't wait for an answer. "Brad's the partner I work with. I was wondering if he's come by in the past twelve hours or so?"

John nudges my foot out of the way with his own. "Sorry. Can't help you."

"Hey, listen, I'm not looking to upset you," I answer, easing my tone. "And I'd like to apologize about yesterday. Seriously, why don't you let me in; let us have a real conversation about things?" I'd like to think he hears some sincerity in my voice. "You've got to be at least a little curious about what's going on."

Reluctantly, John unfastens the lock. Without a word, gestures me inside. Barefoot, clad in a faded Chicago Bulls t-shirt and pajama bottoms. I see towels all over the floor, sopping up the water damage from the previous morning's incident, while stacks of prepackaged bottled water rest near the entrance to his kitchen.

Did the poor guy have to bathe with this stuff last night? Doesn't he have any friends who'd let him crash on the couch for the evening?

He gestures towards his loveseat. "Okay, yeah. Um, have a seat."

"Well, John, I'm going to level with you. My husband and I run a business, and Brad, as absurd as this might sound, really can… He talks to spirits. We've been looking into one specific spirit, and we felt that you were very likely one of her targets."

"You're talking about Alex."

"Yes, and the reason why—"

"You're talking about that sweet girl who keeps me company in the evenings," he interjects, still not facing my direction. "Who tries to make me laugh and gives me little pep talks when I'm feeling down."

"John, the reason why I spoke to you yesterday, and I'm sorry about the lies, was to verify if you're one of her targets. This girl is not your friend, John."

"What makes you say that?" Now he's looking at me, wearing an expression on his face I probably had at fifteen when Mom forbade me from dating our eighteen-year-old neighbor. "I—I'm supposed to take *your* word?"

"I realize you don't have many reasons to trust me, but John, I'm telling you this for your own good. You don't understand what these spirits are capable of. This girl isn't your buddy, she's trying to seduce you. She wants you to feel comfortable around her, wants you to feel special, so that she can get you into the right position."

"Which would be…?"

I don't know, what kind of position do these spectral skanks enjoy? Reverse cowgirl? Can these ghouls look their marks in the eye? "Which would be… Ready and willing to give in to her, uh, charms, and consummate your relationship."

I can tell I've embarrassed him a tad. Didn't mean to, but how else do I get through to the guy? "And why would she want to do that, aside from, y'know, the reasons why anyone would like to do, uh, such a thing?" he asks.

"That, I don't fully understand. But I do know what these spirits, these succubae, do to you after they pop your cherry. Okay, the hours of explosive climaxes seem fun in the beginning, but guess what follows?

"Depression, anxiety attacks, headaches, teeth worn down from all of that god-awful *grinding*, loss of appetite, loss of sex drive— for any *live* girl, that is—it's only the beginning. The insomnia and obsessive thoughts usually lead to self-harm, and eventually suicide; assuming you haven't starved yourself to death first."

Closing his eyes and waving his hands, John says, "This is ridiculous. I don't want to hear you… you lying about this girl."

"Of course you don't. Because she's already given you just a whiff of that honeypot hasn't she?"

"Don't talk about her like that!" he ejaculates, nearly punching the wall.

"Well, John, I can see we didn't reach you in time." I consider offering him my card; we've encountered some marks in the past who were willing to pay the big bucks, just to be free of the merciless succubae invading their lives. And it's not as if John here needs to know what Alex's family is already paying us. "And I'm sorry about that, I am. But right now I need to know what happened to Brad. He hasn't come by here, didn't try to call you?"

Come to think of it, almost always, it was the *female* marks who were the ones with enough sense to get free of these beasts, so technically I'm speaking of *incubi*, not succubae. Brad's always so adamant I get the nomenclature right.

I look in John's eyes and instantly realize that, whatever womanly charms we employ, even from the afterlife, they're damned stronger than the squishy chill I felt for the soccer player next door as a kid.

"Only call I've gotten was from my boss, wanting to know when I'm coming back to work," John tells me, standing. "I haven't heard from your husband. All right?"

I follow John to the door, dreading where the next step in this search will take me. "Fine. But he's my ex-husband for what it's worth."

"Not what you said earlier, but whatever," he says icily, making sure I'm out of his apartment.

"No, John. I'm positive I said *ex*-husband, okay?"

The door slams. I decide to leave my card in the door's crevice anyway. What the hell.

CHAPTER THIRTEEN

INTERLUDE II

Nancy doesn't know about Cara.

Doesn't know about the conversations you have with her in the living room after she goes to bed at the too-sensible hour of 9pm. Doesn't realize you've told Cara things you've never revealed to Nancy in the past twenty-two years.

Nancy doesn't know what it's like to brush your fingers against Cara's shoulders, even if the contact is fleeting. She doesn't know that you dream about Cara, that the few occasions you still make love to Nancy, she's acting as Cara's stand-in.

The abject boredom and anguish induced by Nancy's family gatherings: she should know about that by now. You used to make this known, back in the days when you still cared enough to argue. But it's never stopped her from dragging you to these things, has it?

Nancy doesn't know that Cara is making an appearance now, here in the guest bathroom of her aunt's house. Doesn't know Cara is delivering a message to you, even as your pants are wrapped around your ankles. A cryptic message, but one of great importance.

Why are you still wiping? You have to leave this place, *now*.

Get in the Hummer, fight that traffic, and drive like a madman to where Cara is guiding you. The intersection of Golden Avenue and Pierce Street, its image emblazoned in your mind.

Nancy's calling. Turn the phone off.

You're going to be approaching a red light. Cara tells you to ignore it.

For an ephemeral moment, you question your new love. You catch yourself, thankfully. Castigate yourself for the doubt. Beg Cara's forgiveness.

She grants it to you, as you T-Bone an innocent Ford Fiesta, then keep on plowing into the opposing lane of traffic.

CHAPTER FOURTEEN

Bradley Burns

"I see someone was able to talk me out of my pants. Wish I could remember everything that happened after that."

I'm lying in a bed that looks like something out of the Niagara Falls honeymoon suite. There's a scent in the air, spicy yet sweet, undeniably feminine. My last memories are fuzzy at best, but I seem to recall something about the backseat of a stranger's car.

"Don't flatter yourself," Alex says. I wasn't expecting to see her, or this much of her, when I awoke. A diaphanous gown, the color of a pink rose, her hair now flowing freely in thick, long curls. The image that greeted me upon arousal was this cherubic face, lording over my body. "Your clothes were nothing but tatters when you arrived; we had to remove them."

"And here I thought you were trying to deflate my ego," I groan while moving to the side of the bed.

"We removed them when cleaning your wounds, that was my meaning. Notice your shoulders aren't covered in boils and blisters anymore?"

I look down, confirm she's telling the truth. "Ah. So I suppose you guys have some magic elixirs or whatnot to alleviate the wicked work of… *Her*, do you?"

"You probably don't want to be speaking so flippantly." Alex offers a hand as I navigate my way out of bed. "She's the one who told us to clean you up. It's not as if anyone here has any love for you."

"And why would you say such a thing? Just who are your friends?" I have a look around and question if I've landed in the bedroom of Vlad the Impaler's teenage daughter. "And where's 'here' anyway?"

"You're the one with the fabled connection to the afterlife, aren't you?" she smirks while handing me a robe. "Don't you already know?"

"All I know is that when I was twelve-years-old, every time I was down in the basement, trading baseball cards or sneaking glimpses of Russell Conner's stolen copy of *Oui*, I heard a voice. And no one else could hear this voice, only me." Alex gives an *'uh-huh'* bob, gesturing me out of the bedroom as I continue. "When I was alone, not only would the voice be louder, but visions would accompany it. Visions of a woman—a real beauty—I'd never met, but who sure wanted to get to know me."

"And how long did it take you to realize she was a departed soul?"

"A few weeks. Hey, I was a kid; what did I know? Her name was Dolley. At first our encounters were just… fun. But maybe not the kinda fun a kid should be enjoying."

Leaving the bedroom, I'm speechless as we enter an expansive hallway, that spicy-sweet smell now cloying, our feet treading a regal red carpet. I sense I'm inside a castle, one that doesn't exist in the physical world but feels real enough at this moment.

There's no hint of the strange in-between, of an endless void, here. This place is as solid as any structure I've ever entered, with its ram's head torch-bearing wall mounts, ancient stone wall mural, and ostentatious floral displays adding a pop of color to the landscape. And the art on the walls… kinky.

If Skeletor ever captured Castle Grayskull and reopened it as a high-end brothel, this would surely be his design inspiration.

"Anyway," I respond, after Alex nudges me in the side, "things between Dolley and me started to get… complicated. And Mom was questioning why I so rarely left my bedroom. One day, Dolley pushed it a little too far. And Li'l Brad didn't know how to react. Things got… messy."

"And you made it your mission in life to harass people on the other side from that moment on?" she asks, in a playful tone I know is reserved for her marks, yet remains charming in some sick way.

"Oh, child, I was a wayward youth. One who viewed these abilities as a novelty at times, a curse at others. But one day, after sweating my balls off in the middle of a heat wave, mixing up the details of the 2002 Mercury Cougar with the 2003 Lincoln Town Car, and getting my ass chewed out by my manager, I made a decision to stop screwing around and take full advantage of my gifts."

"And make a few dollars off the families of the dearly departed."

We continue down the winding path. In the distance, I see the hallway opening to reveal another room. "That doesn't make me a villain; I think you people, or ex-people, are clearly the bad guys here. You think I don't know what happens to the marks you target?"

"You don't understand half of what you think you do, Brad, but that's irrelevant. Now, She wants you to watch this." Alex gestures towards a steel cauldron, the centerpiece of this hellish room. The base of the cauldron is engraved with numerous nude forms: all ladies, all engaged in acts of ribaldry that would turn Larry Flynt a shade of crimson. I'm encouraged to look into the water, look past the choking smoke.

"What exactly does the missus think I need to see? You demons get the premium package here?"

"You need to be quiet, and look into the scrying pool. Do you understand?"

I humor the girl, and see in the water an overhead view of a reasonably-priced hatchback approaching the intersection of Golden Avenue and Pierce Street. And simultaneously, somehow, I'm also given a vision of my nearly-lifeless form writhing in agony in the backseat. And a view of the anxious Trina, her head on a swivel, trying to keep an eye on this pitiful, damaged body behind her and the road all at once.

I'm worried she might have an accident, but the girl's sharp enough to apply the brakes and respect that soon-to-expire yellow light. The car immobile, only a foot or so past the white line, she turns back to me and nervously asks if I'm still awake, if there's a number she can call when we reach the hospital. I garble out nonsense in response.

The light changes. We move on.

No, we try to. A quarter-second after passing that white line, our hatchback is viciously t-boned by a Hummer SUV, a holdover from the *Ah-nold* era, perhaps driven by our illustrious former governor himself. The mystical camera isn't offering an alternate view of the offending driver, although it's generous in providing multiple angles of my personal misery.

The intersection is showered with metal and safety glass as our car does a somersault; the inattentive Hummer is plowing on through, colliding with another unfortunate automobile in the opposing lane of traffic.

I'm thrown from the backseat, landing on the asphalt... skidding, actually, for a few yards until I finally, officially 'land'. My personal blood smear can be traced directly to the point of impact. I'm the lucky one.

The victim of a direct collision, Trina's internal organs likely didn't survive the initial impact. Her subsequent ejection from the vehicle, via the passenger side window, was even more likely a fatal injury.

"This is garbage," I tell Alex, when I'm finally able to speak again. "I... I'm not going to believe this."

"You know what you saw, Brad."

I turn away from the cauldron and wag my finger at her. "I know that you spirits live by deceit. You lie worse than politicians, and I can't trust one damn thing you tell me."

She brushes my accusatory finger away, in a manner both gentle and authoritative. "You need to look at the water, Brad, and open your heart to the truth. The scrying pool cannot deceive. Trina is dead and, even though you think I'm some kind of monster, you don't understand how much her loss pains me. But I recognize that death is only the first step, and—"

"Is she here? Did Trina end up in this awful place?"

"Do you sense her here, Brad? You, of all people, realize that only a handful of souls get lost on their way home, correct?"

"So, you're saying you're happy for your friend?" Trina. My God, she didn't deserve that. I pray that was a lie. I pray this is all a dream.

Alex hugs herself, takes a moment before answering. "I regret that she can't serve our mistress... But I'm content, knowing she's now at peace. And you, Brad; do you recognize how precarious your situation is?" she asks, now placing her hands on my arms.

"Would you stop talking like that?" I reject the embrace, turn away from her. "I researched your whole life, kid. I know you're not some Victorian-era countess, you're just some farm girl who moved to the big city without ever watching one of those movies about what happens to sheltered, small town kids who come out here."

"Brad, this is no joking matter." Alex's hands are on my shoulder, guiding me back to the cauldron. "Would you like to see where your mortal form rests at this moment?"

Against my better judgment, I take another look inside the water. What I see is an image of myself, eyes closed, lying in a hospital bed, seemingly none the worse for wear. Yet, the doctors surrounding me are scribbling notes and exchanging bewildered looks.

"Don't you realize what's happened? You nearly passed into the light on that asphalt, but She saw fit to pluck you away before you could begin the journey. Our elixirs have healed your physical form, but so long as your soul rests here, She will be able to keep you out of the corporeal realm." Alex says the next sentence with barely repressed glee. "Whatever nuisance you've been in the past, those days are done."

"And you brought me here to gloat about it?"

"She wanted you to see this. Wanted you to realize that you have no bargaining position... And yet, She is merciful."

At this moment, I feel a presence—a dark, ominous one—enter. I turn to face Her. Tall, and naked, as ever.

"Alexandria, I think that will be enough," the mystery woman says in a motherly, yet cold, tone. "I do believe you have some business on the other side to take care of, yes?"

Alex bows. "You're right, madam. I'll see to it."

The young spirit offers her goodbyes. I can't help but to be reminded of how sheer that gown is, a fact I'm sure Alex is well aware of as she intentionally brushes past me.

And now we're alone. Just me and the mysterious 'She', or 'Her', depending on the proper pronoun usage.

"Hullo, Bradley. We meet again," the ghoul says with an indifferent grin. "I notice that your burns have healed nicely. Is my benevolence not worthy of thanks?" She's tussling my hair now.

"I'll send you a card later. You like Garfield?"

No, okay. I don't say that. I *think* it, because to be honest, I can't say a thing. This is the beast that casually turned the upper portion of my body into a landscape of boiling, festering wounds and, at this moment, my brain has refused to transmit any sardonic remarks to my lips.

"I was hoping, Bradley, that we could have a civilized conversation. Even though I happen to have the better of you at this moment," she says, lightly stroking my trembling face, "I hoped you'd recognize I'm not motivated by spite. I wanted the two of us to talk. Talk, like civilized human beings."

"Human? That only describes one of us, lady." Again, I'm thinking this. Too terrified to breathe right now.

She places her palms against my chin, forcing my head up and down. "Yes? So, Bradley tell me... Where do you think our interests align?"

"I-I'm sorry?" I eventually whisper.

"What I'm asking is... don't you believe the two of us could find some tiny patch of common ground? Some way to move past all of this acrimony and live in peace?" Fingers squeeze my cheeks; nails are burrowing into my flesh, deep enough to make a point, not deep enough to break the skin.

"What I'm asking, boy, is if you would be opposed to striking a bargain?"

CHAPTER FIFTEEN

John Horton

The woman didn't realize what she was doing. Was that supposed to dissuade me—teasing me with the details of utterly mind-blowing spirit intercourse? Silly lady; any sensation good enough to upend your life has got to be worth at least a taste.

Needlessly glib? Maybe. I am curious about touching more than hands with Alex, but there's more to it than that. Whatever monster this woman thinks Alex is, I know from firsthand experience she's wrong.

Not my girl. Maybe there are dark spirits out there, teasing the lonely and withering their souls away with their sensual charms, but no way does that sound like Alex. At worst, the girl has a temper, and that's only when provoked. And that display from yesterday morning, as outright freaky as it was, was most certainly provoked.

Alex doesn't have the capacity to harm anyone or anything. No one with a smile that sweet, a presence so warm, could do the things Sandra described. But, if only a portion of what she said was true, if it's possible for Alex and me to truly join together…

A few months back, I was introduced to the best thing in my life. And now I learn the kindest girl I've ever known can also give me lovin' so good it'll practically melt my face off?

Yes. I want that.

So, I spent most of the day searching online, learning how to take this relationship to the next level. Turns out, spectrophilia is no joke. Yeah, some born-agains have pages warning of these sinful, fornicating spirits, but most of the information available is first-hand details on how to attract a spirit's love.

Specific instructions: a clean bedroom, breathing exercises, candles and romantic music to set the mood—but no burning of sage, as this frightens them for some reason—chanting, repeated visualizations of your ghostly love, and finally, an hour of quiet meditation before calling out to the spirit.

With diligence, I've followed every step like the former Boy Scout that I am. Now I'm lying in bed, questioning if my selection of Marvin Gaye was perhaps too hackneyed, simply waiting for that touch. Minutes, perhaps hours, pass.

Then I feel a brush against my chest.

Now hands on my shoulders. Fingers through my hair. Little pecks against my neck. Lips so soft, I know they just have to be…

I open my eyes, and she's there. Smiling, revealing dimples I've never noticed before.

It's a vision. It's everything I've ever wanted, but thought I could never have. It's the answer to every longing of this solitary soul: not only the prospect of transcendent carnal pleasure, but the emotional connection to a heart so genuine, so pure, that I find myself unable to express my gratitude.

Yet, for some reason, I'm hearing the high-pitched, strangulated vocals of Jack White.

Danger! Danger! High voltage!

"Is something wrong, dear?" she asks. "Why are you moving away? Isn't this what you wanted?"

When we touch, when we kiss!

I brush her hair over her left ear and place my hand against her soft face. "I'm, uh, sorry. Just wasn't even sure if this could work. That we could be…"

"Lovers? Intimate? It's okay, Johnny," she tells me, drawing a shape with her finger on my chest. "We can be anything you want us to be. Don't be shy. You called me here for a reason, didn't you? I came as fast as I could…"

Danger! Danger! High voltage!

"No, honey, that's great. I just mean… Well, I've been reading about relationships like ours. Just taking things in. And I'm starting to wonder if maybe this, that maybe it…"

"That it's unnatural? Dangerous?"

"Something like that, I guess."

"Tell me, how have all of the natural, *safe* relationships in your past worked out? Would a little danger really be so bad, Johnny?" she asks, kissing, then biting my lower lip. "Don't you trust your darling Alex to guide you through the experience of a lifetime?"

I tell myself that early 2000s indie rock was vastly overrated, opting instead for The Prince of Soul to remain the soundtrack for this evening. Tomorrow morning, I'll check and see if my face is a puddle next to the bed.

CHAPTER SIXTEEN

Sandra Jones

"Brad? Yeah, we see each other every now and again," says Tiffany, the twenty-four-year-old dental hygienist that my ex first listed as a contact three years ago, according to his phone. "It's been a few weeks since I've heard from him, though. Who did you say you were again?"

I'm the person he once pledged to do all that love, trust, and honor stuff with, until I chose to stop ignoring his tendency to chase every wayward piece of strange in the tri-county area.

"I'm Sandra Jones, and I'm Brad's partner. He didn't come home last night, and I'm trying to locate him." And I didn't spend fifteen minutes guessing my way past his phone's lock screen just to stalk the guy, either. I'm simply following whatever leads I have, holding on to the hope that this disappearing act is merely bim-related.

"Partner?" she asks, still removing rollers from her butterscotch blonde hair. "Oh, you're his assistant who helps him with that ghost hunter stuff?"

"No, I'm his *partner*. And if you happen to hear from Brad, or can think of anywhere he might be, please let me know." I hand Tiffany my card. I hope she'll notice it does not read 'assistant'.

"Okay, sure." I'm a millisecond away from leaving, but the way she's examining that card leads me to believe she isn't quite ready to return to her morning routine. "Now, forgive me if this is too forward, but by 'partner'… Are you talking business or, like, married but, y'know, not willing to make it official?"

With a plastic grin, I reply, "Actually, we've been divorced for a little while. Still work together, though. Anyway, any help's appreciated." I really am turning to leave this time, although I have a hunch another question is coming. A part of me would hate Tiffany for *not* asking. The other…

"Okay, so one last question," she says, flicking the card with her candy-apple red nails. "If you don't mind me asking… Um, how long ago did you guys split up?"

Watching her deflate is, I confess, more satisfying than I thought. "It was just over a year ago, Tiffany." As the bim reworks the math in her head, I wave my goodbye. "Well, nice to meet you."

To her credit, she did want to know. And, yeah, she should know. She deserves to. I shouldn't blame *her*, and I try not to, but forgive me if I'm in something of a snitty mood, considering what I've been through the past two days. It's not as if I wanted to hack his phone—I've *never* been a snoop—but considering that his one male friend has been traveling Europe for three weeks, and Brad has no family in town, I had to start somewhere.

Discovering evidence of around eight affairs I was previously unaware of shouldn't have been a shock. And I've tried to keep any irrational jealousy in check, tried to remind myself that none of this should wound me today, since it's why we split in the first place. But having to track down and *talk* to these horrid women, having to give a polite smile while explaining to them who I am, all in the hopes that *maybe* one of them has seen him since yesterday, in who knows what kind of precarious-and-sticky situation… That's a hard one to forgive.

Not that I plan on doing it. I'll do what I can to find the lunk, and of course I'll call the police if it comes to that, but I'm not going to buy any of his pathetic excuses this time. If he thinks I've been acting 'cold' towards him lately, wait until I tell him that it's time for him to move out.

And that, after we've collected enough money to get out from under this IRS nonsense, it'd be a good idea to end the partnership once and for all. Go see if Tiffany is willing to depart the exciting world of fluoride and tartar scrapers for a chance to chase wayward spirits. I'm sure she'll be thrilled.

I'll keep mentally cursing him out, keep scrolling through the addresses of these cocktail waitresses and beauty school dropouts, keep repeating that it's just Brad acting out again. Acting out worse than ever, unfortunately. I won't think about yesterday morning, about what those beings can do. I won't tell myself that maybe he's gotten in over his head this time.

I'll keep thinking of Brad the Horndog, Brad the Louse, Brad the Crappy Partner, and try to stay appropriately pissed yet unconcerned and certainly *not* a nervous wreck.

CHAPTER SEVENTEEN

Bradley Burns

What could you possibly have to offer me, you depraved ghoul?

That fiery interrogative is translated by my mouth as "Wuh—What?"

She squeezes my cheeks again, but this time it feels more like a grandma pinch. "I'll speak in as plain a manner as possible," she tells me, her pointer finger in the air, "avoiding any of the colloquial vulgarities that might be associated with the subject matter. This is polite company, of course."

Talk normal, ya crazy demon broad.

This comes out as "Uh-huh."

"You have made a nuisance of yourself for several cycles now, Bradley. I grow weary of your interference," She says, her hands now moving down my chest. "At the moment, I clearly have you at a disadvantage." Her palms press against my nipples. "Yet, I am not a malicious queen. I understand the value in respecting a foe. What I seek, Bradley, is equipoise."

And what I seek is that word-a-day calendar you're hiding somewhere on your very nude person.

"Y-you… want…?"

"What I want, Bradley, is for you to *behave*." She lifts me to face her eye-to-eye. "And I believe I've discovered a way to accomplish that, one that could please us both. Tell me, boy, is your reputation as a lady's man undeserved?"

I don't know. Call your mama and find out.

"M-maybe…?"

My feet quietly return to the marble floor. I look to my left, then my right, and discover a harem of her followers, all dressed in the sheer gown sported by Alex earlier, have entered the room. "And do you suppose, Bradley, a life here in my home, surrounded by my loving daughters… Could this arrangement possibly bring peace to both sides of our conflict?"

Did… Did you just offer me unlimited blammin' for all eternity?

"P-pretty…"

An evil, condescending grin. "Yes, they are all beautiful, aren't they?" Her pointer's back in the air. "Or would you rather return to your flesh and live out how many of your mortal years remain… With the understanding you're never to interfere with my work again?

"Don't answer at this moment; I realize you've been through so much. Ladies, why don't you escort our friend Bradley to his quarters?"

She gestures to her followers, who form around me, all wearing expressions like Pam during her heyday of *Playboy* covers. No one physically lays a hand on me, yet I'm clearly being herded in the direction of that bedroom.

Still overwhelmed by this cavalcade of absurdity and questioning just what this evil She has offered, I say nothing as we travel the hallway. One of the ladies—the one with the wet, dark red hair that's brushed over her left eye—places her hand on my cheek.

"Missus didn't do you any harm, did she?" asks the ghoul-in-training. "I could make it better. We *all* could, Bradley."

The pale blonde who's been keeping to my right reaches behind me. "You've never known 'girls' like us before, I'd wager."

I'm tempted to swat her hand away, but then I remember the unholy form Alex took a few hours—days?—ago, that moment I got on her last nerve. I suppose there are worse things than an unwanted goosing, but goodness, I feel like such a piece of meat right now…

I stammer out a rejection. Even when I was fifteen and treating the hall bathroom like a Florida timeshare, I wouldn't have taken bait this obvious.

"More fool, you," says Blondie, removing herself from my earlobe. She snorts, turns to her friends. "To think, sisters, he views us as common harlots. Tell me, Bradley, could a plain female from your realm offer… *this*?"

'*This*' is her tongue down my throat, her soft, perfect hands cradling my face, and her firm legs wrapped against mine in quite the provocative fashion. When she pulls her body away, perhaps a full minute later, I have to confess a part of me doesn't want her to let go. God help me, I'm not even grossed out by that string of spit that's still connecting our faces.

"That… I didn't ask you to do that," I tell her, wiping my mouth.

One of her friends, the apple-cheeked Asian girl who's taller than I am, plays with my hair. "Bradley, what you just tasted is only the smallest of morsels. Pleasure on a much grander scale, pleasure greater than several lifetimes, is yours… You have but to ask."

I break away from the crowd, point towards the bedroom I've been assigned. "I'll, uh, keep that in mind. But, hey, we're back at my room, and I'd hate to keep you ladies from seducing whatever poor mope you have on the schedule to torment tonight." I grab at the door. We can talk about unholy sexual blackmail in the morning.

Flopping on to the bed, I exhale, catch my breath. Try to erase the thought of Blondie's tongue massage.

Did She really think this would work? Like I'm so utterly enchanted by the thought of sexual conquest I'd let myself be played like one of their marks?

Hey, I enjoy the actual act as much as anyone, but She's confused the same way Sandy always was. I'm not acting out of malice towards women, I slip up *because* I like them so much. Not just the physical pleasure they offer, but their presence, the indescribable energy that surrounds them. It's so tender, so gentle… So completely different from men and our dimwitted, Cro-Magnon ways of interacting with each other.

Yeah, there's a sense that a little is never enough. A voice that screams, *'Looking, flirting: pal, you need more than that.'* Of course their allure makes me act a fool; that's what it's done to men since the beginning of time.

Oh, geez. I tried explaining this to Sandy once. She just sneered, "So I should be *flattered* on behalf of us ladies that you can't keep it in your pants?" I guess she wouldn't get it.

Anyway. Not relevant now.

What I *do* know is that their psycho head priestess is desperate to get rid of me. And, for some reason, She hasn't decided to light my body in unholy blaze again. I appreciate the thought, but her motives remain obscure.

Does this have anything to do with the vision of the hospital I was shown? Am I in some unique in-between stasis… assuming I can even trust anything I saw in that pool? But if I'm not in a coma, how did I cross into this world? Elements of it remind me of that void I entered through an astral form, yet it's so much more… *real.*

And who is their den mother anyway? I've heard the succubae reference a 'She' or 'Her' over the years but had largely dismissed it as a scare tactic.

If they are serving this beast, if they're not wholly responsible for their actions, what's her motivation for any of this? What does She get out of watching these harlots drive men into unknowable misery?

And where do the incubi fit into this? I'm guessing they have their own eleven-foot representation of masculinity compelling them to seduce the cat ladies on Earth, all for similarly arcane reasons.

Yup. Tall naked dude, commanding his army of necromantic

Chippendale dancers. Oh, man, what if I'd been kidnapped by their dude leader? What would he offer to entice me to stay out of his hair: an endless supply of Buffalo Wild Wings and daily Super Bowls? Okay, I am far off-topic.

Sleep doesn't clear my mind. She… She… She… Inhumanly tall, major player in the afterlife, surrounded by female slaves, derives unusual pleasure from human torment. What else? Has a look in her eye like I'm less than a dust mite to her, yet still gets a kick out of watching me squirm.

Why am I suddenly reminded of my college girlfriend? There's a shame: used to be a sweet girl, until she got 'zapped'. Was never the same after she brought home all of those pamphlets from that women's music festival. The one with the henna tattoos, guerrilla haircuts, and menstrual painting courses… Damn, she got so mad when I accidentally shrank her Indigo Girls t-shirt.

Oh, my sweet Lord. I remember what they called that tour now. No, that can't be. And yet, it fits, doesn't it? Admittedly, I don't know the Apocrypha from, well, the Bible itself, but I still remember some of that empowering language from those leaflets she left by the bed.

Adam's first wife, her name banned from history… refused to be subservient to her husband… cuckolded him with an angel… later dismissed as—if I'm remembering the term right—a 'night hag' by the writers of the Old Testament.

Lilith.

I'm still piecing together the significance—and I'll confess, patting myself on the back for being just that clever—when I hear a knock at the door. I tell myself I have no reason to answer, given the circumstances.

My resolve weakens when I hear the fragile voice on the other side.

"Hey, Brad? You're in there, right? They didn't hurt you, did they? I, uh, this is kind of embarrassing, but I really need someone to talk to. I can totally understand if you want me to go away, but I was hoping you could, maybe, give me a minute?"

It's Alex. And before I realize what I'm doing, the door is open, her pristine face greeting me with a shy smile.

CHAPTER EIGHTEEN

John Horton

"You realize you're four hours late, pal?" Peterson barks as I take my seat in his office. The top of his bald head has sunburned since I saw him last. Ordinarily, I'd be envious of whatever outdoor activity he'd been engaged with—most likely tennis with that exec he absolutely is *not* nailing—but that was before my face was metaphorically melted off yesterday. "After telling us you'd make it in today, you think it's okay to waltz in here *four hours* late?"

"Sorry. My place is, ah, still a mess and I'm not through dealing with the water issue."

My voice cracks as I give the answer. As loathsome as Peterson is, most of this disgust is directed inward. Not for being late— that happens, I guess—but for ever allowing this human slime to intimidate me.

After taking a moment to digest my response, he suddenly explodes with "Why wouldn't you answer the phone? I've been calling you all morning; you have no idea the crap that's been dumped on us today."

I didn't answer the phone because I was recovering from the most magnificent experience of my life, you human bulldog. People are allowed to sleep in the next day after something like that, right? Realizing he actually wants an answer to his asinine question, I provide a predictably lame one.

"My phone, uh, wasn't charged. What 'crap' exactly did you mean, sir?"

Sausage fingers curl into a fist. "The birth scenes in the past three episodes; there's a new head at Standards, and he refuses to air *any* of them. Claims they show too much… well, everything. And guess who has a marathon of all-new episodes debuting next week?"

I answer reflexively. "Okay. You are the one who directed the cameramen to 'really get in there'." I notice my voice doesn't crack.

"And you're the one who edits these masterpieces, Horton," he says, ignoring my tiny act of defiance. "Get back in your bay and make sure we see about seventy percent less hoo-hah." I stand, dreading whatever hour I'll be leaving here tonight. As I reach the door, I hear his voice behind me. "And don't even think about coming in late like that again. Just so you know, I'm writing you up. HR will have the forms this afternoon."

Never been written up at work before. Can't imagine I've ever been late, either. By the time I'm in the edit bay, I realize how much I don't care. I load up the first episode for re-editing and consult the censor notes on what needs to be changed. In a word: 'everything'. I take a sip of my coffee, crack my knuckles, and get to work.

*

I assume I got to work. I'm looking up at the screen, and down at my empty coffee, and I'm going to guess something got done before I fell asleep. Who am I kidding? My mind's not on this stuff today; it's on my girl. And, yeah, she wore this stud out yesterday.

I decide another shot of caffeine will help, so I beat a path to the commissary. While standing in line, I catch myself nearly falling over. Did I eat last night? Or this morning? Wow, I can't honestly remember. Have to remedy this with a *Big Texas* cinnamon roll or two. And of course that tall cuppa. Way to leave a man drained,

Alex, you little minx…

Headed back with my nourishment, I'm cut off at the commissary's exit by a lanky female with medium length, corkscrew hair. Looks like she's going for dark brown with red highlights: cute, maybe she did that as a fiftieth birthday present for herself? Sorry, but it can't compete with the way Alex's thick auburn locks cascade down her shoulders.

"You John Horton?" she asks.

Nodding, I notice the lady is dressed for business, but not quite the type of business we do here at the studio. Her suit looks off-the-rack from Macy's, not exactly the *haute couture* I'd expect from one of our execs.

Stoic, she produces a badge and introduces herself. "I'm Detective Amash. Do you have time to talk, Mr. Horton?"

I motion towards the nearby *EXIT* door, the one normally used by smokers during their hourly breaks. None happen to be here at the moment, yet the musky scent of their vice still lingers around the patio area. If I weren't half-asleep, my mind would likely be running a million miles a second. What does she want? Am I in trouble? Did Mom finally kill Dad for hiding his toenail clippings in the bottom sock drawer? That kind of thing.

At the moment, I have only two thoughts: Alex, and sleep. And now I'm thinking of a third option, falling asleep with delicate Alex in my arms. The stern expression on Detective Amash's face, directing me to have a seat on the patio table, wakes me up a bit.

"Mr. Horton, I don't plan on keeping you long, but we need to talk."

My head bobs again. Her face goes even tighter, I guess irritated by my lack of perspicacity.

"Sir, are you familiar with a Sandra Jones?" she asks, lording over. Is that why she wanted me to have a seat? Like she isn't tall enough already? Ah, is she trying to intimidate me? And what was the question she asked? Why is she asking me about this lady?

"Uh… No."

"That's funny, because she seems to know *you*. Her ex-husband has gone missing, and she gave us your name as someone who might be able to help locate him."

What on earth is this woman… Oh. "Ah, okay. Sandra Jones. Sure. I just met her a day or two ago, that's why I didn't catch the name." The truth, but I wonder if Detective Amash will believe it. "She was asking me about this Brad person. I feel bad for the lady, but don't know why she'd think I could help her out."

Amash folds her arms. "According to what she told us, you might've crossed his path during one of his private investigations. Any truth to that?"

Did Sandra Jones also tell you that her ex-husband investigates *ghosts*, not adulterous real estate agents? That he has some weird vendetta and thinks he can make a quick buck off the poor spirits? "Nope."

"You wouldn't have any motive to lie about something like this, would you, John? You've had no contact with a Bradley Burns?"

"Nope."

Amash stares me down for maybe a second or two, and admittedly, were I not in severe need of a caffeine injection, I'd likely be unsettled by her experienced glare. Presently, my mind is already drifting back to those earlier two thoughts.

"Fine, Mr. Horton. But if you hear from Mr. Burns, or if something jogs your memory, please call us, all right?" she says, handing me her card. The detective tries to leave through the *EXIT* door, not realizing there's a press-key lock attached. Gentleman that I am, I get up and type in the code for her. She nods her thanks, I nod goodbye, then return to the patio table.

The sheer absurdity of the exchange dawns on me as I open my coffee and take a sip. This Sandra Jones… What was she thinking? Why was my name in that woman's mouth? I've never even met her ex-husband… You'd think the woman could find some better clue to chase.

After a few more sips, I open my wallet and search for a place to house Detective Amash's card. Have to remove some of the other useless cards I've accumulated lately to make room. And guess which one is selected?

Sandra Jones - Manager, Burns Paranormal Investigations

84

CHAPTER NINETEEN

Bradley Burns

She enters with a panting desperation that could melt any skeptic's heart. "Brad, thank you… Thankyouthankyouthankyou *so much* for answering the door," she tells me, no longer in her peekaboo gown but dressed instead like any girl you'd see standing outside a trendy boutique on Ventura.

"I realize I don't have any right to—" She places her nervous hands on my shoulder, looks up at me with puffy eyes. Considering the prior events of the evening, I have a visceral desire to pull away, yet I remain still. The rest of the harem oozed sin and chicanery but, at this moment, the girl seems as threatening as a butterfly.

"It's okay, Alex. I couldn't get any sleep anyway," I say as she catches herself and removes her hands. "'Talk' sounds like a safer proposition at the moment than the other four-letter word your sisters were offering."

"I… I don't even really understand what the plan is for you, Brad," she claims, implying with her tone she might tell if she could. I remain skeptical, but notice I haven't kicked her out of my room yet. "Her ways are mysterious. I just needed to talk to someone, and I don't think this is something the others would understand."

"Maybe you could float into one of your mom's dreams and see if she's up for a heart-to-heart," I state as my opening gambit, pouring myself a drink from the antique water pot on the vanity. I offer her a glass, then catch a look on her face. Oh, have I hurt the darling's feelings?

"If I could talk to my mother," she replies, after collecting her thoughts, but still not looking directly at me, "have a real conversation with her, and not just pass through her dreams, I would. You seriously thought I was trying to hurt my own mother?"

I hand her the glass. "No, I was… Fine, I wasn't sure what you were doing. Look, I'm not trying to be insensitive. I'm sorry you can't speak to your mother."

She takes a seat on the edge of my bed. "If I could… You have no idea how much that'd mean to me."

"Do you speak to Her about things?" I gesture towards that room with the magical TV pool.

"Sometimes, but this wouldn't… Brad, all day I've been thinking about Trina. Even though She told me not to, even though she 'cleansed' the grief from me…"

I position myself next to her. Some incredibly stupid impulse longs to put my arm around her shoulder. "Everyone needs time to grieve, Alex. I only knew Trina briefly, but I could tell how close the two of you used to be."

"Oh, like sisters. Such a goodhearted person. She's from here— well, there, not *here*—and she did a lot to help me out when I first moved to the city. Tried to look after me; even though we were getting into the same things, things we should've stayed away from, I could tell how much Trina worried about me."

"Yeah, she seemed like a decent girl." She did. So, is Alex genuinely mourning her friend, or is this just another angle for her mistress to exploit? I certainly can't assume the best about this girl… or 'girl' who exists now as a pawn for the ruthless demigoddess that's determined to remove me as a nuisance.

"And when I heard her voice calling out to me, it's like I just remembered, like a part of me that'd been dead for ages had suddenly been awakened. I mean, parts of my past, they're impossible to erase." She wipes away some snot, starts to get animated with her hands. "My parents, the house I grew up in, that lake behind my grandparents' place where we used to go swimming… but so many years were just lost to me, after She took me in. So hearing Trina's voice, having those memories return." She looks at me, doesn't turn away this time. "Brad, it was like heaven." Are they allowed to use that word here?

Alex abruptly stands, makes a grand gesture towards me. "And then I saw her with *you*, and when I thought about how you were using her… Everything went red after that."

"Just doin' my job, ma'am."

"It's okay," she says, with a small laugh. "I'm glad, in a way, because at least I had one last chance to see her, even if things didn't work out so great."

"One way of putting it."

Her face drops again. "That's not funny."

I raise my hands in defeat. "Okay, retracted. Don't want to hurt any feelings: don't want you flipping out, turning into that hideous she-beast thing again." She gets that I'm testing her, right?

Then again, am *I* really so clever? If I successfully prod and prod and bring that beast out again… Fine, I've proven a point, but what then?

"Brad, I'm sorry, I don't think I can explain that." She retakes her place next to me. Were I willing to drop my skepticism, I might even say her following words carried genuine remorse. "It's like… Everything, my entire life, stopped making sense that day when I collapsed," Alex says, holding herself. "Trina was there, you know. She was so worried for me. She's the one who called 911, and when she thought they weren't coming fast enough, Trina was ready to throw me in her car and take me herself."

"Imagine that."

Alex nods. "She would've, too, but finally, the ambulance came."

Oh, did she seduce it, too? Man, Sandy would laugh her ass off at that stupid joke.

I notice that Alex seems to be drifting off. "Not that they could do any good. I know the official time of death, but the truth is, I remember floating over the bathroom floor twenty minutes before that. I knew it was over. But, then, it turned out not to be."

I take a sip. "Uh-huh. Maybe you should've been a good little girl and gone into the light like most decent people?"

"Brad, unless you go through it…" Alex starts, then stops the sentence. This tiny barb did seem to get to her. She thinks for a moment, then turns to me. Puffy eyes still have a trace of sincerity in them. Using her hands again, she tries to explain her actions, as if my lowly opinion matters a helluva lot to succubae.

"Look, I realize the light is supposed to be comforting," she says, both hands open. "But to me, it was the scariest thought in the world. Me, *dead*? No way. And the more I thought about it, the angrier I got. Yeah, I was up to stuff I shouldn't have been doing, but I'd had ex-boyfriends who could do eightballs all night *every* night, and they never crashed. And purging? That's nothing unusual today; not even that unusual for girls I knew back in the eighth grade.

"But now, me? *I'm* the one who has to pay a price for it, when I knew people into far worse, *way* sicker shit?" She wipes another tear. "I'm not gonna lie, that pissed me off. And just when I was tempted to move away from that light, that's when I heard a voice…"

"*Her* voice."

"She told me I didn't have to accept that fate. That she had a better plan for me. I could be like her daughter, and she would look after us, keep us safe from scary thoughts like dying."

"Did She try to nab Trina, too?"

"She did," Alex affirms, biting her lower lip. "A part of me wanted her to… I wanted to be reunited with my friend, of course. But She told me Trina was gone in a heartbeat. At that moment, I was furious. Trina, my girl, taken from me again?" Alex sighs. "Now, though, I'm relieved."

"Why?"

"Because Trina deserved the light. Even if it does separate us.

She shouldn't have to live this way. Shouldn't have to do what I did a few hours ago."

I'm genuinely curious. "Which was?" Alex gives me a look. Not that demon hag face from earlier, just a normal female reaction to a thoughtless male comment kind of look. "Ah. Okay."

"Anyway, I've probably wasted enough of your time," she tells me, standing again. "I think I just needed to speak to someone who knew her, if only for a little while."

I walk Alex to the door. Again, I have to fight this urge to place my arm around her shoulder. "Don't worry about it. Now, do you think you could do a favor for me?"

"I guess so."

"I'm going to say a name, and I want you to tell me the first thought that comes to mind."

The arbitrary nature of the question seems to cheer her up. If the girl only knew… "Well, fine. Shoot."

"*Lilith*," I say, making sure every short syllable is properly emphasized.

Alex's eyes widen, then point up. "Hmm… Can't say for sure," she says, fingers tapping on the doorframe. "Wasn't she the mom on *The Munsters?*" she eventually responds while closing the door.

Now, discerning how much of Alexandria Abernathy, the person, still exists might be an impossible task. Those stories she just told would make her a Streep-level actress, were they fibs. But that look right there? That tone of voice? On the subject of the 'L' word, there's no ambiguity.

Alex is lying.

CHAPTER TWENTY

Sandra Jones

"Hey, Ms. Jones…? That was, ah, kinda messed up. You giving my name to the cops like that. You need to leave me, and Alex, alone… Okay?"

Meep.

"Hello, we're trying to reach Brad Burns? This is Darlene Abernathy. He told us there'd be an update on our, ah, situation by now, but we haven't heard from him. If he gets this message, please let him know how important it is for him to get back to us. Okay. God bless. Oh, yes, my husband is, well, rather adamant you understand he's not sending that second check until we have some confirmation that… Well, anyway, please get in touch."

Meep.

"Ms. Jones, this is Richard DeVreiss at the Internal Revenue Service. I notice that you didn't respond to our most recent mail correspondence, but it's imperative I speak to you as soon as possible. You must understand that we're talking about a potentially significant penalty, in addition to—"

Meep.

The third '*meep*' was me pressing that red phone icon early. I'm sure Mr. DeVreiss has a fascinating spiel about how thoroughly his agency is prepared to ream us, but the reminder isn't that necessary. I'm well aware of the absurd amount we owe you—*we're working on it*—and yes Mrs. Abernathy, I realize that we're not going to get that second check without your 'closure'.

And as for you, John What's-Your-Name, so sorry I listed you as someone Brad might've had contact with. That's the question the police asked me, and I gave them the most honest answer I could. If it makes you feel better, I also gave them the contact info for the future Armenian trophy wife last seen batting her eyelashes at my ex.

Oh, I guess I should expect a voicemail from her in my future, too. *"I'll have you to know Brad and I are only friends, and you probably shouldn't care so much about what he's up to in the first place, and anyway I saw him leave on a party bus with this class of graduating Moreno High seniors the next morning, after we woke up from an entire night of being 'just friends' together, so I can't help you, girl."*

Anyway, this has been a fun thought exercise as I'm sitting on the curb, watching the nice tattooed man from Southern California Repossession Services attach my specially ordered Chevy Malibu with the heated leather seats to his tow truck. I knew I was behind on payments, but had no clue I'd hit the four-month mark.

Funny that I'd lose track of all of those notices, considering how many I mailed out when I worked for my dad. Guess I'm the worthless deadbeat taking the food off someone else's table now.

Or, I was, until this fine man in the tow truck relieved me of my burden.

It's not the end of the world. I can drive Brad's car until he turns back up again. Which is hopefully soon.

Of course, just knowing he left his car in the garage and his keys on the coffee table, with no explanation, no warning, does nothing to help my anxiety. Brad could be thoughtless, he might even disappear for an evening on a few random nights, but he's never pulled anything like this before.

I go through my phone, seeking info on the aforementioned 'friend' Brad was making the day he disappeared. Girl hasn't answered her phone any time I've called, and no one was home when I visited. I told the police this and the detective just "uh-huh"-ed and scribbled something down. She was more interested in whatever gambling debts Brad had racked up, or whose wife he might've gotten too close to.

I told her he was an innocent babe in terms of dice and cards but, if she really wanted a list of his female acquaintances, I'd have to compile an Excel spreadsheet.

I'm inside the house, enjoying the air conditioning—and praying I remembered to pay the electric bill—when I finally find the bronze-skinned sex kitten's ridiculous surname in my contacts. Trina Haroutunian: there's a name that's going to look great on the movie screens, I'm sure. I call and receive the usual non-answer.

Brad, Brad, Brad… It's not like my life revolves around you, man. I need to take my mind off you and do something productive. Like sit down at the table and work out the rest of these unpaid bills. Bills for the house, and business, I share with you.

That's the plan, at least. Instead, I find the bottle of Moscato that's been hiding in the back of our increasingly barren refrigerator. I have two glasses, listen to a mix of appropriately miserable Elliott Smith tracks, and collapse on the bed.

I could've kicked him out. The house is in my name, thanks to Brad's credit score. But Brad found one excuse after another.

It's the address on our business cards. Can't confuse clients, can we?

Look, it's so hard to find a place out here, especially an affordable one. You looking to make a man homeless?

And, hey, don't you feel safer here in the big city with a man in the house? Not just any man, but a paranormal CrossFit enthusiast?

Yes, I am crying by this point, but Brad shouldn't try to claim exclusive credit for the tears. Damn it, I really liked that car.

An hour later, I'm awakened by the phone. "Hi, Sandra Jones? This is Detective Amash; I've been looking into your ex-husband's disappearance? Do you think it would be possible for you to meet me at Riverside Community Hospital?"

My heart skips. "I… I don't like the sound of that. Can you tell me why?"

"Ma'am, I would rather not discuss this over the phone. Do you think you could meet me here in the next hour?"

*

Forty minutes later, I'm a trembling nervous wreck standing outside a hospital room. Detective Amash is joined by Dr. Pitts, a balding gentleman with a bent nose and excessive ear hair, standing nearly a foot shorter than the detective. He doesn't say much after we're introduced, leaving Amash to go through a few rehearsed lines.

"Ms. Jones, we're not looking to upset you, but we have good reason to believe your husband was admitted here two days ago. We'd like to know if you could identify him."

I blurt out, "Is he dead?" because that's the thought that's driven its claws into my brain for nearly an hour now. Apparently it couldn't wait to escape.

The doctor shakes his head and ushers me into the room. "Not at all. He was admitted with severe injuries, however. At the moment, he's in stable condition. But—"

"Then why don't you ask *him* who he is?" I shoot off, still nervous.

"I'm trying to tell you, Ms. Jones, that this is a unique situation. This man is in a coma..."

The curtain is drawn, I approach the bed, and inches away is the man I married, sleeping peacefully in the same pose he'll one day assume in his funeral casket. And why is my mind going there? Hesitantly, I stroke his cheek. The skin is cold; so cold, I'm tempted to repeat my initial question.

"...yet the injuries he sustained healed rather miraculously within minutes of arriving."

Looking back at the doctor, then the detective, I try to digest the information. "Accident?"

Amash jumps in. "Ms. Jones, is this your husband?" she asks in a tone that's just curt enough. I nod, then repeat my question. "Unfortunately, Ms. Jones, your husband—*ex*-husband, sorry—

was the passenger in a severe accident not too far from here. According to the doctors, they weren't optimistic about his chances when he arrived but, within a few minutes, his body underwent an amazing recovery."

"And yet," Dr. Pitts asserts, "he's remained in this coma. Medically, we can't explain this." The doctor looks back at Brad's body, then again to me, his face exposing his bemusement. "If the wounds from the automotive accident have healed, he should've awakened hours ago. And yet…"

My brain continues to process. I blurt another question, "Who was he in a car with? What happened to her?" And why do I just know it was a *her*?

The detective places her hand on my right shoulder. Like her introduction at the door, I can tell this is a practiced maneuver, probably something she took a three-day seminar to learn. "Ma'am, do you remember the young lady, Trina Haroutunian, you asked us to look into? Well, we ran her name and discovered she was taken to this hospital after a serious accident. She was riding with a man who fit Bradley's description."

I am *almost* tempted to make a sarcastic crack along the lines of, "Surprise! He was with a bim!" Instead, I do the decent thing and ask, "And how is she?"

Detective Amash's hand squeezes my shoulder. "She was… not as fortunate as your ex-husband, Ms. Jones." We exchange a look that confirms the detective's euphemism. An equal mix of shock and guilt confront me, but there's only one clear thought emerging: *That poor girl.*

"And, unfortunately, Ms. Jones, I'm afraid your husband's news might not be much better," the doctor says.

"Why? I thought you said his body was fine? Right now, it's like he's just asleep, isn't he?"

The doctor squints, then shakes his head. "I'm sorry, Ms. Jones, but the difficulties associated with a comatose state can't be ignored. I realize television has created the impression that someone in a coma is merely asleep, but the truth is, a comatose patient rarely lasts more than two to four weeks. We've already seen some deterioration in brain activity, I'm sad to tell you."

And as I'm replaying these words, looking for some loophole in Dr. Pitts' diagnosis, some way for those syllables not to mean what I think they mean, the doctor breathes in and drops the next bomb.

"And, sadly, the longer he's in this state, assuming he ever awakes, there's a possibility of him facing permanent brain damage. Unfortunately, ma'am, there's a real chance that the Brad you knew is gone forever."

CHAPTER TWENTY-ONE

Bradley Burns

I awaken with a plan.

Actually, I'm awakened by the sensation of knuckles nudging into my back. I turn and confirm my living / unliving alarm clock is indeed Alex, who apparently doesn't need permission to enter my room after all.

But, still, I do have a plan. And I'm not entertaining any moral quandaries about executing it.

It's not a bad sensation. The knuckles. Girl has a way with her hands.

"It's getting late. She has asked me to wake you," Alex says. I notice she's back in her gown. "You can join us for a late breakfast, if you like."

"You guys eat meals like we do? Any decent breakfast cereals here in the not-quite-afterlife?" I yawn, rub away more eye snot. "It's not all *Boo Berry*, is it?"

Alex, no prompting, draws back my sheets. "She wishes for us to have a comfortable, familiar existence, when possible. She is a loving mistress."

I scoot my butt to the edge of the bed. "I guess that's something I'll find out, during this eternity I'll spend here as a piece of communal man-meat. Assuming I give your mistress the answer she wants, I guess."

Alex continues to strip the bed, as if I haven't left it yet. "I can't tell you what to do, Brad. The choice has to be yours."

Taking the hint and making a final scoot out of bed, I try to coax a better answer out of the girl. "You could at least offer me some guidance on the subject. If I reject your mistress, will this end with her boiling my body alive, only this time for all eternity?"

"Her ways are not for us to judge…"

"And why are you talking like Emily Brontë again?" Alex, folding the bed sheet, doesn't answer so I invade her personal space, grab her arms, force her into eye contact. "C'mon, Alex, this is *me* you're speaking to."

A moment passes. "What should that mean to me? You've been a pest, trailing me for weeks," she says, abandoning the stony indifference. "How do you know I wouldn't be happy to finally be rid of you?"

Bradley Burns, you just hit the jackpot.

"Because I know that wasn't the true Alex I saw in those flashes of anger. I have a sense of the real you, the person that Trina told me about. The person who came to my room last night, in tears…" Alex turns away, embarrassed; I'll have none of it. "*Listen*: in tears because she hates what this horrible woman is forcing her to do."

Should've realized this sooner; but, hey, near-death is somewhat distracting. I'm still the paranormal desperado, aren't I?

Still able to herd these body-less souls in the right direction. Still in possession of a silver tongue those of the spectral persuasion cannot resist.

"I shouldn't have told you those things," she says, facing the opposite direction, returning her attention to that sheet. "It was a moment of weakness."

Alex has to drop the Renaissance Fair lilt when it's the two of us because—hey, like I said—it's *me* she's speaking to.

"It was a moment of *truth*, girl, and we both know that." See, not just any near-dead schmuck could've elicited such a response out of the girl.

Something human remains in Alex. And my only shot at the

moment resides in drawing it out.

"And if you know more than you're letting on, Alex, which you *do*, then I can't let you stay quiet. This is my life we're talking about, and forgive me if I don't want that literal demon you serve to have the upper hand in our negotiation."

Alex finishes folding the sheet and tosses it on to the bed. With an expression of arrogant annoyance—or annoyed arrogance—she examines me for a second. "*Fine*. If you want to know more about our home, I'll just have to give you a special tour."

Taking me by the hand, Alex opens the door and looks both ways down our baroque hallway. Like a kid leading her younger sister through the house early Christmas morning, discreetly checking on the presents under the tree, Alex puts on a show. I'm nearly convinced she shouldn't be taking me through these various passageways: the way she's looking over her shoulder and cautiously approaching each intersection.

Eventually, after taking a tour of one needlessly-ornate passage after the next, we arrive at a flight of stairs, pointing perhaps all the way down to Hell itself. Without a word, she guides me down the stone steps, leading to one final, sparsely decorated hallway. No need to impress the visitors here?

At the end of the hall stands a wooden door, taller than a redwood, accompanied on each side by two torch-bearing beasts. Every design element of this place has been a sick blend of creepy and horny, but this dead end is less joyhouse and more slaughterhouse.

Perhaps sensing some reluctance, Alex tugs me onward. "Come on. You need to see this."

As we approach, I get a good look at those torch mounts. Two goblins; they seem to be moving. Seem to be whispering something, in fact.

"Looks like we got us another one, huh?" I think the first says.

"I hope the ooooh-na-na was worth the price, buddy, heh," laughs the second.

Alex breathes into the lock, coaxing the door to crack open. She then shoots a look at the mouthy pundits. "Real mature, assholes." She flips the little imps off, dragging me behind.

The scent hits first. The rest of the castle has the smell of a funeral, a real *sexy* funeral—yes, it's hard to explain—but this place truly does stink of death. And a backed-up toilet. My eyes adjust to the darkness; I soon realize we've entered a dungeon, the anguished wailing of the prisoners begging whoever's just opened the door to please, for pity's sake, end their suffering.

"Everyone, *quiet*," Alex barks.

The room obeys. The buzzing flies do not.

She whispers, "So, Brad, what do you think?"

I get a look at the prisoners. All men, all nude, all emaciated. Rats scurry across the floor, taking morsels of gruel from the filth-infested plates. Iron bars keep the inmates in place, yet none of these poor souls could possibly have the energy to escape anyway.

The men, the ones with the strength to move, stare at me, gaunt, bug-eyed, riddled with disease. Surprising myself, I draw Alex near.

"Why did you bring me here?" I growl, motivated by a primitive, instinctual desire to leave this hellish place.

"Because you needed to see this, Brad. You needed to see what She'll do to you."

"Okay, Alex, you made your point. I'll do it. I'll reject your mistress. God knows how she'll react, but it can't be any worse than this."

"No, Brad… You don't understand," Alex says, her expression almost breaking again. "This is what will happen if you *don't* accept her proposal."

"*What?!*"

Her eyes narrow. "If you reject your place here, return to your body, you're just going back to your old life. And you remember what that was like, don't you? Only now, She's going to be targeting you, every second of your existence." Alex gestures to one of the shivering victims. "If you think these people have it bad, wait until you receive the full force of her wrath. It'll be pleasurable for a few days—it'll be the best you ever had—but once it's over, you'll be no better off than any of them."

"Who… Who are these men?"

Her look implies I'm the crazy one. "Our 'victims' as you call them, you've never tried to contact them after they passed, have you?"

I give her an honest answer. "None of them ever came back to harass anybody, so I didn't need to."

"None came back because they couldn't. Because they're *here*, Brad." It's that last line that gets to her. I can hear her voice start to crack, hear even more of the real Alex coming out.

I'm in no mood for sympathy, though. What this girl has shown me is beyond inhumane, and someone needs to answer for it. "What… What are you sick ghouls doing to these men?" I ask, my voice breaking now. "Why are they even here? Why didn't they go into the light?"

"Because, by the time they reached their end, She owned their souls, Brad. There was no light for them." Alex squeezes my arms. "These men are her sustenance. And this is your future if you reject the offer. I realize you don't want to believe this, but She was acting out of mercy. You can either stay upstairs as a willing plaything… or you can go back home, *maybe* wake from that coma, enjoy a few weeks of living, and end up here soon enough."

Tears in her eyes, she asks a final question. "Not even a eunuch could resist someone my mistress has targeted… What hope do *you* possess?"

CHAPTER TWENTY-TWO

John Horton

I don't know why I yelled at the lady. She was just doing her job, after all.

Can only think of a few times in my entire life I've lost my temper like that. Dad unplugging the TV just as I hit the final level of *Yars' Revenge*, ordering me to go get some fresh air for a change? That was definitely one of them.

But, yeah, coming home to discover a different lock on my door, that'll probably put me in a mood, too.

Now, I'm sitting in the front office of my apartment complex, waiting for the manager to return my call. Betty, the wide-eyed receptionist, possibly didn't deserve the verbal abuse I doled out when I stormed into the office, but whatever… I was *pissed*. Twenty minutes ago, I was calming down, and Betty was kind enough to offer a cup of coffee, perhaps the fifteenth I've had today.

So here I am, questioning why none of these caffeine jolts have worked all day, avoiding connecting eyes with Betty, fending off those irritating, anxious thoughts… Fun.

No apartment doesn't mean no Alex, does it? She's not bound to this place, is she? That can't be right. I realize she's kind of trapped in a circumstance beyond her control at the moment, but she wouldn't abandon me simply because I had to move, would she?

Anxious fingers tap against the coffee cup, creating a machine gun rhythm. Or is that the sound of my shoes rapping on the chair leg?

A phone rings. Not mine: the office phone. Betty answers, and I notice her hand is still shaking. Was I really so bad?

"Yes, Mr. Grady. No, sir, he's still in the office. I did tell him when he could collect his possessions. No, he wants to speak to you. He was, um, adamant about that, sir," she says, taking secretive glances at me. "Yes, I'll put him on."

She gestures towards me; I could almost swear she flinches when she hands me the phone. C'mon, lady. I inhale. Exhale. Try to remind myself to stay calm.

"Yeah, I'm here," a voice snarls. I grasp it's mine. "Mind telling me why I can't get into my damn apartment?"

"Sir, do you have to ask that? After what happened to the pipes and light fixtures earlier this week?"

"None of that was my fault. It was all, ah, shoddy wiring and bad pipes, Grady. And you told me that it could all be fixed."

"Eventually, yes. But when the workers called me in this afternoon—after you *refused* to let anyone in this morning, I'll add—I saw the state of the bedroom. I have no idea what you did in there last night, but it's not happening ever again. Not in my building. Honestly, I don't know if we'll ever get the smells out."

What I did in there last night? There aren't words for it. And if this snot thinks he's going to keep me from ever having that again, then I'm going to reach through this phone and personally chew his dick off.

"I'm sorry, Mr. Horton, but you're going to do what?"

Ah, did I say that last bit out loud? "*Listen.* All that's important is that I get my apartment back. I'll pay you whatever I have to pay for the cleaning, I'll pay you extra for any inconvenience, but I'm *not* going to let you evict me." I realize now anger is a far greater stimulant than caffeine.

"You don't have a choice in this, Mr. Horton," the pissy voice on the other end shoots back. "You've violated the renter's agreement and, considering the state of the place, I hope you're not expecting that safety deposit back. Now, if you don't leave the premises this instant, I'm afraid my assistant will have to call the police."

The line goes dead. Two seconds later, I watch the cell on Betty's desk vibrate. It's Grady, sending texts to make sure I've left. To make sure I haven't done anything stupid, or maybe even hurt this girl.

What a joke. I turn and exit the door—admittedly, after slamming my fists into her desk and throwing that phone at the wall—then snarl the loudest obscenity the neighborhood has ever heard.

I realize I've been pacing the parking lot for maybe ten minutes or so, Betty spying on me through the office blinds, before I've calmed down enough to return to my car.

Opening the door, I look up and notice the outer window of my former home. A man's home is his castle, and only recently have I discovered what it feels like to be treated like a king. As I smash my fists into the steering wheel, I grasp how quickly that 'calm' has left me.

Soon, the anger transforms into tears. "Alex," I cry, snot running into my mouth. "Don't tell me this is it."

I feel a hand on my back. I look to my right, and through the haze of tears, see her face. The sense of relief is inexpressible, but so is the embarrassment. How could I let her see me like this?

Those full lips draw into a smile as she whispers, "Johnny? Buddy? Things are going to be just fine." That hand goes up and down my spine. "Just fine, I promise. C'mere." She reaches over. "C'mere. Just let me hold you. We'll get through this. I promise." I bathe her dark cinnamon hair with my tears. She emits a soft moan, then says, "Everything's going to work out, baby. Hasn't sweet Alex always been good to you?"

An unknown amount of time passes. A gentleman wouldn't describe what transpires between us. The words likely don't exist anyway. Suddenly, I hear a tapping at the window. I collect all the air I can; realize Alex is gone. I turn around, a flashlight greets me.

"Sir, would you mind stepping out of the vehicle?" asks a man in blue.

CHAPTER TWENTY-THREE

Bradley Burns

There is a way out of this. And, if I have to wrap a spectral plaything around my finger to save the life of that pale human body back home, so be it. This is my new mantra, as I march towards Alex's chambers.

I sense her mood. Hear those tears a good five yards before hitting her room.

I knock on the door. "Alex? It's me. Are you feeling okay?"

I overhear her blowing her nose before she clears her throat. "Don't worry about me, Brad. I think you should go back to your room."

I test the door. It's unlocked, but I resist the temptation. "We can talk if you'd like. I, uh, won't be set ablaze if I walk in here, will I?"

Her footsteps grow closer. "You're so paranoid," she says, nearly laughing, as she opens the door.

"Wonder why." I offer what I hope is a reassuring smile. "Can we talk?"

She invites me inside. Her quarters are essentially the same as mine, only smaller. The fruit and floral decorations are no different from what I see in the hallways. Not a lot of room for individuality in the evil ghost harem, I suppose. I do notice she's wearing a trendy tank top and ripped leggings, however, and not the naughty nightgown.

"Sorry I was so loud." She takes a seat on the edge of her bed. "You must think I'm the biggest baby, always crying like this."

I sit opposite her. "Don't worry about it. I take it you had another bad night? Anything you want to talk about?"

She shakes her head. "Anything *you* want to discuss, after our field trip this morning?" she asks, after taking another second to suck in more snot and compose herself. "I realize that was… intense, but you needed to understand how serious this situation is."

"Alex, are you okay with what we saw down there?"

"How I feel is irrelevant."

"Not my question."

"If I saw it through your eyes, of course it would terrify me." She bobs her noggin a bit. "But I'm not of your world anymore, Brad, so I can't. And I think that was my point. Even if you're able to return to your world, that fate is what inevitably awaits you. I realize you hate the thought of giving in to death, of becoming any kind of slave, even… *that* kind of slave," she says, grinning. "But She was gracious. She offered you an alternative to the hell you witnessed downstairs. Is this such a hard decision?"

"You're changing the subject. The things going on here, the things you're doing with these men… They don't disturb you? Some part of you knows this is wrong… Right?"

"Concepts like 'right' or 'wrong' can't apply to me anymore, Brad." She stands, heads for the door. "And I appreciate you taking the time to check on me, but I have an errand I need to run before bed."

I refuse to move. "Oh, yeah? You guys have to go out for milk just like us ordinary mortals?"

"There's somewhere I'd like to go, and I doubt it's something you want to see."

"Of course it is. Take me with you." She'll be stunned by my brazenness…

"What?"

Yup. Stunned. But I detect no anger in her response. Excellent.

"Hey, I know your kind pretty damn well, and I doubt there's anything you'll show me that's gonna turn my hair white. Let me go with you, let me see what kind of mystic tough chick you really are."

She chuckles in disbelief. "It's nothing that dramatic, Brad. But if you're so curious, and you promise not to get in the way, I suppose She wouldn't mind…"

I stand, clap my hands. "Great, it's settled. Where to?"

Alex walks over, we touch hands, and suddenly there's a flash of light. When my eyes adjust, I realize we're no longer inside the castle. The lilac scent is gone, replaced by… Absolutely nothing. No smell, no sense of air currents, or even heat from the sun, despite the fact we are now outdoors, and it's clearly around midday.

We're standing in a field, a pumpkin patch to be more accurate and, within a second or three, I understand it's the farm I visited less than a week ago. Standing in the distance, alone, is an older woman staring off into the expanse. She's standing in profile, too far away for me to discern any facial features, yet I instinctively sense her despair. Her identity isn't a mystery for long.

This is Alex's mother.

"So this is where your mother is still catching glimpses of you."

Alex turns to me. "Yes. Didn't you think this was horribly offensive? Like a girl shouldn't try to connect with her mother?" She has this look, this superior *So what you think now, huh?* expression. She knows how to play her hand, though, because it comes across as more playful than condescending.

And the way those eyes flash at you, when she's showing some of her personality and not putting on that zombie sex goddess act… Yeah, it's something.

"I'll let you in on a secret, Alex. That was at least partially for show, to get a reaction out of you, make sure I could connect with your translucent hotness."

She nods, with a sarcastic kind of enthusiasm. "Oh, it worked. You figured out quick how to piss me off."

No one says anything for a while, both of us silently enchanted by the lonely spirit on the other end of the field. Alex isn't attempting to draw her attention, while Mrs. Abernathy never seems to turn our way.

Maybe she'll see us, maybe she won't. Maybe she's so deep in her subconscious she'll forget every second of this by morning. All we can be certain of at this moment is the solitude, the hopeless ache surrounding this poor woman.

"Alex, it wasn't all an act. There is something cruel about coming here, letting her have these glimpses, and then fading away."

"It's not cruel," she answers with a polite sort of insolence. "It's the only way we can see our families again. And most people aren't attuned enough to notice us, anyway. Usually, it's mothers dreaming of their daughters." Alex takes another look at me. "They're calling out to us, too, Brad. Is it so wrong that someone would seek us out without a paycheck involved?"

"Ouch. So why don't you speak to her? Why not, hell, why not just lie to her and say you're happy and there's nothing to worry about?"

She silently inhales before answering. "Because I can't. You're here as my guest… and right now, probably more dead than alive, in case you didn't know." Nice reminder. "But Mom? She's just a decent, ordinary lady, one who lost her baby girl and can't help thinking about her at night. Of course I come and see her, Brad. It would be cruel not to."

"But, *why* can't you speak to her?" Does Alex realize I'm pumping her for information? Does she care?

"Because She forbids it."

"And if you disobeyed Her?"

Alex shrugs her shoulders, but doesn't look back at me when she answers. "Would you disobey the laws of gravity?"

I'll acknowledge I have no idea how to answer that. So, I take the next gamble. The big one. "Alex, can you go anywhere on this plane?"

"I go where I'm called."

"But if you weren't being called, could you travel anyway?"

She ponders this. "I suppose so. Why do you ask?"

Not sure if I should answer yet. Across the field, Mrs. Abernathy is cradling herself as she ambles through the pumpkin patch. She looks up, and having now turned our way, catches our image in the distance. She's momentarily stunned, but soon enough, her face takes on this quiet resignation. Her head bobs, and mother and daughter exchange a sad smile.

Seconds later, she's gone.

Alex continues to gaze at the empty horizon. I give her a moment of unrequested, but deserved quiet. Perhaps a minute passes before I make my appeal.

"Alex... Take me to my body."

CHAPTER TWENTY-FOUR

Sandra Jones

It's far too late, but I'm still here. Still waiting for some sign of life.

I talked to Mom about Brad's condition; about how the odds are decreasing by the hour. She tried to be reassuring, to choke down just how much she despised the man, but even my pure-hearted mother could only offer cold comfort.

I repeat as a mantra that Brad can beat this. Keep holding on to the good memories; trying to put some positive vibes out into the universe, or spectral atmosphere, or however that works.

This guest chair I would deem 'granite-like', but somehow my body eventually relents. Sleep takes over, sending me off to that unknowable astral realm Brad once swore was connected to all of his spiritual what-have-you.

"Seriously, San, we all exist as tiny points of light in an infinite universe. The world we know just vibrates differently than the others. Dreams? Merely your soul detaching from its corporeal form, getting that line between the physical and spiritual all kinds of blurry."

Always assumed he was joking. Sometimes, with that man, it's hard to tell.

CHAPTER TWENTY-FIVE

Bradley Burns

Okay, I can do this.

I am the Paranormal Desperado. I am King Badass of the spirit realm.

And I feel no guilt, buttering up this wayward spirit who's falling under my influence. Exploiting her ability to casually stroll back to Earth, sharing a personal moment with the lass, and then directing her to my hospital room.

"I remember how I felt... Looking down at my own body."

"Well, I'm sure it was a traumatic experience, Alex. But, let's remember, you were officially—and I hope you don't mind me saying this—all DOA on that bathroom floor. Me? I'm still possessing a smidge of that ol' thump-a-thump in my veins, so..."

She places a spectral hand on my shoulder. I tell myself it isn't warm; that we're not truly vibrating on the same frequency. That can't be happening because *I'm not dead yet.*

"Brad, I get that it's a hard thing to let go of." Her hand squeezes, voice goes a little more somber. "But, at a certain point... Brad, me holding on so hard, that's what enabled Her to recruit me."

"Sounds to me like somebody has a few regrets, huh?"

She refuses to acknowledge this. Just closes her eyes and keeps going. "I'm not sure what you think you can accomplish here."

I'd like to tell her that I can do plenty. That I'm merely

inconvenienced by a precarious state of near-death. That I'm not like all those everyday folk who only see ghosts on the movie screen. And what I've got planned right here? It's freaking brilliant.

But I'm still seducing lovely Alex here. *Hmm... Right verb choice there, Brad?* Don't want to scare her off just yet; don't want her suspecting too much.

"I need to say goodbye in my own way, Alex. I hope this doesn't get you into any trouble, but I need this final moment."

She offers a morose bob of the head. I remind myself that Alex, in her current state, can't make any claim on being beautiful when she's angry. But when she's sullen, mournful, all-out woebegone?

Sure, the girl's a knockout.

But, more important matters here. I clear the girl from my thoughts. I clear most things from my thoughts, aside from my still form below. Not narcissism, just cool focus.

This slab of meat is me. And yet *I'm* me, floating above. I monitor how my transparent, diaphanous lungs are breathing. Get them in the right rhythm.

This can work. I see spirits; I chase them back home. *I* am a spirit, presently. My body still lives. I can return myself home.

I connect with this slab of meat that is no slab of meat. Repeat a mantra, assuring myself I still exist on this realm. That I have a right to live out my days on this Earth.

Bradley Burns is not a stubborn spirit who refuses to enter the afterlife. He has dividing cells, and flaring neurons, and tiny hair follicles and even tinier bacterial life growing on his skin.

And I can sense that commensalistic bacteria. Practically taste the way it's feeding off fats and cholesterol in this still-living body. Connect to its warmth, its own unique soul glow.

Thank you, microscopic *Propionibacterium* that's currently chowing away inside one of my hair follicles. I recognize your life and slip through your primitive—but quite fascinating—glow and hitch a ride inside my meat form.

Wow, I am good.

The heat of my spirit connects with this pink, wrinkly organ that houses my memories. Those are the key. Those define this piece of meat that is not meat.

Through memory, I reconnect with the human Bradley Burns. Relive the moments that sent him—no, *me*—to this hospital. Relive that late morning meeting with the sumptuous Trina. Relive Sandy's irritated reaction to her company.

But I also have to relive that sense of guilt, when Sandy came back home and told me what happened earlier at the mark's apartment. I relive a mental image of shattered glass nearly blinding this person that I love. The sick sensation of knowing I put her in this position.

And, surprisingly, an emotion buried deep. The impulse to joke my way through. Distract both of us from the seriousness of the moment.

Anything, really, to get myself off the hook.

I have to do this, because I can't let her hate me. Can't let her know how wrong she was to marry me in the first place; to still stick with this ghost-hunting nonsense.

I need her to laugh at my jokes. To roll her eyes at the deep, paranormal truths I lackadaisically drop during conversations. To enjoy the absurdity, the relief from bland everyday life, I bring her.

Her best friend growing up married a patent attorney, for crying out loud.

My life continues a backwards replay. Shamefully, I see myself turning off my phone when Sandy's calling. See myself turn my attention back to some random brunette whose name I can't recall.

I endure annoying club music I pretend to like, pursuing a twenty-year-old model I happened to run into while shopping on Rodeo earlier that day. What was this: three years ago?

A pang of conscience strikes, as I experience again a lie told to Sandra. A pathetic excuse for missing the birthday party her friends spent a month planning.

I see my wedding day; that cold handshake Sandy's father offered me.

We're at a roadside *Applebee's* months before, Sandy and I. On the way back from my parents' double funeral. She hides her shock when I make a tasteless joke, regarding the drunk driver who took their lives.

She knows this is how I cope. She doesn't judge. And I'm reflecting on the brevity of the life we have here as meat. I'm considering now that I should pop that question.

A day earlier, the smell of incense at the funeral mass. A repeat of all the handshakes and hugs from relatives and childhood neighbors. But the steady embrace of Sandy's arm is all that matters.

I'm back at Sandy's kitchen table, inside her tiny apartment, where she's working out the numbers. Telling me I almost have enough to quit that heinous job on her father's lot.

I see Sandy across the table at our favorite Italian restaurant, explaining how someone she knows through her meager Hollywood connections knows a guy who knows a guy who knows the actress who just auditioned to be Tom Cruise's latest girlfriend. And that actress just so happened to move into a condo on Palm Avenue, and she keeps hearing this voice every time she walks into the bathroom… Where the previous tenant drowned in the bathtub.

Could I do something about that?

I see Sandy as I saw her the afternoon we met. That day on the lot, her first day on the job, working the phones inside. I come in, joke with her about nepotism and air conditioning and notice how well she can dish it all back at me.

But I also notice her smile. How her eyes narrow when she delivers a truly brutal punchline.

I see myself in those days before I met Sandy. I laugh at this cornball observation, but it's true. It's like the sky's not quite the same color. Something's wrong with the taste of the air.

I'm on a road trip with my college girlfriend, Miss Indigo Girls t-shirt herself. She thinks it'll be a gas to take me to a Civil War battle site.

Yup, dull colors. Stale air.

Young, stupid Brad is in high school now. I strike up conversations with girls, tell them things about the relatives I see floating around them. There's an abandoned steel plant in the next town. The braver ones, I take on the tour. Exploit the plant's high mortality rate and offer these young ladies an experience with the restless departed they won't get from any football jock.

Sometimes, I can make them laugh. But I realize now, how different it was with Sandy. What it was like to have a true partner and not just a hookup.

Hey, wrinkly pink organ with the firing neurons and whatnot: what's the deal with that? Why was I so determined to chase cheap titillation while a good woman waited at home?

I relive earlier experiences with female classmates. That thrill of pursuit, that inevitable disappointment when the whole experience can't match a moment from my past.

We're getting there...

I'm an even younger, stupider Brad now. I'm twelve, several weeks into the haunting of Dolley, my first. Literally my 'first', as she introduces young Brad to a world he wasn't quite ready for. I relive awkward conversations with my parents, then a trip to the library, researching old newspaper files.

Discovering how Dolley met her end in the Craftsman-style home now owned by my parents, that fateful day in 1951.

My instincts shout to resist her. Not to submit to the short bursts of ecstasy she provides. I'm reliving the day I informed Dolley we were calling things off. Just how she reacted.

I'm reliving the true birth of the Paranormal Desperado, as he takes control of the situation. Shocks the literal hell out of the succubus by forcing her spirit back into that light she'd been trying so hard to resist for forty years.

The psychic backwash ruptured every pipe in our house, but I learned. Got a handle on my mystic hoodoo, as my future love will call it.

And did I just touch on some unspeakable trauma? Some experiences that bent young Bradley in the wrong direction? A whisper I'm a fool for giving up something so unbelievably sweet; something I'll never have a taste of again?

Irrelevant, right now.

This 'deal' offered by Alex's mistress is pure crap. And I'm not playing by her rules. I don't need her help to return to my body: I've been running game on her kind since before my balls dropped.

If She wants to send her daughters after me on Earth, let her. I'm not some random mark; I'm the man more than qualified to fight off the touch of spirits. My bravado isn't diminished by a sudden memory of those gray-skinned husks in that dungeon. The putrid smell of urine and rotting teeth. Nope, it is not.

Come after me: watch ol' Brad fight like hell.

I'll do that and more, just as soon as I inspire this wrinkly, pink organ to wake up the rest of my body. Wiggle some toes, twitch my nose a bit.

Come on. Anything.

Come on, Mystic Badass. Why isn't this working?

"Brad, we've been here awhile now," I hear Alex speak, dreamlike. I fight the pull of that sound; do what I can to remain tethered to this insignificant bacteria nothing that's offered entrance to my meat form.

But a realization hits like bricks. Exposes just how weak that connection is. Just how small a thing I was clinging onto. That flash of memories flames out, is replaced by the aerial view of this hospital room.

In that sliver of a second, I get a sense of my surroundings. A rush of the souls in nearby rooms in various stages of departure from these meat forms. Just next door, a sixty-year-old father of three is now succumbing to his afternoon heart attack.

He's a good man. Doesn't fight it. He's surrounded by those he loves, realizes this is what matters.

What a fool I was for believing this could work. That I could just evade what's waiting for all of us.

And only now, appreciating our view of this room, do I realize the chair next to my bed is not empty. Typical of me, isn't it?

Sandy. I reach out to her in my new, translucent form. Don't even realize I'm doing it at first. Just an instinct to offer comfort, offer one more apology.

The touch lasts not even a heartbeat. But it's enough for me to see all of this from Sandy's point of view. To see how badly I'm hurting her, yet again.

Even worse, I have a taste of *her* regret. A fleeting thought that maybe, if I work a miracle and beat this, the two of us might try again.

The sensation's so fleeting it moves like quicksilver; she'd deny it with all her heart later. But it's there.

I snap back, overwhelmed by the emotion. Suppose I do come back: do I truly think anything will change? Let Lilith send every insatiable soul she can after me. I'll give 'em worse than what Dolley got.

But can I say the same thing about the random dental hygienists and bartenders and bachelorette party stragglers the resuscitated Bradley will encounter?

Can I pretend I haven't just witnessed the life of one severely crappy partner, in every sense of the word?

"Alex, one last favor," I tell her, my hand on her shoulder. "*One more. Promise.*"

CHAPTER TWENTY-SIX

Sandra Jones

Late afternoon on the water. The sun's going down, alighting the nearby clouds that unbelievable hue of dying embers.

The sky just seems so big out here, the colors so vivid, like tastes of something our tiny human minds are hardly meant to comprehend. Fate's way of telling us we only caught this glimpse out of sheer cosmic circumstance, maybe, and we'd better appreciate it.

Nah, it's just a cheesy dinner cruise.

I didn't know why he made the arrangements, but now I'm glad he talked me into going. Out here on the water, enjoying the cool air on the deck with our wine, just the two of us, I'm half-convinced the dope might choose tonight to make some grand romantic gesture, to actually pull out a ring and ask the question. Not that he'd ever do anything so cornball… Not Bradley Burns.

He's been cracking dumb jokes all night, making a game out of the absurd backstories he's created for the wait staff: apparently, they're a motley assortment of evil twins, sex fiends, and escaped Nazi war criminals. None of this stupidity should make me laugh, which is why the jokes are that much funnier.

You'd almost think the eternally-cool Bradley Burns had something on his mind, though, the way he keeps excusing himself to the bathroom. Or maybe it's bad shellfish.

He disappeared five minutes ago. When he comes back, he's

going to offer me a glass of champagne. Right after I notice him dabbing sweat off his brow, and I open my mouth to make fun of him because it's sixty-five degrees out, I'm going to look down and see that ring resting at the bottom of my crystal flute.

I know this because I'm dreaming about the night he proposed. No great mystery why he's on my mind tonight. And since I'm dreaming, I guess I was finally able to stop crying long enough to fall asleep.

My perfectly rehearsed movie goes into bad improv, however, when I see my future spouse walk around the corner looking more sad than nervous. And he isn't alone. His companion, if you're curious, is the vengeful spirit who nearly killed me a handful of days ago.

She looks like she's been crying, but that's only made those sad kid eyes even more inviting. And I hate myself for acknowledging this, but even those modeling photos didn't do her bone structure justice. Just how many reasons do I need to despise this cow?

"What is *she* doing here?" I ask without thinking.

Brad takes in the surroundings and his lips break into a grin. "You know where Alex comes from, Sandra. She's… Well, she's here to escort you to the other side with me." In spite of myself, I gasp. Loudly.

Then he cracks. "No, no… Kidding! Bad joke. Sorry, but that was just too good an opportunity."

The girl speaks up. "Sandra. I realize this is all pretty bizarre and I probably shouldn't even be here." You think? "Really, I'm just here as Brad's guide. And, yes, of course, in case you didn't know, I do feel horrible about the exploding pipes."

"You also threw a toilet at my head."

The girl does this kind of shameful half-a-smile I'm going to assume has gotten her out of trouble with her actual daddy and / or sugar daddies in the past. "I did do that, yes. I… Yes, sorry."

Brad interjects, his tone growing more serious. "Sandy, listen to me. This is all crazy, even crazier than usual, but I wanted you to know… I, uh…"

"You still haven't explained what the ghost whore is doing here."

"Excuse me?" she asks, those hazel eyes flashing anger.

"Why so chummy with one now, Brad? That's what you've always called them. Ghost. Whores."

"Listen, Alex is how I'm reaching you right now. She *has* to be here, okay?"

"'Has to be here' so that you can do what exactly? Ruin another memory for me?" The insult is too grave to be overlooked. Not even here, the place where our life together was supposed to begin, is sacred to this man. I swear to God, his whores follow him everywhere.

"Have you been watching from above? Do you know what I found in your phone, Brad?"

He raises a hand in defeat. "Oh, geez, Sandy. Don't ever look at those photos, please. For everyone's sake."

"What? I didn't even get to the…" I shake my head, try to regroup. "Brad, why are you here?" I ask, hitting each word.

He holds on to a breath and finally answers. "Because, Sandy, this may be it. This is likely the last chance we have to ever speak to one another."

Everyone's oxygen dissipates. The girl, the departed darling who shouldn't be here at this moment, looks away. Perhaps out of respect, or just overwhelming social unease.

"Brad, no. Don't be talking like that."

"I have to, Sandra. We have to be real about this. I'm not in a good place, and at this moment, the odds of me ever returning to you are… Honestly, Sandra, you have to accept that I'm probably not coming back."

As my heart sinks, I fumble for some rebuttal. "Why? What exactly happened to you? Tell me how I can—"

He takes my hand. "It doesn't work that way. And I'm not trying to upset you. I just want you to know that I do love you, still. I always have." His face begins to collapse, and I recognize I'm witnessing something he'd never let me glimpse in our years together. Bradley Burns, the king of irony, is crying.

"And, of course, I'm apologizing for all of the screw-ups," he continues, nearly panting, "all of the lies, all of the times I was chasing something because I was so stupid I didn't recognize what I already had." His voice cracks when he delivers this final sentence, "You're the best thing that ever happened to me, Sandy, and I hate that our life turned out the way it did."

I'm fighting back my own tears when I blurt out, "Brad, don't talk to me like you're already gone. Please, don't do that to me."

He squeezes my hand, but can't look me in the face. "I have to, sweetie. And I'm sorry for that. But odds are this is the last time we're going to speak, and I couldn't spend eternity knowing I didn't say these things to you."

Brad finally looks up, and our eyes meet. That air of hopelessness, that shameful way he looks away from me… This can't be the man I know. But it is. It's Brad, trapped in something he can't escape, can't charm his way out of. He gives me a hug that honestly feels like a final goodbye.

And as he walks away in tears, his new lady friend is there to pat his back. She offers me a drawn-out, apologetic look over her shoulder as they literally fade into the sunset.

How nice of her, silently asking forgiveness for defaming this place, this moment, with her foul presence.

My mind races, but the mood that eventually settles doesn't match Brad's departing waterworks. More than anything, I'm furious at the man-child for not only bringing *her* here, but for opening his *long* overdue apology with a dumb joke at *my* expense, for never saying those things when they could've made an actual *difference*, and for even getting himself into this wacked out situation in the *first* place.

It's her face, that haunting sulkiness, as she comforted the man I was supposed to be growing old with, ushering him into what could very well be the hereafter… *That's* what loiters in my thoughts.

And, rather than cursing the girl, I start to wonder if she just might be useful in some way.

CHAPTER TWENTY-SEVEN

John Horton

My first demand was an Egg McMuffin. And coffee, black. Don't judge me.

"And how did you know I'd been arrested?" I ask, the muffin crumbs tumbling into my lap. My companion shoots a dirty look she quickly tries to conceal. I'm going to clean it up, lady. It's not as if I want to waste any of this.

"The woman who works at your apartment complex told me. Watched the whole thing through the window." She pauses, waits for me to say something. I don't comply. "Nice lady. Wanted me to know she's praying for you."

There's a thought. "Uh-huh. At least someone is," I mumble.

"Are you so alone, John? There isn't anyone who would've bailed you out?"

I'm tempted to snap at her for asking such a personal question. It's not as if I know this Sandra—Jones, was it?—so well. I appreciate her making my bail and providing some breakfast, but truthfully I would've been content sleeping in that cell until the hearing. At least when I'm asleep I'm not anxious about when I'll be able to see Alex again.

"I'm not so pathetic, Sandra. I do have some friends." *Work acquaintances*, corrects a tiny voice. Zip it, tiny voice. "And my parents are good people. No way I'd ever make a phone call like *that* to them, of course."

Sandra removes her orange juice from the cup holder and takes a pull on the straw. "I guess I could understand that. But, John, you've got to understand… They *do* target loners. I don't fully understand why they do what they do, but their pattern is usually darned consistent."

"Okay, I'm a pathetic nobody who couldn't even land a job directing adult diaper commercials, I'm stuck working on a nauseating show that I hate, and, yup, I have no social life, so I deserve what I get… Yes, fine."

"Not what I meant, John," she sighs. "I just wanted you to know that your shyness, your unwillingness to ever ask for help, that's what led you here in the first place."

"And you're offering to help?"

"Wasn't I the one who warned you about all of this days ago?"

"What makes you think I want to be free of her?"

"Has this relationship worked out so great for you so far?"

I admit, I have to pause before responding. "I don't blame her for this. She's not some monster, she really isn't."

"Listen, I don't doubt you believe what you're saying. And, hey, maybe this Alex isn't so bad after all. But John, we're just normal people, and you're messing around with some scary stuff."

"And how do you propose to help me with this, um, *perceived* problem?" I ask, balling up the empty wrapper, deliciously slick with fast-food grease.

The hints of a grin appear on her thin lips. "I think, first of all, I need to speak to Alex."

CHAPTER TWENTY-EIGHT

Sandra Jones

You'd think the little prick would show an ounce of appreciation. It's not as if there was a line of folks at the jail waiting to bail his sorry butt out. And, woo boy, I hate to think about what the check I just wrote is going to do to our balance. But, no, the first thing he had to do after he walked into the room was demand *McDonald's*, or else he wasn't getting into the car.

At least he's coming out of his shell a bit.

I think I knocked the wind out of him when I asked to speak to his translucent girlfriend, though. Thankfully, he didn't immediately squeal *"Stay away from her! You can't speak to my precioussss!"* or anything like that. He did get uncomfortably quiet for a while, though, before finally now asking:

"Why?"

"Why? Because maybe she can help me find Brad and, since you're the person on our plane she's made a connection with, I'm going to need your assistance."

"And I guess that detective lady wasn't any help?"

"Not especially, no." Not a total lie, but enough of one to bug me. Detective Amash might not be the warmest of souls, but she has taken this case seriously and managed to locate Brad as fast as could be expected. But a situation like this, it's not exactly something the LAPD covers at the academy.

No, I need help, the kind she can't offer. And while I'm still unsure of every step of this plan, I know that I have to make contact with that… thing hovering around Brad last night.

"Won't you at least consider connecting us, John?"

"I'll… think about it. Right now, I think I'd just like a shower and change of clothes. Can that be arranged?"

"Yeah, I'll swing you by your—" No, dunce. John was in jail because of that exhibition he put on after they kicked him out of his apartment. And, oddly, a public indecency charge got thrown in there. "I'll take you to my place. You can freshen up and we'll talk about things later, okay?"

*

An hour later, we're standing outside my hall bath. Wrapped in a towel, a freshly scrubbed John is examining my ex's year-old Rick Owens t-shirt and a pair of jeans he saved for painting the bathroom. We *could* have sold these clothes on eBay before resorting to pawning some of our appliances, but Brad was adamant… "Isn't this one of those t-shirts that costs like two hundred bucks?"

He had to say something, didn't he? "Brad tends to have expensive tastes."

"Because you know they sell packs of tees at *Target* for less than ten bucks, right?"

"John, I need you to calm yourself, and think of some way you could call Alex."

"You realize you severely pissed her off last time, don't you?"

"I do, and… and I want to apologize to her."

He turns away, heads towards the living room. "Oh, please."

"Hey, John, I'm not going to pretend that I don't have selfish motivations," I say, following, "but I do feel bad about how I provoked her, and if we get a chance to talk, I *promise* I'll apologize."

125

Another hour later, I'm wearing that ridiculous potato-sack jumpsuit again. Thankfully, there's a different girl at the desk, so she doesn't recognize me as the woman asking about John Horton earlier.

No, I'm merely an employee of *Carmine Plumbing Solutions*, one of a dozen or so blue-collar workers who've entered that apartment in the past few days, doing whatever's necessary to undo the damage left by Alex, the Mischievous Ghost Skank.

"Nah, you don't need a key," she tells me. "Door's open: they're still airing the place out. I think the last cleaning crew went out for lunch, so you've got the place to yourself right now."

A lucky break from the big guy upstairs? Maybe. With my clipboard of gibberish tucked under my armpit, I head back to Brad's Dodge Charger. "John," I shout. "Coast's clear. Move it!"

John emerges from the car in a matching jumpsuit, his face partially concealed by a well-worn *Angels* ball cap, fished out of the closet earlier today. He doesn't say anything, but he dutifully follows behind.

As soon as we enter the hallway, the stink hits. How could I ever describe that horrid blend of sulfur, brine shrimp, and bleach?

"John, buddy, you proud of yourself?" I ask, forgetting I'm trying to stay on the weirdo's good side.

"It's uh, not that bad," he answers defensively, covering his face with the top of his uniform.

Fully prepared for this possibility, I brought along a few sets of Smiley's nose plugs: they ain't just for swimmin' anymore. I might not have the 'gift' like Brad, but I've learned a few tricks over the years.

"Take a pair of these," I advise my companion.

He complies and, with some trepidation, guides me into his former place of residence. "I'm not sure what kind of condition this place is going to be in."

"Don't worry about it. All that's important is that Alex makes an appearance."

We enter the apartment, nearly tripping over the toolkits, cleaning supplies, and rearranged furniture obstructing most of the floor. The pipes are now exposed throughout strategically-placed holes in the wall and floor, mid-repair, reinforcing the savagery of Alex's tantrum.

I grab the edge of John's sofa, then gesture towards the door. "We've got to barricade the entrance until we're done." And, yippee, trap ourselves inside with that odor. "Help me move this."

After we drag the sofa into position, I lock the door from the inside. "Okay. So, when you want to talk to Alex, how does this normally go?"

John, taking in the sights, perhaps reflecting on how much this "relationship" has cost him, is too distracted to answer.

"John, this is important…"

He lets out the bad air. "Yeah. Typically, she's the one who reaches out to me. We're connected like that, you know? She understands when I'm down, and when I need a friendly ear to gnaw on."

"Sure, but… If you *really* wanted to see her, isn't there some way you can call out to Alex?"

"There's the list of things I read online. That seemed to work, yeah."

"Great. Let's do that; but *fast*. Because I don't know when those workers are getting back."

"It's not exactly something you can rush."

"Right now, it's gotta be, bud. C'mon. First step. What do you do?"

Rubbing this right thumb against his left palm, he slowly responds, "I would have to meditate for a while… Concentrate on Alex, think about what our relationship means to me…"

"No time for that. Next step."

"It's not like a shopping list, Sandra," he says, exhibiting more of that snotty attitude I witnessed this morning. "It's more like a mood I have to be in."

"Okay. What gets you into this mood?"

"Some music could help. In bed, the right music, I could zone out real quick and get into a place where I'm ready to, well, accept her. Last time I put on some Marvin Gaye…"

"Little hackneyed, but whatever works, I guess."

I'm ready to kick myself for letting that one slip, but to my amazement, the smartass remark actually seems to perk him up. "No, see, I thought the same. Like, that is a damned obvious choice." John turns his hands over. "Then again, he's the go-to reference for this kind of thing because he was so good at it, right?"

"Yeah, I mean, he did a lot more than that. Probably did as much as Smokey Robinson to popularize smooth R&B, before it turned into elevator music. And of course the Motown era is a classic."

John agrees enthusiastically. "Right. But, now, it's like he's only remembered for that one album, and any time some stupid movie or commercial needs a shorthand for 'mood music,' you get either Marvin or Barry White."

I *mm-hmm* my agreement with John while gently nudging him into the bedroom. "All true. But not important right now. Unless you want me to pull up some Marvin or Barry." Thankfully, no one's removed his bed, although the sheets have been stripped, most likely in an attempt to do something about that smell.

"I realize they've packed most of your stuff up, but I've got plenty of music here on my phone," I tell John while handing him the model I spent far too much on, in those pre-audit days. "Scroll through and see what you think will get the job done."

"Well, no, I'm not looking to do *that* right now. Not with you around, at least. We just need to talk to her, right? It's not about sensuality, it's more about the mood Alex inspires."

John thumbs through the screen, making sometimes snide, sometimes supportive remarks about the music on my playlist. He gasps with disbelief after hitting one particular track.

"Sandra… You're kidding. Seth Timbs, *'Overlong'*. Really? How could you possibly know about Seth Timbs?" Dropping the phone to his side, he stares in disbelief. "I thought I was the only person outside of his mother who'd ever heard of him."

"You kidding me? I saw Fluid Ounces open for the Features ages ago out in Nashville. Damn near changed my life. Keep scrolling; I've got the 'Overlong' demo Timbs was going to release as a Fluid Ounces track."

John sighs with disbelief. "Didn't even know that. Huh. It's such a beautiful song."

"Sure. Maybe this is what you need to help find the right spirit?"

With no words, John positions himself on the bed. Stretching his body the length of the mattress, crossing his arms, and without looking down, he's clicked on the phone's speaker. I take a seat on the floor.

It's a song about falling asleep under the stars, bundled up next to the person who means more to you than any other thing in the world. About recognizing in a sober moment just how much they've changed your life, chastising yourself for ever taking them for granted, and fearing those dark impulses that might ever cause you to blow this whole thing up.

John is quietly singing along. I realize at the start of the second verse that I'm joining him.

The pace picks up towards the end of the ditty, singing of a Technicolor landscape, the voices of doubt, drowned out by emotions that can't be silenced. Then there's a brief pause, and the vocals resume, a cry of longing, of a love more powerful than the singer could have ever remembered.

*

Not so long ago, those words could bring tears to my eyes. With the song on its third repeat, I'm resisting the sensation, squeezing my eyelids shut. When they open, I see a lithe figure standing before me, facing John. She's clothed in the hottest fashions of two years ago.

Alex.

CHAPTER TWENTY-NINE

John Horton

A vision of beauty. And she isn't even trying.

"Hi, John," she says, almost laughing, perhaps a mite confused. "I take it you wanted to see me?"

I sit up, the enthusiasm impossible to disguise. "Alex, honey. It's so good to see you. I'm sorry about the way we were interrupted the last time..."

"Oh, that. Don't worry, babe." She would say that. "No, no. You don't have to pretend. That had to be humiliating for the both of us, although I guess you have a knack for escaping embarrassing situations." She smiles, nods agreement. "And the way I was acting when I called out to you, I don't even know what I was thinking. I didn't want you to see me that way."

She moves closer, places her hands behind my ears. "John, dear, you have nothing to apologize for. No secrets between us, right?" I murmur an affirmative. She kisses the top of my head before turning to the side. "So, that in mind... Why don't you tell me what *she's* doing here?"

"Hi, Alex," calls out Sandra, still sitting on the floor. "Nice to see you while I'm fully conscious."

"What's that supposed to mean?" I ask.

"Don't worry about that, hon," Alex replies, without looking my way. "Now, Sandra, is there any reason why you've entered this place that's so special to John and me?"

"I… I told John that I wanted to apologize," Sandra says, any sincerity in her voice debatable. "About the first time we met here; even though I wasn't able to physically see you then, and was trying to do my job, I have to admit that I was extremely disrespectful towards you."

Alex is off the bed now, standing over Sandra. "You were."

"And that was wrong… and I'd like to say that I'm sorry."

"Fair enough." To my surprise, Alex takes a seat next to Sandra on the floor. "And, in that spirit, no pun intended, I'd like to apologize if I offended you last night. It was a favor to Brad, and had I known what… What you were dreaming about, I probably wouldn't have—"

Sandra stops the sentence by raising her hand. "It's possible I was too emotional about the whole thing." She pauses, but everyone can tell there's more she wants to say. After a few seconds, Sandra continues. "But, speaking of last night, I have to ask you about Brad."

"I can understand why you're worried, but it's not really my place to speak about him."

"But you do talk to him, right? That's how he convinced you to contact me?"

"We have spoken, yes."

Sandra grows more animated. "Well, can you convey a message? Can you try to… Get him out of that mood? Talk him into fighting back?"

"Fighting back against…?"

"You heard him last night, Alex. He's given up. He thinks that he's never coming back again. Can't you talk to him?"

"And what would you have me say? What if he's prepared to make a decision, and it isn't the one you want?"

"But he needs to know that I don't want him to quit. Yes, I'm mad at him, but that doesn't mean I want him to throw away everything. Alex, if there's still time; if you have any sway in this, is there any way Brad…?"

"That he can come home? Sandra, you don't realize what you're asking," Alex responds, with a note in her voice implying she'd rather Sandra not finish that thought.

What exactly happened between these two last night?

Sandra hasn't picked up on the hint. "So, he's going to linger like that and then… What?" A panic enters her voice. "He'll just float off forever with you?"

Alex closes her eyes, breathes, and—is this possible?—seems to whisper a brief, silent prayer. When she opens her eyes, she straightens up some. Places her hand on Sandra's shoulder.

"He'll be treated justly by my mistress, Sandra. Truthfully, She has shown him favor that few others would receive."

"I know this sounds ridiculous, but is there some way I could speak to him again?" Sandra asks, growing either more frustrated or more desperate. "Was last night really our goodbye?"

Alex leans closer. "Do you wish to see Brad in his new home? Would that ease your mind?"

"You mean you can take me with you?"

"If you come willingly, that can be arranged." Her voice—it's Alex, no doubt—but she sounds so mature now. Like she isn't just this silly girl who stops by and cheers me up; somehow, she's so much more than that, something people on our side simply aren't meant to comprehend.

One aspect of the conversation only registers with me now, however.

"Hey, hey, what was that?" I climb out of bed. "Alex, are you saying there's a way for us to follow you back home?"

"Is this something that interests you, dear?" she asks with a grin.

"Babe, you've gotta ask?"

Alex rises, extends her hand. Do I hesitate? Of course not. "I suppose it's been decided, hasn't it?" she says, taking me in her arms. "Sandra, John, with your consent, I would like to escort you to my home. Do you accept?"

Alex reaches out to Sandra. With no words, Sandra nods and takes the offered hand.

133

CHAPTER THIRTY

Bradley Burns

My guides escort me to the castle's throne hall, decorated as you'd imagine: a raised chair lined with velvet cushions, overlooking engraved steps, resting under a canopy of silk. On the throne sits the mother of my misfortune, a lady servant pouring wine into her goblet.

"Bradley. Your visit is not entirely unexpected, but undoubtedly welcome." She dismisses the aides, then sips her vino. "I take it we have matters to discuss?"

Yeah, I'm here to discuss how you've set me up in this no-win situation and thoroughly screwed me for the rest of my life, you sadistic demon from Hell.

Assuming she isn't telepathic, she hears none of this. I do nod, however.

"Because I understand you've been quite busy lately. Roaming about the place, unescorted. Traipsing through the dreamland; no permission required, apparently." She pauses to make sure I register what she's saying. "Yes, Bradley, I know of such things. And I'm not upset, I assure you. You require time to make your decision, and perhaps one or two moments to say goodbye to your previous life. All understandable."

Yup. I'm sure buying this. If there's one word that describes the Queen of the Succubae, it's 'magnanimous'.

"But I think you've come to realize your time is limited, haven't you? And after reviewing the terms, you wish to tell me your decision?"

Unfortunately, yeah…

"Your choice, Bradley?" She asks, raising an eyebrow. "A life here with my daughters, all anxious and more than capable of fulfilling any concupiscent fantasy that rests in your heart." Leaning back, she says with a snort, "Or, perhaps, you'd wish to return to your mortal form? So long as you keep yourself removed from my affairs, you have nothing to fear from me."

The Mystic Badass, unable to rejoin his mortal form. Dependent on Queen Succubus for his bus ticket back to Earth. Where, let's face it, he would be condemning the only person who truly cares about him to an extended version of that slow car wreck they call a relationship.

She stares for a moment; I gather it's my turn to speak. Clearing my throat and steadying my nerves, I manage to get this out: "I have thought about this. And I think that, really, back home I could be causing more harm than good, were I to… Yeah." With a deep, reluctant breath, I close my eyes, finally finish the thought. "Assuming that I have no other options, I will accept your offer."

Not good enough for her.

"Speak it, Bradley." Just a hint of that serpentine lisp. "What do you accept?"

Eyes still closed, I screw up the courage to say the words. "I'll stay here. With you. And your daughters."

"Oh, delightful," She erupts. I open my eyes and the demon's standing over me. "Come closer, Bradley. Our covenant requires ratification."

"What does that mean?"

She grasps both arms, forces me to turn back to the entrance. "You're no child, Bradley. Surely you know of what I speak."

Standing in the doorway is Alex, draped again in the sheer robe, a lone flower over her left ear. Has a look on her face that reads, *'Yup. Here we are.'*

"Hi, Brad."

Our host titters. "She's so shy at times. How endearing. Well, if the two of you desire privacy, I'll respect your wishes." She gestures for Alex to join me as she returns to her throne. "Alexandria, escort Bradley to his chambers. And, once the formalities are seen to, perhaps the two of you could join us for a celebratory dinner tonight?"

So, this is it, huh? My choice made, the less terrible of two options chosen. And Sandra, I pray, is spared more heartache. Hooray for everybody.

Alex, her face displaying a mix of regret and resignation, takes my hand. We've moved five feet before I turn back. "Oh, hold on a sec. Your Majesty, do I have permission to approach the throne?"

"Is that sarcasm I detect? Come, Bradley. You may approach."

Not even sure how I've found the balls to do this, but I guess I officially have nothing to lose now. What is She going to do at this point: scald my flesh to the bone right after I've given Her what She wanted? And enough of this 'She' crap…

I keep a steady stride up those engraved steps, then ask my new queen for her ear. She obliges, leans forward with a patronizing smirk. I move closer, nearly brush her ear with my lips.

Whisper a small act of insubordination.

"Enjoy your victory… Lilith."

And that's when she explodes with laughter.

CHAPTER THIRTY-ONE

Sandra Jones

"Look at this one," I say to John, gesturing at the demented ceramic cherub resting in my palm. "Disgusting."

He looks up from his book, a leather-bound collection that appears to predate the *Kama Sutra*, only this volume introduces goats into the fun. "It's just a cute baby angel."

"Who's hung like Lexington Steele's horse, in case you didn't notice. And those aren't angel wings, see? Evil, nasty batwings." I return the devil-angel to the bureau. "These people are sick."

John sighs, closes the book, and drops it on the bed. A painting, featuring a scene out of primeval Babylon that straddles every conceivable line of good taste, hangs on the wall behind him. I'm not a prude—I couldn't be less of a prude, I promise you— but every piece of décor in this room is sickeningly perverse. "Regardless, we're in their home now," he says. "And if you want to see your husband again, you're going to have to play nice."

"*Ex*-husband. And I have a feeling your girlfriend just played both of us for suckers."

Maybe I shouldn't be snapping at John; he's actually been a decent companion during all of this. Turns out, the guy graduated from the film school I once considered attending and, a few years back, he directed a friend of mine in a commercial for a local law firm. *"Big trucks equal big bucks!"* I still remember Patty exclaiming, happily displaying a fanned-out stack of hundred-dollar bills, cartoon bandage on her forehead. They ran that thing at least fifteen times a day.

But it's hard not to redirect some of this anger at his girlfriend. She was supposed to take me to Brad, not dump me in Aleister Crowley's private boudoir. John and I spent ten minutes deliberating whether or not to leave the room and, even though I submit that I won the debate, I've yet to muster the courage to reconnoiter whatever lies outside that door.

So, yeah: I'm a little scared and kind of freaked out.

"Okay, I'll admit this place isn't what I was expecting," he says, "and I'm not sure why Alex bailed on us as soon as we arrived, but…"

I snap. Again. "What do you think this place *is*, John? It's somewhere people like us weren't meant to visit." Gesturing towards the demonic candlestick holders which are designed to simulate a certain act we were once shocked to discover was occurring in the Oval Office, I drive the point home. "Maybe this isn't Hell, but it's some corner of the afterlife, and we don't have any business here."

"Is that what you believe, Sandra?" asks a voice, a female voice of indiscernible origins, from behind. The air sucks out of my lungs.

"Who are you?" I gasp, turning around. "And how did you…?"

"You are in my home, beloved," the woman, a true exotic queen, tells me. I'd place her at over eleven feet tall, perhaps of Middle Eastern origin, with dark, shimmering hair that'd make any girl envious. Even in a world of restless spirits of the undead, I'd say she's the strangest—and most breathtaking—sight I have ever seen. "And as my guest, I ask of you to alter your tone. As for your friend," the mystery lady adds, granting John her attention, "his touch is known to me."

"It is?" John whispers.

"I know of you through my daughter. Isn't she quite the beauty?"

John's speechless. I ask the obvious. "You're Alex's mother?"

"In a… manner of speaking. But we needn't concern ourselves

with such matters now. Sandra, might I petition for a few moments of your time? I feel we have matters of import, best discussed immediately." She doesn't wait for my response; I have a feeling that she isn't used to being told no. "As for you, Johnathon, might I offer you a means to relieve your boredom?"

The door opens, revealing a bevy of indescribably fetching ladies, all garbed in *sheer*—and I mean literally sheer, as in *'Why did they bother to get dressed in the first place?'*—gowns. John, to my amazement and relief, doesn't seem particularly enthused by their arrival.

"I… No. Alex, I… couldn't do this to her," he says, hands raised apologetically.

Our hostess invades John's personal space and, as casually as I'd stroke my parents' pet calico, she's running her fingers through his hair. "Johnathon, my dear, the mores of your world don't apply here. This is something your sweet Alex understands now." She pulls John's face up, so close it nearly touches hers. "You'd be well served by divorcing yourself from the puritanical echoes of your past life… and opening yourself to a different, far healthier, carnal understanding."

Lord, could John be foolish enough to fall for this? Is it so hard to guess what these women are? "John, I'm not sure if this is the best—"

"You, my dear, are not granted a vote." Our hostess turns to face me, her stern expression more than sufficient to evoke an involuntary bladder release. "Now, come with me. You've forced me to repeat myself, an action I'd ordinarily avoid." Approaching slowly, she hisses, "I *wish*… to *speak* with you."

Who could resist an invitation like that? She places her chilled hands on my shoulder and escorts me out of the room. I glance back at John, who looks as if he's a freshman nerd being cornered by the entire football team after school in the locker room. These waifs probably lack the muscle mass to crush a grape, but I suppose there is more than one form of unwanted touching.

As laughable as it is that John wants to stay 'loyal' to Alex, shouldn't his wishes be respected? Should I do something to stop this? *Can* I?

"Don't dawdle," my host scolds. "Your friend will not be harmed. You, however, would do well to learn a few manners."

The door slams, even though no one touches it. Rationalizing that everyone's safest play at the moment is to avoid rocking the boat, I allow the mystery brunette to offer me a tour of the facilities.

"Okay… 'manners'. You know my name. Should I know yours?"

Did she just giggle? "Not entirely necessary. Many of the subjects identify my person as 'She'. You may do so as well."

Kind of the answer I expected. I'm thinking back to the stories Brad's told me over the years; I seem to recall some of the succubae referencing some sort of 'She'. So is this who I'm facing? It'd make a certain amount of sense.

"Do you care for my home, love?" She asks, interrupting the silence. "I'm told mortals find it quite inspiring."

We walk the royal red carpet of this spacious hallway, the stone walls evoking the interior of a Middle Ages castle, if not a palace from even earlier in time. *Much* earlier, like maybe we've barely taken steps out of prehistory. The décor isn't as obviously obscene as the guest room, but there is still an aura of tawdry sex permeating the halls. Even those ram's heads mounted on the wall have a sense of barely restrained sensuality to them. Offsetting their overpowering masculinity are some truly impressive floral displays: hugging each wall, producing a scent more intoxicating than the priciest perfume.

Have I stepped into some Old Testament house of ill-repute? Is Samson's severed head on display in the lobby?

"Tell me, Sandra. Do you love your former husband?"

"What… What's that supposed to mean?"

Allowing a small amount of irritation to surface, She continues, "Is there room in your heart for the fool? Do you think you could find forgiveness for the man?"

"If you're asking if I'm going to forget what he's done, then no," I tell her, unsure why I'm giving the mystery ghoul an honest answer. "But that doesn't mean I hate him, or wish him harm. I still care for him, I still enjoy spending time with him, usually. But we're not getting back together, if that's what you're asking."

"Then why travel here? Why go through such great depths to pursue him?"

"I don't even know. I thought he… needed me," I respond, not fully realizing what I've said until it's too late. "God, that sounds ridiculous. But when I saw him in my dream, saw him so dejected. Just defeated, like he was going to give everything up, and I'd never see him again, that this would be my last image of Brad…"

"And you felt *you* could rescue him?"

"I… I guess I did. Or, at the very least, I could have a chance for a real goodbye. One final moment to tell him that even if our marriage couldn't work, and even though I don't regret ending it… Yes, I do still love him."

She stops in front of a closed door. I could be crazy, but it sounds like muffled screams are coming from the other side. "Fascinating, the way the heart works, isn't it?" she says, grinning far too wide. "Well, Sandra, I won't hold you any longer. Behind this door is your former spouse, and whatever final words you wish to speak to him, I shan't stand in your way."

I examine my host, then that doorknob, far longer than I'm sure She likes. Is Brad really on the other side? Is he okay? Lord, it sounds like someone's being mangled in there… Has this twisted bitch sent him to some torture chamber?

The door cracked open, I receive an answer to a question I mused about earlier. No, succubae aren't given to reverse cowgirl. Turns out, they're into plain ol' boring missionary.

But, not surprisingly, remain on top.

"Oh!" She says as a taunt, reaching for the door; only after she's certain I've caught a glimpse of Alex writhing on top of my husband. Ex-husband. "I believe he's rather preoccupied at the moment, isn't he?"

CHAPTER THIRTY-TWO

Bradley Burns

"So I guess it would be naive of me to ask how we're going to 'ratify' my agreement with your mistress?"

Alex rubs my back. We've been sitting on the bed for five minutes now, getting the formalities out of the way.

Do I feel lower than dirt, giving in like this? Not even a question. Is a part of me relieved that a choice has been made, even if it's a bad one? Sadly, yes.

But, as crazy as all of this is, I hope, in the end, it's the best choice for Sandy.

"It'll be okay, Brad," Alex tells me in a tone I've likely used on a partner or two in the past. "Well, trust me, it will be five thousand times better than 'okay'. No, seriously, what I mean is—"

"I know what you mean. You won't hoover my soul out the first time our naughty bits bump. Mighty gracious of you."

"What I'm saying is," she continues, head resting on my shoulder, "any guilt or anxiety you feel won't last for too long. Any emotion attached to the act isn't, well, relevant here. It's just a part of our lives." She says that last part with a *whaddaya gonna do?* tenor. I'm not sure if I'm supposed to find that endearing.

"And do you believe that, or is it something you've convinced yourself of by now?" Her hair, a bit wavier and bouncier than normal, is falling over my shoulder, nearly down to my lap. "Or maybe Queen Lilith forces you all to chant *'It's Just Sex. No Big Deal. Pass The Ointment'.* every night before bed?"

Alex's genial expression shifts. "You really don't want to be throwing that name around, Brad." She removes her head from the bump in my shoulder. "And I'm telling you the truth. We have a purpose, and we fulfill it." She squeezes my hand, looks me intently in the eye. "I'm not entirely certain what role She intends for you, but you'll accept it soon enough."

"Don't I sound lucky? You think there's some significance behind Her choosing you as the method for the 'ratification'?"

"I assume She senses we've grown close these past few days. That you recognize I'm not the monster you were so quick to believe I was earlier." Alex picks a stray eyelash from my cheek. "Or, hey, maybe she realizes you're hot for my perfect body."

A shameful flash agrees with that sentiment. Her body is impeccable. So is that face. And those ruby lips, the eternal pout, that extra curve resting over her upper lip… I guess I should hate myself, but how can I pretend I don't notice these things?

She's positioned her body even closer to mine now, arm rubbing against my back, and I think the top strap of her gown just dropped from her shoulder.

I clear my throat. "Alex, if we are going to be intimate in this way, don't we owe each other some honesty?"

"Okay," she smiles. "Shoot."

"I'm… not really one hundred percent sure I'm doing the right thing."

Her pointer finger lightly traces my bottom lip. "But, if you had to do this with any girl, aren't you glad it's me?"

"I… like the real you. Not the *Masterpiece Theater* crap."

"Okay. You're not going to be charmed by my ethereal nature… If anything, given your past, you're repulsed by it. You just want someone normal to speak to in this situation." She kisses my cheek. "Fine. I'll be that."

I laugh off the advance. "But do you ever wonder why your mistress has you do these things?" Both of those straps are now down.

"We don't have to talk about Her." Alex moves her hand from my shoulder to the bare skin beneath the robe. I should be thinking of what her mistress did to that skin not so long ago. I *should* be, yes. "Not right now. This is our time."

She maneuvers herself so she's directly facing me. Petite thighs, curved just enough to enhance her femininity, wrap around my waist. "Face it, Brad. We need each other."

We kiss. Some hands move. Maybe a tongue is slipped; who's keeping track of whose?

The inevitable occurs. I'm not normally one for theatrics, but this excursion turns out to be worthy of more than just a few quiet moans. I'm not even aware I'm making those sounds at first, to be honest, but eventually just decide to go with it.

And Alex, she's everything I could've hoped for in this situation. Not some detached erotic dream, but more like a companion, fully sympathetic to the curious circumstances, doing what she can to help me through this. More like a friend than some dumb, horny fantasy.

An equal in this awful but magnificent dance. A partner.

I had to think of that word, didn't I? But when the guilt surfaces like a bat out of the darkness, I fight it off with my prepared mantra: I'm doing this for Sandra. She can't be hurt anymore. It's all for Sandra.

Sandy.

And, as if on cue, I hear the door creak.

CHAPTER THIRTY-THREE

John Horton

A new set of footsteps enters the room. And unlike the tiny footsies that belong to the tittering gaggle of *unusually* eager females calling out my name, this pair carries a heavier step. The other voices in the room grow quiet as she enters.

It's her again, isn't it? That colossal goddess creature who brought those temptresses into my room, mocked the love that's given my life meaning, then sicced her minions on me. Encouraged me to betray my girl, to abandon 'silly' concepts like monogamy.

Well, joke's on her. I didn't give in to the temptation. I stayed on my best behavior… here, underneath the bed. And any floozy who tried to pull me out, she'd be sure to find a fresh pair of dental imprints on those slender, well-manicured fingers. Absolutely no hanky-panky under this mattress.

Through my limited field of vision, I see a Manute Bol-sized pair of bare feet approach. "Johnathon, darling. It's okay," says the voice, calm like a mother talking her child off the top of the jungle gym. "You can come out of hiding now."

"I-I'd rather stay here, if that's fine with you."

She bends down to face me. Her features are honestly striking, although I maintain her 'daughter' still has her beat in the looks department. "Do you truly fear my lovelies, Johnathon? Because I've been watching you, my dear, and I've yet to see you exhibit such pusillanimous behavior in the past. This does not reflect the man Alexandria speaks so highly of."

"Alex talks about me?"

She exhales. "*Endlessly*. The baby seraph simply adores you. She's waiting for you at the table. Won't you join us?"

"You guys eat dinner here?"

"Certainly," she says, offering her hand, twice my size. "A veritable feast awaits you… and not the lascivious kind you were promised earlier, lest you be confused."

I allow the mystery goddess to pull me from underneath the bed. I realize now I likely had no choice in the matter. "I guess I could go for a bite. I mean, if Alex is waiting."

She escorts me out of the room, my rejected harem offering giggles and a few pitiful tugs at my clothes as I walk past. Okay, it's something of an ego boost, but surely these ladies have to know by now that my heart belongs to only one female.

My hostess says nothing as we walk the halls, all decorated like something one of the really *bad* Old Testament monarchs might enjoy. The ones hung up on sacrificing babies and crafting false idols out of elephant tusks: one of those creeps. None of them were female, however, and I'm pretty sure they didn't waltz around in the nude.

Entering the dining hall, my eye is drawn to the ridiculously long table in the center, raised on a dais. Only three are seated at the moment. The breadth of the room is amazing: mile-high ceiling, a massive bay window offering views of pitch-black sky, and a chandelier overlooking the table, sporting over a hundred individual candles and an unbelievable array of hanging crystals.

All lovely, yes. But there's only one image of beauty at the moment that concerns me. Her name is Alex, currently seated across from Sandra, and a man I recognize from the various photos around Sandra's home. The seat between them is empty and, judging by their body language, I'd hate to be the poor bastard stuck sitting in that spot.

The goddess gives a push between my shoulder blades, directing me to my seat. Guess which one it is?

"Ah, I guess we're doing the arranged seating deal?" I take my time, pulling out the chair. "Would it be okay if I sat next to…?"

"Don't be rude, Johnathon. That is your seat," I'm told by the host. "The meal begins shortly."

I muse this isn't so bad; stuck between this busted up ex-couple, radiating foul vibes, I can at least look Alex in her gorgeous eyes now. As I take my seat, more of those creepy sex-starved mistresses in sheer robes are filing in. I look to my love, formulate a question about just who these ladies are… and notice she's wearing the same inappropriate outfit.

"Hello, John," Alex says as a greeting, an unusually formal one. "It's an honor for you to join us."

"Yeah, thanks. You feeling all right?"

"I'm wonderful, John. Why do you ask?" Our dinner companions, not the two stiffs pretending they don't know each other, but those girls surrounding the entrance, apparently find Alex's question amusing.

"You just seem more… formal than I'm used to."

"Dinner with our mistress is a formal event, dear. Will you forgive me for displaying the proper deference to our hostess?"

Our hostess has an unusual conception of female formal attire, I take it. Not a shock, given her own minimal taste in clothing. "Oh, not at all. I, uh, wish I knew. I would've gotten dressed up." Whatever that means for a guy in this place. I examine my hand-me-down clothes from earlier in the day, then turn to my right for a look at their original owner. Only now do I realize he's draped in a baby blue bathrobe, legs crossed, hairy thighs exposed to the world.

I turn back to my love and give her a smile. "But I guess I'm not the only out-of-towner disobeying the dress code."

The goddess takes her place at the head. Seconds later, I realize Alex is the only 'daughter' seated at the table. The rest of the goddess' followers are walking into the side rooms.

When they emerge, they carry sterling silver serving trays, golden chalices, and antique bottles of wine.

"Tonight, we dine in honor of young Alexandria. No words need be spoken of her deeds, so none *will* be," our host says, giving Sandra a nasty look. "But just know that the lass has greatly pleased her mother this evening."

Some might say a dozen attendants servicing a dinner for four is overkill, but those jerks don't know my Alex. She deserves all of this and more. As a server pours my wine, and a second dollops out the meal of roasted lamb and steamed vegetables, I try to regain eye contact with Alex. "So, dear, it's our first meal. And it's all in honor of you, huh? A special occasion, wouldn't you say?"

The only other male in the room pipes in: "'*Dear*'?" He looks me over, then his face lights up. "Hey, I have a shirt just like that! Rick Owens, his Fall line, like two years ago…"

"Heh. Funny story about that." I look over to my left. "Has Sandra told you the details yet?"

"No, I don't believe Sandra and I are on speaking terms at the moment."

Sandra finishes her—lengthy—sip of wine before answering, "I suppose we aren't. And I can't imagine why…"

"Anyway," Brad continues, his tone just shy of friendly, "how do you know Sandra?"

I chuckle nervously, then gesture towards my girl. "Hey, Alex, do you think you could dole out the deets to our friend Bradley here?"

"How do you know my name?" he interrupts, the irritation growing. Looking past me, he asks, "Sandra, what's going on here?"

She doesn't respond.

"Uh, anyway. Alex…?"

Alex, with an eerie calm, gestures towards me. "Brad, this gentleman is John Horton. I believe you know him by reputation, if not personal experience. And he's traveled here, by request, with your former love, Sandra."

"All right." Brad takes a sip and leans back in his chair. After a noticeable moment of silence, he continues. "Still doesn't answer all of my questions. So, I guess you were in contact with Sandra following that incident at your apartment? How'd that end with you in my clothes? What were you doing in my closet in the first place? Are the two of you…?"

"No! It's nothing like that," I shoot back, hands raised. "I'm already, well, spoken for." I look back to Alex. She doesn't offer any affirmation.

Brad takes a breath, then in a conciliatory tone says, "I mean, if it's true, you don't have to deny it. No judgment. I just wondered if maybe Sandra had already given up on me as a lost cause…" He turns to the woman who's been so quick to declare herself his *ex*-wife. "I don't know, I'm just saying, if you want to move on, I'm not trying to hold you back."

And this is the moment Sandra explodes.

Slamming her glass down, refusing to look in Brad's direction, she says the following with gritted teeth: "We split up over a *year* ago, you load. I've been free to 'move on' ever since then." I'm hoping she's said her piece, but unfortunately a second later I feel her eyes burning through, attempting to penetrate Brad's detached exterior.

"Ever since the first time you caught an errant piece, I've been free to find someone else, really. And trust me, I've had opportunities, as much as that might shock you."

Our attendants have no visible reaction to the display. Me, I'm ready to crawl out of my skin, but Alex stays cooler than a cucumber. A quick glimpse at our hostess, however, confirms how much she's enjoying the show.

"Whoa, now. No need for the hysterics."

Sandra's fist hits the table. "And there you go with *that* again. Any honest discussion, any talk that can't be dismissed with a joke, and all of a sudden I'm in 'hysterics'. And Brad? Brad stays the calm, reasonable one. Because God forbid you spend a second thinking about what you've done. God forbid we *talk* about your obscene actions, and how they killed our marriage."

Brad puts on a game-show-host smile, stretching his arms out. "Well, folks, you've just been granted a glimpse into why the Burns got that divorce. Anyone else have any dirty laundry they want aired in public?" He looks over his shoulder, to a lovely young lady with pale blonde hair. "Hey girl, you driven any poor souls to suicide lately? Interested in giving us the backstory on your own premature demise?"

But the girl says nothing. Sandra, meanwhile, isn't letting this go. "Oh, so you're not going to be addressing *her*, are you?" She points to Alex, who does nothing in response. "No snide remarks for your new buddy?"

"Now isn't the best time for that, Sandra. Seriously."

Before I can ask for any clarification, Sandra doesn't hesitate to jump in. "Okay, now you're ready to drop the jokes? Why? I thought we were all just having a great big laugh. Right? Everyone's just in *hysterics*, aren't they, Brad?"

Brad doesn't lob any comebacks. Instead, he places his hand on my shoulder and says, "Anyway, John, maybe it'd be best if *you* finish the story."

Sandra's back to her wine; I'm still waiting for someone to explain how exactly Alex is his new 'buddy'… but maybe we've hit an awkwardness threshold for this meal. Pressing the issue is tempting, but after catching another look at our hostess, that sickening expression of glee she's not even trying to disguise, I won't provide any more of a show. If there's something Alex and I need to discuss, that can happen later. In private.

I try my best to finish the story. "Well, I guess you could say I was having some problems at my apartment, and Sandra was pretty upset after you disappeared, and that led to the two of us hooking up." Eyes widen. "Not like that! But, y'know, she needed my help, and I guess I wanted to do the right thing."

"I still don't see how you could help her in this situation," Brad says, eyes never leaving my shirt. His shirt. His ridiculously overpriced, designer shirt I'd never buy in a million years.

"Sandra—being quite intuitive, I have to say—figured that Alex could be the key to reuniting the two of you. And, since I'm the lucky fellow that Alex has made a connection with on the other side…" I say this while offering Alex another smile. She barely responds. "…I called to her on behalf of Sandra, and Alex being generous enough to offer to take us along with her, well… I guess we're all here now, aren't we?"

"Yup. Happy endings all around," Sandra interjects. "Though, I guess only one of us so far can make that claim, am I right, Brad?"

Brad seems to wait nearly a minute before he says anything. And when he does, it's in a whisper, as he stretches out of his chair and leans past me. "Sandra, have you given any thought to this? You *chose* to come here? With *her?*"

This seems to nab Alex's attention. "Bradley, are you implying something?"

"Yeah," Brad says, moving back into position, "I'm saying, good egg that you are, you still exist to harvest souls."

Excuse me? I'm ready to defend my girl's honor, but no words come.

Brad turns back to his former bride. "Sandra, did you think this through? You could be—"

A voice from the head of the table intrudes. "Guests, this little drama has carried on long enough, hasn't it?" The tenor in the goddess' voice makes it clear that she isn't soliciting responses. "I suggest we enjoy the rest of our meal in silence. Any objections?"

She grins macabrely, taking another sip of wine. "I didn't think there would be…"

CHAPTER THIRTY-FOUR

Sandra Jones

I'm enjoying another glass of the *shekar* provided by our host. Maybe enjoying it too much.

But I'm not enduring this meal sober. Not pretending the sight of Brad and his latest bim isn't enough to turn my stomach.

You shouldn't have to, my lovely.

It's the voice of our hostess, seated in her chair, silently sipping the wine. But it's also emanating from my slice of lamb. And the chandelier. Maybe the walls, too?

I'm everywhere, dearest Sandra. This is my realm.

"Well, I don't like this. Just too freaky," are words I don't believe I state aloud.

Oh, apologies, Sandra. Would a remembrance from your realm be preferable?

And now, the ornate dining table long enough to serve every member of Congress has morphed into the round kitchen table of my childhood. Yup, it's Tuesday night, which means it's meatloaf, green beans, and an optional serving of coleslaw.

Dad's upset because a new dealership is scheduled to open directly across the street. Has heard rumors the owner is looking to poach his best salesmen.

Mom's upset because no one's noticed she's spiced up the green beans with red pepper flakes. And, hey, she's not looking to push the issue but no one's asked how *her* day went, yet again.

Cold, passive aggressive comments are exchanged. One goes too far. Voices are raised, old grievances return to light. I'm nine, but even at this age I know the only passion in this marriage erupts when the fights break out.

And you're determined this will never be your life, aren't you?

The dining hall has melted, transformed into the living room of the Gruber family. I'm fifteen, surrounded by my clique of degenerate friends. They have parents with liquor cabinets. Parents who don't lock the things when they leave town for the weekend.

I'm seventeen. Still chasing cheap thrills. I'm dating a boy behind my parents' back. I'm borrowing a motorcycle from my weird uncle's new girlfriend. I'm wearing pants for three weeks during the summer, paranoid my mother will notice the road rash on my legs.

Yes, and now you're twenty-one, aren't you? And your father has offered you a job on his lot, hasn't he?

And, even on the first day, I know this is a tedious nightmare. Glued to a desk, typing numbers into a computer, calling up a list of deadbeats.

And it's blessed hot on that first day, yes? And there's a young salesman who comes in for a drink, isn't there?

And he busts my lady-balls about how lucky I am to work indoors. To have a rich daddy who can just hand out a job like this. I give it right back to him.

He likes this. And I like him.

And, two weeks later, he tells me he can talk to ghosts.

But it was no happy ending, was it?

Is there such a thing? Maybe the best case scenario is my parents' life, with their twice-annual arguments over nothing and their early bedtimes and Meatloaf Tuesdays and all those intensely quiet dinners.

With Bradley, it's exciting, at least.

The landscape has shifted, remolded into my living room. And I somehow know it's the day Brad sent that wrong text. When, heart on the floor, I mentally collected the clues. Admitted to myself what I'd been denying for weeks.

Brad's a cheater. A philandering piece of garbage.

And this tears you up, doesn't it?

But I find excuse after excuse to stay with him. To keep our silly, but fun, lifestyle going. Even after the divorce, I let him talk me into staying at the house.

Because you can't bear the thought of truly letting go. Because, even when he breaks your heart, you're feeling something, *aren't you?*

Not anymore. I am officially done.

Would you think me a skeptic, if I were to doubt this latest proclamation?

Are you judging me, Queen of the Naked and Damned?

Oh, not at all. Merely enjoying the presence of your company...

CHAPTER THIRTY-FIVE

John Horton

I keep telling myself that I'm doing this for Alex. That I didn't have much of anything to live for back home, anyway.

An enlightened perspective, Johnathon.

And now the dining hall is liquefying. Colors blend, then reform as a new locale. I'm sitting on the floor of my childhood home. And the voice of the creepy nude woman Alex apparently serves is coming from the walls.

Does this disturb you? Do you find my presence so disconcerting?

I try to ignore the voice. Just focus on tiny me over there, glued to that old *Zenith* set on the floor. I'm watching my afternoon cartoons, engrossed in the adventures of my heroes.

It's an appealing thought, isn't it? To be needed. To be the one who saves the day.

Probably wasn't the pickiest of kids. It could be *Blue Falcon* and his canine sidekick *Dynomutt, Dog Wonder*, or an ancient rerun of Clayton Moore as the *Lone Ranger*. But I loved my heroes.

And what became of this child who worshiped heroes, Johnathon? Has perhaps a cynical perspective entered the heart of this innocent boy?

The landscape gets all goopy again, reforming as my high school courtyard. I see kids smaller than me being picked on. A fourteen-year-old with acne and a bad stutter receiving hell from a friend of mine. I say nothing.

Then there was the day you journeyed to a new town. Left behind those friends of old.

And now I'm two blocks away from my first apartment in Boyle Heights. Walking home with a bag of groceries. And I know this is the day I'm jumped by some random punk.

Yes, now I taste the blood against my teeth. Feel the sting of the punches.

The police will later tell me, from my hospital bed, that it was likely a gang initiation. Whoever happened to be passing that street corner would've taken the same beating.

But those physical wounds eventually healed, didn't they? Surely you didn't allow this random experience to color your view of the world?

I see myself alone in that apartment, six months later. A classmate from film school is calling; she's friendly. Wants me to join her group of friends for a night out. I'm not answering the phone.

I see myself six years later in a new apartment. I'm watching a DVD collection of one of those old hero shows. Outside my door, I overhear my neighbor's ex-boyfriend drunkenly pounding on her door. Demanding she let him in.

The shouting intensifies. I turn up the television, drown out that racket.

Had you learned by then, Johnathon, that you are no hero? That you're far more comfortable standing in the periphery?

It's no sin, playing it safe. Protecting what you've already got, regardless of how meager it is.

Oh, of course not. Admirable, truly, to recognize what you are.

And I find myself asking this dark goddess what I am. She's kind enough to answer.

A bit player, at best. But, Johnathon, not everyone enjoys the privilege of playing the hero.

This is followed by a laugh that chills my marrow: but also warms my spirit. And, even though I recognize the dark goddess is playing some twisted game, I find myself thanking her for the attention.

For confirming what I truly am.

CHAPTER THIRTY-SIX

Bradley Burns

Sandra was the first to go down. I mean, I guess it's understandable, her turning to the comfort of fermented drink during the Dinner from Hell.

But my lovely ex-bride should've realized the vino was spiked. Really, we all should've guessed that. But, no, we had to sit here awkwardly, ingesting the lovely meal and granting Evil Queen Succubus a show worthy of *Jerry Springer* in his heyday.

Spiking the wine, sending us to this foggy oblivion, truly does border on overkill. But, as she's explained previously, this is a land of excess, after all.

Were I forced to guess, She's doing this to all of us simultaneously. Appearing before us, warping the surroundings into a melted psychedelic tapestry, forcing us to relive horrifying moments of our past.

Yes, yes. I see the day I received that call about my parents. Oh, look, it's the first time Sandy confronted me over my wayward unit. And there's Dolley, introducing Li'l Bradley to a forbidden world of carnal delights.

Oh, and there's the sense of shame and confusion that followed each encounter. Followed up with a flood of guilt, condemning me as a nightmare husband. Mustn't forget that.

Guess what, genius? I did this to *myself* the other day.

Oh, I know, dear, I hear that sweet yet spiteful voice speak. *Merely enjoying a taste of my latest prize. But, only a taste. I've already indulged myself so much tonight.*

CHAPTER THIRTY-SEVEN

Sandra Jones

"He did attempt to speak to you, to explain himself."

She's addressing me from her throne. And, as per the introduction provided before that utterly fantastic dinner—the one with that foggy final course I'm having trouble recollecting—'She' is this broad's name. Not too pretentious, nope.

"And you realize that your marriage vows were broken ages ago, correct? His coquetries should no longer concern you."

Maybe I shouldn't care, or even be surprised by where his prick leads him. One point to you, freaky giantess. But seeing him like that, in this setting, giving in to *that* woman, this had to be his new low. And when our hostess made it known that 'no' wasn't an option, I soon found myself seated at Her table, avoiding eye contact with my ex *and* his new playmate, finding more than a little solace in the vino.

"And while I've been worrying myself sick over him, he's been here on the other side, boning ghost chicks and having the time of his life." That old liquid courage. Looks like I still have a tad. So how's nude demon lady going to respond if I do step on her freakishly large toes? And why's she so protective over Brad, I wonder?

"Sandra, perhaps these matters aren't so simple? Did it ever occur to you that Bradley made this decision after no small amount of soul searching?"

"Uh-huh. You offered him an eternity as a sexual plaything, and I'm sure he did everything in his power to resist you, didn't he?"

She crosses her legs, leans back on her throne. "Believe what you wish. The question now remains… What's to be done with you?"

Is *that* the question? I pause, decide to show a little more humility towards my host. "I only came here to say goodbye to Brad." Perhaps genuine emotion helps. Maybe she has empathy for us fleshy creatures. "Actually, this is a joke: to maybe talk him into fighting back and coming home, if that was possible. I didn't mean to invade your territory. Not the best irrational decision of my life, I've gotta say."

She looks at me the way my family's calico studies a canary. "Ah, but your presence does present a conundrum, dear. You asked to travel to this place. I granted permission. Did you not consider that the journey would have its cost? Are you my guest, or are you now a servant of my will?"

Or am I simply a pawn in this game you're running on Brad? Maybe you're all-around nasty and conspired to bring me here just for that one moment outside Brad's bedroom? "That's ridiculous," I spit, forgetting my manners once again. "Are you saying I sold you my soul or something? Doesn't that entail a few parchments signed in blood, maybe an oxen sacrifice or two?"

Eyes squint just a tad as she smiles. "Perhaps the legalities would work in your favor. Perhaps not. Regardless, you are now in my realm, not some hostel where you're free to leave at your leisure."

"So I'm your prisoner here?" A prisoner for life thanks to a dumb, romantic split-second decision that I should've known I'd regret?

"Let's not get ahead of ourselves. Were I to send you back to your home, would you be willing to return a favor?"

"Well… maybe."

She then asks, "Would you be prepared to travel to a certain place, and see to a few errands on my behalf? I'm not able to traverse the realm of humans so easily, as you might've surmised. Having you as an aide might be… advantageous, I suppose."

"And what would these 'errands' consist of?"

"I'll compile a list within the hour. Come see me then. In the meantime, you're free to explore the palace." I turn to leave, but she adds, "Mind you, if you take a liking to our home, I would be open to more negotiations…"

I have to stop myself from making a crack about those gowns. Yes, I could pull one off, but I'd hate to make those other bims jealous. Speaking of which, two members of the concubine appear to escort me from Her chambers. None of our electronic devices journeyed with us to this realm, so I'm left to guestimate the length of this waiting period.

An hour to kill. I could take in the sights, appreciate the vile pornographic glory of the décor, but opt instead for a nap. Yes, I have at least one goodbye I know I need to make, but the plan is for that one to stay as short and sweet—or 'sweet' in quotes—as possible.

I spot a familiar, gaunt figure lingering in the hallway. "Kinda hiding in plain sight, aren't ya, pal?" I ask him.

John, lost in his own world, looks in my direction. "Sandra, hey. Hiding from what?"

"More of your groupies, of course."

"I'll take my chances. Alex said she'll meet me here. Said she needed to tell me a few things."

Sure, nothing about that sounds ominous.

I touch his arm, try to offer comfort. "John, listen, be careful. This is, clearly, a place where 'mortals' like us don't belong. And I'm in the process of negotiating my way out, just so you know. Maybe the rules are different for you, I don't know, but you ought to consider asking for *some* exit." I force a smile, adding, "If you'd like, I can speak to the naked boss lady and see if she'd include you in my deal."

John squints. "Sandra, I don't want to be rude, but… haven't you been paying attention? I didn't make some spur-of-the-moment decision to come here, and I didn't plan on a quick stay for the sake of one conversation. I *want* to be here."

"John… Are you sure you know what you're saying?"

"I want to be with the person who makes me happy; happier than I ever thought I could be. If this is where we're fated to stay, then I'm fully prepared for that." Both hands open, he adds, "If there are conditions, or some red tape attached to… whatever all of this is, I suppose I'll deal with that, too. What matters is, it's going to be me and Alex. If I have to make sacrifices to make that work, then—know what?—I'll be glad to make them."

I'm willing now to admit that I do, in some odd way, like John. Maybe his social skills aren't the best, but his heart seems to be in the right place. I probably would've liked to have met him in a different context, maybe at a club show for some obscure indie act, or waiting in line for tickets for a superhero movie we both know is likely going to suck because Sam Raimi is really the only person they should let direct the things.

But, sweet baby hay-zoos in the manger, he's about as pathetic a mark as I've ever seen. "John, you do remember that second time we talked, don't you? When I explained to you what someone like Alex is capable of? What that 'love' can do to you?"

"Make me act irrational? Forget my own best interests?" He crosses his arms. "Crazy thought, huh?"

An uncomfortable silence lingers for too long. Unsure how to answer, maybe even unable, I give John a hug goodbye and continue down the hall. These hallways can be confusing, but I'm sure if I make a left here, I'll be a few doors away from the room John and I were assigned.

So, why am I moving straight ahead? Why am I moving towards the room our nasty hostess escorted me to, just to get that reaction out of me?

And why is that skank whore coming from this direction?

When Alex recognizes me, she puts her head down in shame.

As if I'm going to let her off that easy?

"Congratulations," I tell her as we pass. "You've got another one on the line, ready—*eager*, actually—to be reeled in."

She stops, looks up at me. "I suppose that's one way to repay a favor," she says, cold.

"Say what?"

"I seem to recall," Alex continues, "only a few hours ago, you were desperate to follow me home. I also remember warning that you might not like what you find here."

"Oh, okay, sweetcheeks," I tell her, still not letting this go, because I shouldn't have to. "Guess you've got a point. First thing I do when I get back home, I'm heading to the *Walgreen's* to pick up a *Hallmark* card. *'Thanks for guiding me into the afterlife to say one final farewell to someone I should've abandoned years ago. Fun times. And, P.S., way to put a hurting on his Irish shame down there. Nice technique, sister.'* I'll try to find one with Snoopy on it."

And now I've inadvertently dragged up a memory of a game Brad and I used to play. Every holiday, we'd each find the cheesiest greeting card at the store and, with a creative use of *Sharpies*, revise the saccharine messages into the filthiest declarations of lust allowable in most states.

Whoever managed to corrupt the sweetest cartoon image the worst was declared the winner. And the prize just so happened to be, no questions asked, a recreation of whatever depraved act the winner had scribbled onto the card.

Perverted, yes. But I can guarantee we had a more memorable Arbor Day than most.

"You think I'm some kind of monster, don't you?"

"No, no. Heavens, no. I think you're a poor, lost soul, who accidentally came into my life, invaded my dreams, and then slept with my ex-husband. You also threw a toilet at my head. But I guess you apologized for *that* one, huh?"

She collects herself. I'm fighting it, but I'm beginning to see more of the girl who visited my dreams the previous night. "Sandra, I know I scared you during our first encounter, but you have to

understand that, as much as I'd like different, I'm not one of…
you, anymore." Some hurt's pooling in those eyes. "My reactions
aren't the same. And, even though I am here on the other side, that
doesn't mean that I can't feel things."

I should stop myself, maybe, but I can't let her get away with
this. "Mm. So that was all *my* fault?"

"I would say the blame falls equally in that circumstance. As for
Brad, you must realize that no one was looking to hurt you. Just
the opposite, in fact."

"Oh, really. I should feel flattered, I guess. I don't know what
kind of magic you have working downstairs, but it must be damn
strong." Yeah, who cares about what you see in her eyes. Probably
another con she's running. Probably thinks she can just cry her way
out of the guilt. "Brad *despises* your kind. Yeah, he might be a louse
and a cad and all that, but you ghost whores outright sicken him.
That game you were playing in your mother's dreams, breaking her
heart every night, tearing open that wound when all she wanted
was to rest? Brad told me about it, told me how badly it disgusted
him."

"No. That's not true."

"It is. Said it was typical asshole ghost behavior. Yet, somehow,
you've twisted him around. Gotten him to taste the ultimate
forbidden fruit, right?"

For a second, I think she might cry. Instead, she chokes
something down, then steps closer. "If you must know, all of this
isn't exactly my ideal picture of the afterlife, Sandra." Directly into
my eyes, she makes this clear: "But it's reality now, and I'm dealing
with it the best I can."

I shoot out my answer before giving it any thought. "Sure. Poor
demonic Alex, she's the victim in all this. Listen, if you want to
prove you're not a sadistic monster, won't you at least give that
poor woman some peace at night?"

Cheap shot. Maybe I'll feel bad about it later. I'm in the process
of officially walking off in a huff when another thought lands,
however. Let's say, hypothetically, I am home within the hour. And

Brad's not there with me. Don't we have this one last case to clear, regardless?

"And if you happen to come across a bright tunnel of light," I say, over my shoulder, "try floating your pert little ass up into it, okay?"

CHAPTER THIRTY-EIGHT

Bradley Burns

"Oh. Sandra."

Didn't mean for the words to come out like that. Truthfully, I was more shocked than anything. Was hoping we could have a chance to talk, away from the psycho-queen, but the beast has been hovering over Sandy since the moment she arrived.

"Expecting your favorite bubbly succubus, were you?" Sandra says, not waiting to be invited inside the room. "Sorry to disappoint."

I tried to pull her aside, leaving the dining hall, but she was swooped away by more of Her followers, while I was politely 'escorted' back to this room.

I was going to find Sandra, try to apologize, try to work out some way to get her out of this. I swear that I was… After I figured out precisely how to string those impossible words together.

"Sandra, actually, I'm glad you're here," I say as she brushes past. "Well, okay, I'll be honest. I *hate* that you're here, and damn worried about it, but I'm glad I have a chance to talk to you… Y'know, about…"

"What I walked in on? Your latest little affair?"

"'*Affair*' implies infidelity, which would also imply that we're still a couple." Shit, what's wrong with me? Why do I always say the wrong things to her at the worst times?

Before she can even react to that one, I add, "No, wait, Sandra, I'm not looking to fight. And I'm sorry I got so defensive during dinner, but you've gotta admit that was just prickly for everyone involved."

Since my room has no chairs, I invite her to sit on the bed with me. Her face exposes her reluctance but, after an internal debate, she makes an effort to seat herself as far away from me as possible without landing on the floor. "Look, I appreciate you coming here to see me again, and I'm sick that you walked in on… what you walked in on."

"Of course. Always filled with regret, as I recall."

Okay, buddy, good luck with this one. "But you don't understand… I didn't exactly have a choice in the matter. Well, there was a choice, but the alternative would've been even worse. For everyone. And Alex, I have to say, was doing everything she could to help me through this."

"Yes, I caught a nice glimpse of how helpful she can be." That pissy tone is muted a tad after she breathes in and starts again. "You know what she is, Brad. You know what she's already done to that poor schmuck down the hall, what she's probably already done to a dozen before him. You know these beasts, Brad, you know not to fall for the pretty face and perfect body. Why…? *How* could you ever let something like that touch you?"

I've been working on an answer to this question ever since I caught a glimpse of Sandy's silhouette in the doorway, that moment Alex and I were 'indisposed'. And I still haven't come up with a suitably non-creep explanation.

"Oh, I'm supposed to guess the answer," Sandra says, not waiting for the response. "Okay, this time I guess we'll go with *'I was weak, Sandy. You just don't understand the temptation, how hard it is to refuse that touch, to turn down that feeling they can give you…'* Close enough, right?"

Not where I was going. I wanted to tell her I viewed this life as penance, as a form of just desserts after so many years catting around. I know what these women are; never wanted them touching me.

I didn't realize Alex would be my 'first', though. Didn't know she could find a way to make the experience bearable. Not that I can ever tell Sandra this.

Instead, I have to say, "Sandy, believe what you want, but this is where we have to say goodbye. So, you can rehash old arguments or you can—"

"No, buddy. Uh-uh." She stands. "I'm not letting you off that easy. You're coming back home with me."

"What?"

"You heard me. If She's willing to let me go back home, then she'll do the same for you. Assuming her mighty nakedness doesn't expect us to do anything too offensively gruesome, I'm going to tack on your release as a condition of mine. Just don't expect us to share an address anymore after we get home."

Sandy holds out her hand. "And, hey, if I'm on a lucky streak, then we might even be able to drag Sad Sack Jack out of here with us."

"Ah, Sandy… No. It's not going to work like that."

"What do you mean?"

I'm still staring at her hand. When I look away, she finally retracts it. "My fate is sealed, Sandy. There's nothing I can do. I'm destined to stay here, with Her and her servants, for all eternity."

"Get out."

"I can't. I literally can't. An offer was made…" And for the thousandth time I consider telling her everything, but stop myself. Exposing how weak I know I'd be on the other side, how certain I am I'd keep on hurting her… is that really going to help? "…and I had to go with best option in front of me."

"And you can't get out of it?" she asks, more angry than sad. I hope. "You can't plead your case?"

"A covenant was made, Sandra. I've given my word. And the agreement ratified."

Twice, actually. And, truth be known, Alex and I were in the midst of a third ratification when Sandra made her entrance. Something else I'd rather not tell her.

Sandy says her goodbye with a middle finger. The door slams. I, regrettably, shout a curt expletive, one I know she'll hear on the other side of the door.

CHAPTER THIRTY-NINE

John Horton

I recognize Sandra's heart was in the right place, and I hate to be rude towards someone who, in her own way, was trying to help. I can appreciate what she was trying to say.

But get with it, lady. Did she really think I was going to abandon an eternity with the woman of my dreams?

Is this situation freaky as all hell? Of course. But, as I keep repeating, it's not as if courting a spirit was going to be an ordinary dating experience. And who needs 'ordinary' anyway?

"Any reason why you wanted to meet here?" I ask my love, as I spot her down the hall. From this distance, it looks as if the poor girl's ready to cry. She doesn't say anything when we meet: just a squeeze of the arm and peck on the cheek. After collecting herself, Alex finally smiles. The thought that maybe, just maybe, I could be for her what she's been to me sends my head reeling.

I try to remind myself I'm at least a little upset with the girl.

She takes me to the manor's library, bookshelves lining every wall, stacked with ancient tomes. I know Sandra was unnerved by the furnishings in our guest room, but this seems to be a fairly typical study.

That's what I tell myself, until I catch the lone piece of furniture in the room, a sofa resting in the middle, its decorative pillows depicting an obscene act that involves five different people.

Alex, for her part, is far more engrossed with these twenty-foot-tall bookshelves.

"John, there's something in here you need to see," she finally says.

"Okay… But I thought we were going to talk about some things."

"Sure, Johnny. What would you like to discuss?"

"Us, of course." As much as I adore the girl, we're going to have to address these things. "I'll be frank, this isn't what I had in mind when I volunteered to travel here."

"That's… understandable, John." She motions for me to join her at the nearest bookshelf. "But, please listen. There's something I wanted to show you."

"And, there's something else, Alex. What was that between you and Brad back there? All that talk about the two of you being buddies? Because, I've gotta be honest, that's the kind of thing no man wants to hear about his girl."

Quiet, Alex reaches for a book. "John, you need to take a look at this." She hands me a leather-bound volume, one that looks like something Indiana Jones would've rescued from an ancient excavation in Tunisia. The portrait of the man on the cover is obviously from modern America, however, right down to the trendy mustache I attempted—and failed—to grow last year.

I read the cover copy aloud. "*Franklin Parks. Medina, Ohio.*' I don't get it."

"Just keep reading, Johnny."

Inside are painted portraits representing this anonymous Franklin's life. His idyllic '80s childhood. A Las Vegas wedding ceremony. A second one in a church, the role of the bride recast. A moving van, the parking lot of my apartment complex. Images of him alone, miserable, a *Jim Beam* bottle half-empty on the coffee table.

And, a third of my way through this tome, the arrival of Alex. Taking a seat beside him on the couch, calling his name. First image, he refuses to believe some invisible figure is nearby. He's nervous by the third. Infatuated by the fifth. Ten pages after my love's arrival, she's granting this Franklin Parks the kind of supernatural ecstasy that, foolishly, I thought Alex would only share with me.

When my heart slows its pounding just enough and I'm finally able to speak, I ask, "You… slept with this man?"

"I joined with him, John," she says, with a tenor that nearly sounds like pride. "Made him complete."

What did she say? "Why… Why would you show me this?"

Coolly, Alex returns to the bookshelf. "Here, Johnny. Look at this one."

The volume's cover has a similar portrait, another man who could be just some guy I went to high school with. I read aloud the words "*James Flatt. Narragansett, Rhode Island.*"

No, four years of mediocre public schooling isn't what James and I have in common. I flip through the pages and see the same basic beats repeated, only the names and faces changed. "Alex… Another one? How long have you been doing this?" I realize I've slammed the book shut. "Why are you showing me these things?!"

"John, this shelf is devoted to my accomplishments," she tells me, left arm stretched to indicate that row. "It's a meager collection, compared to others, but She has been pleased with my work so far." Approaching me, Alex closes her hands and says with an unnerving sincerity, "And having you here with us, joining us willingly, before your natural time, I can't tell you how honored we are."

She has her hands on my arms, but I can't respond. "Understand? These are your brothers now, John. And soon you'll be bonded with them."

"I'm supposed to be happy about that?" I snatch the book from her hands and, I'm not proud of this, but the next thing I know I've slammed the thing onto the cold stone floor. "Alex, I love you. I… I don't want to share you."

"You have to understand that all of these thoughts about possessing someone, keeping her exclusive to you, that's from the culture we were born into," she says, shaking her head and placing petite hands on my chest. "But it's unsuitable for this world. Here, no one owns anyone."

"But, Alex, I don't want to share." I reject her embrace for a second time. "And the thought of you being with other men, having them touch you… Lord, I think I'm going to be sick."

I turn away, deny her the tears forming. She gives me space, but within a moment I feel a hand on my back. "No, John. Don't give in to that. This is a different world, Johnny, a more honest one. We don't hoard love here."

She's caressing my upper back now. I remember the massage she gave me as a prelude, that first night we joined together. "I still care for you, love. I've never known someone as pure-hearted as you," she continues, in a voice that could soothe any wounded child, while also evoking thoughts of the most forbidden of acts. "I know how life's disappointed you, but our visits, what we have…"

"Alex, don't do this."

"Johnny, you mean the world to me. I recognize this wasn't exactly what you had in mind, but ultimately, didn't you want the two of us to be together?"

I turn to face her. Cheeks are moist, but she uses her fingertips to dry them. "Yes. You know that's all I wanted. But—"

"And are we not together now? Johnny, do you remember what it was like, those first few weeks, when our skin couldn't even connect?" Her hands head south. "Don't you want to feel my touch now, Johnny?"

"I… I love you, Alex. But this is too much…"

She takes my hand, guides towards the sofa with the mischievous pillows. "Please don't reject me, Johnny. I'm here now, offering myself to you," she says, breathless. "No one's ever made me feel the things you made me feel. Don't cast me out, my love."

Her lips, her full, ruby red lips that always make me quiver, brush against mine as she whispers, "I couldn't bear that."

I can be magnanimous, I tell myself. I can be forgiving. I can open myself to the sweetest love imaginable. And, for better or worse, I give in.

We fall asleep in each other's arms.

Sometime later, I'm awakened by a chill. I spend a few seconds transitioning from dreamland to reality—or whatever we're to call this place—and soon realize my body's resting on the icy floor, my view obscured by iron bars. On the other side of my prison, I see Alex making a surreptitious exit into the darkness. And, I could be wrong, but in her right hand there's what appears to be a glass vial.

Disoriented, still trying to make sense of what's happened, I examine my cage. Realize three strangers are my roommates. My muddled grunts have disrupted the sleep of the nearest gentleman. He pulls his head away from the pillow he's made of his arms, curses at me, and then resumes his sleeping position.

I did get a decent look at his face during that brief, profane lecture, though. Wouldn't you know it? My pal is none other than Franklin Parks of Medina, Ohio.

CHAPTER FORTY

INTERLUDE III

She again ached to see the one who birthed her. Selected another sacrifice from the pit downstairs. So many developments the mother must hear of.

Their conference is not going as planned. Her mother, her mistress, has been paying attention. Has a list of concerns. She, naturally, feels no embarrassment expressing them.

The daughter tells her mistress to not worry about this Alexandria. Says the girl is only sowing her oats, clinging to the last vestiges of her old self. Alexandria still performs her function, still has the love in her heart.

The mistress corrects her offspring. Expresses misgivings over the way the diviner is saddled up next to that girl. Their bond is… unusual.

She counters this has only worked to their advantage so far. Says this with the proper deference. Subtly shifts the subject. Wants her mistress to know this woman, Sandra Jones, has pricked her finger. Signed the agreement with blood.

This Sandra Jones will soon awake back in her birthrealm. Will have no choice but to live out her end of the bargain.

She wants her mistress to share her amusement over this inconsequential mortal. Of how this Sandra Jones, in a peculiarly human state of anger and heartbreak, walked directly into their trap.

But her mistress is too anxious to submit to levity. This Bradley Burns, she's heard the words he speaks. Knows the name he so casually tosses about.

The servant seems embarrassed. Tries to reassure her mother of the diviner's obliviousness, apologizes for briefly finding his haughtiness amusing. We'll have what we need of him soon enough, she promises.

The affront is not a tiny one; the mistress is adamant she understand this. Know this, sister-daughter, speaks an indefinable voice: he's not one to take lightly. The plan hinges on this cad, and he's practically laughing at us.

The little bastard knows the true monarch's name, speaks it so casually. At the proper moment, the queen's Queen fully expects him to pay for this blasphemy.

CHAPTER FORTY-ONE

Bradley Burns

First time I entered this chamber, all I wanted to do was run the hell away. That feeling isn't nearly as prodigious now, but I must acknowledge the urge has yet to abate.

That's a smarty-pants way of saying I'd rather be anywhere than here. *Anywhere.* Yet, persistent pangs of conscience demand I at least make a social call.

"Hey," I tell John, who's on the opposite side of those iron bars. He's sitting, legs crossed, on the floor, fingers playing a solitary game of tic-tac-toe with the grime underfoot. Two other men occupy the corners of his cell, both asleep, both horribly malnourished. "I'm not even sure I'm allowed down here. I just found out about your, uh, predicament, though, and thought I'd check in."

He doesn't bother to look up. "That's big of you, I suppose."

"If you don't want the company, that's fine. No hard feelings." I wouldn't mind an excuse to leave. The stench down here is, there's no other word for it, overpowering.

"No, you can stay a while if you like. If you don't mind the ambiance."

"So, are you doing okay down here? Or is that a stupid question?"

John brushes his hands and gets on his feet. "We sleep most of the day, which helps to kill time. When we're not, as you know, being called forth to be 'drained'," he says, now facing me. "I don't seem to be as fatigued as the others, which might be because I'm the rookie. Or maybe because I chose to enter here willingly."

"That's something I've wondered about. We're all chumps for being here, but are we in a different position from the ones who had their souls slowly whittled away?"

"Cleary, the two of us *aren't* in the same position," John says, his hands on the bars.

"Yeah, fair point. Well, is anyone here decent company at least?"

"When my cellmates are awake, usually they just whisper 'kill me' over and over again." He snorts. "Glad you asked?"

"If it's any consolation," I say, pretending I didn't hear him, "I'd help you if I could. I'm still trying to figure out what their Queen's game is, and if there's anything I can do to stop all of this."

"You sure about that? Your time isn't elsewhere occupied?"

"Meaning what?"

With a smirk, he asks, "Meaning, your 'buddy' isn't distracting you from your top secret mission?"

I suppose I could tell him. Let him know that it was Alex who told me he'd been sentenced to live in this hellhole. How full those precious cheeks were, as she tearfully told me the story of leading him down here. My lips open, I try to form the words but… Nothing.

"Look, it's probably best if we don't discuss the Alex situation, John. And I realize you're probably angry right now, but I think her situation is more complex than you understand."

"Heh. She got to you, too, didn't she? And Sandra thought *I* was the most pathetic mark she'd ever met."

"To be fair, Sandra didn't fully understand these circumstances, either." A nice opportunity to change the topic. "She did manage to finagle a way out, by the way."

"Yeah, I remember her saying our 'Queen' was offering her some escape."

"Uh-huh. 'The Queen.' John, you ever hear of the legend of Lilith?"

He squints, then says, "Wasn't she the ex-wife on *Frasier*?"

"No, I'm talking about the woman from prehistory; the ancient Hebrew myth. There's an old joke—I mean, horribly sexist—about her being the first feminist, in a way."

"Ah. You think the Queen's bargain with Sandra was some form of exclusive sisterhood deal?"

"What do you mean?"

John rests his arms on the horizontal bar that connects to the lock. "Think about it: what good is a mortal woman in this place? *We're* the ones she wants."

"And that's what I still don't understand. What do they need us for?"

If John has an answer, he doesn't offer it. After a few seconds of silence, he speaks, his voice now distant, "I just wish I'd listened. Sandra, she tried to warn me. Tried to make me realize what a fool I'd been."

"Yes, she's pretty good with that. Not that I've ever been any better than you, in terms of listening to her."

"Well, hopefully, she got back home okay. And whatever happened here hasn't scarred her too much."

"I'd like to think she's totally forgotten it. All of it." Is that so much to ask? That Sandra just thinks this was all a dream? And whatever happens to me in that hospital bed, she'll be able to view as one of those random, inescapable tragedies we all have to suck up and endure?

"Maybe. But I think we both know how hard it is to let certain things go." John taps against the horizontal bar. "You want to know what's really sick? When Alex drops by, singing my name, when I feel her fingers on my skin… Even though I know what she's doing to me, how twisted her motives are, I still can't resist her touch. I still can't bring myself to hate her."

CHAPTER FORTY-TWO

Sandra Jones

"You're out of your mind, kid. *Vick's* is just gonna make the smell worse."

That's the first voice. The gruff one, belittling the younger man who's brought along a tub of that slimy gunk Mom used to cover my chest with, those nights my allergies got to me.

"How so?" asks the younger, gentler voice. The darkness is subsiding, but the images remain an indecipherable blur.

"It opens up your sinuses, dumbass. You're gonna be inhaling even more of this toxic shit in a minute." I hear the footsteps of this older man waltz past my head. He's wearing some off-brand, relaxed fit dress shoe that's evidently been selected for comfort over style. "Your best bet would be nose clips… or you could do like my old partner, who put tiny dabs of snuff up his nostrils."

"No way. *Tobacco* snuff?"

I can make out his features now. The older one is fatter than he probably ever expected to be, considering how much of his gut is hanging over those slacks. "Just a pinch of *Smokey Mountain*, he'd tell me. That'd make any crime scene bearable."

My new friend squats above, then turns back to his companion. "Another option would be to remove that tampon and just take the stench like a man."

The younger one snorts. "Sure thing, Huffman. And I'm gonna

pretend I didn't see you cursing out Sternenberg for not sharing his ammonia poppers?"

"Feh. Sternenberg pees sitting down, too," says the rasping voice. When he looks back my way, eyes bug out of his head. "What the fuh…"

And that's when I appreciate I'm staring directly into his eyes. Apologies, sir. Didn't realize the journey back from the netherworld would leave me so out of sorts.

Disoriented, I pull myself off of the floor. Allow my vision to adjust to the light… and inadvertently crush these tiny numbered flags planted in an outline, surrounding my body. Not my intent to disrupt the workings of the LAPD, but I'm a lady on a mission, and it doesn't include just lying around here.

Wherever here is.

Clearing more gunk out of my eyes, I finally gain a clear view of the room. It's John's apartment, the last place I happened to be on this Earth before foolishly deciding to chase a succubus. We were in John's bedroom, correct? Yes, there's his bed, behind the younger, cuter detective with the buzzcut and designer dress shirt. Resting on top of the mattress is a body that clearly no longer belongs to this world.

Are the maggots causing that stench, or is it the ozone that surrounds all ungodly paranormal activity?

I instinctively begin a silent prayer for John, but stop myself. That couldn't be him. We departed at the same time, and even if he's not coming back, there's no way… There's no way he could be the decomposed cadaver rotting into that bed.

I tell myself that, at least.

This Detective Huffman can't stop swearing long enough to form a coherent sentence. His junior partner maintains his cool, to a certain extent, and stammers out this gem: "Lady! Y-you're supposed to be dead!"

I wish I had a witty *bon mot* to toss back at the fella, but I don't think my lungs, throat, tonsils, etcetera, are working at this time. I just gurgle something indecipherable out of the back of my throat, knock the dirt off my clothes, and head for the exit. Older, fatter detective is still too shocked to move. Younger, cuter one extends his hand to stop me, but I unconsciously swat it away.

Bouncing off the doorframe, I exit the apartment, passing through a dozen or so crime scene investigators before staggering into the elevator. I see the junior detective emerge in the hallway, commanding me to stop, right as the elevator doors close.

So, what was I supposed to do again? Something about Mesopotamia? Does that sound right? No, She told me I'd know it today as Iraq. Okay, sure. Makes perfect sense. Who doesn't want to go to Iraq nowadays?

As the elevator descends, I think about John. No, I'm haunted by that decaying corpse in his old bedroom, I'm *not* thinking about John because that isn't him. Even if his body has passed on, we weren't gone that long, were we? His body couldn't rot like that in only a few hours; there's no force on Earth that could do that…

Ah. Maybe I just answered my own question.

And immediately, thoughts turn to Brad. Whatever debauchery lies ahead for John in the afterlife, Brad's already gotten a taste of it. Is his lifeless, rotting cadaver currently being prodded by a team of confused doctors at the hospital right now? All crowded around, cracking jokes about the stench and questioning just how this stiff got so ripe so quick?

No. I push the thought away. Can't obsess on these feelings because I have things to do. An agreement signed in blood, a quest, an *adventure* that doesn't make any obvious sense, but it's going to keep my thoughts occupied for the next few days. I'm not dwelling on that sickening sight from upstairs. I'm not twisting myself into more knots, obsessing over what fate lies ahead for Brad.

He made his choice. The bastard made his choice.

I'm free now, I tell myself as the elevator mercifully dings. Not entirely. I still have that list of nonsense to see to, but at least I'm back home, and able to start some kind of life again.

"Freeze!" shouts the officer, firearm drawn, who greets me as the doors open.

*

Four hours later, I've answered all of their questions, which didn't seem to vary much between "Why aren't you dead?" and "Seriously, lady, why the hell aren't you dead?" During Hour One, I explained to the investigators that John invited me, as his friend, to help collect his things… and goodness, fellas, I hope we didn't break any laws sneaking into that apartment after he'd already been evicted.

Did I see anyone assault John? I absolutely did not. Did I see a body in the bed when I entered the room? Negative.

Could I explain what happened? Are you kidding me?

My memory of that other realm, of that last conversation with their queen, remains cloudy. I know that I have things to do, and some whisper in the back of my head keeps cursing at these cops for standing in my way, but I hold the irritation in check.

There's no chance freaking out is going to resolve this situation any faster. Maybe my best bet of getting out of here is playing it cool; act as if *they're* the crazy ones for thinking something weird is going on.

Riding to their headquarters, one of the uniforms poked me with his pen to prove that I was real. After the first hour the absurdity of the situation became something of a joke around the stationhouse, and by the third hour some of the police were actually asking to have their photo taken with me.

One of the investigators walks in with a file, asks if I'm the same Sandra Jones who filed a Missing Person's Report on her ex-husband. Yup, and thank you good men and women of the LAPD for your help locating Brad. I tell them I'd like to be excused, because I'm the only visitor the poor soul has in the hospital.

Eventually, a consensus is reached. Not being dead is no crime.

On my way out, I catch one of the cops at the bulletin board, scribbling a note on the bottom of the Polaroid they took of me. How cute that the desk sergeant still had one of those cameras. The officer tried to cover the words while writing, but his hands were too slow.

"The Living Dead Girl!" reads the note, devil horns sketched atop the capitalized "D."

CHAPTER FORTY-THREE

John Horton

Not surprisingly, we don't count the days in this place. I'd estimate the day's Friday, but I've lost count of just how long I've been trapped in this realm. Lack of sunlight will do that.

I'm presently polishing the obscene bits of an obscene statue that decorates the hall. One of Alex's sisters has informed me that, as a new, healthy recruit, it's my duty to perform these menial chores.

'New and healthy' is polite demon speak for 'not quite drained into a lifeless shell', by the way.

The sister who recruited me for the task stopped by ten minutes ago to check my work. Told me I'd accomplished all I could with the rag. That it was time to prove my devotion. To use my moist, pink tongue.

My revulsion at the thought had to battle excitement over the cheap titillation. The thrill of knowing I'm serving my mistresses so well. I suppose that's how this starts: the degradation of a human soul. My first step into becoming the withered nothings I'm currently bunking with.

Footsteps approach. I brace myself for the return of my nearly-nude supervisor.

"John, hi," says the surprising voice of an angel. No. *No.* Stop thinking of her that way. "Been looking for you."

I collect myself. Pretend she didn't just catch a glimpse of my tongue touching a certain place on that statue. "Alex… You've gotten what you wanted. Don't… It's cruel, keeping this game going."

"It's no game, John. How could you believe that?" She touches my arm. "What you have—"

I'm shocking myself, jerking away. "I know. Mortal minds can't comprehend it. Maybe I'll appreciate the sheer depths of all this when I'm as hollow as my cellmates."

"You're still early in your days here. Still healthy enough for the chores. Serving our Queen; this doesn't please you?"

Can't even look her in the eye now. "Alex, how could you fall for this? Why can't you see that demon for what she is?"

"That's… Johnny, don't use that word for her."

"It's the perfect word, girl." A rush of pride as I finally stand up for myself. But it's immediately followed by a mental rebuke. A warning to watch what I say. I try to fight this off, to spit out the rest. "And w-whatever's good inside you, she's twisted it to serve her bidding. To garner more souls to feed her sick appetites."

Sorry, Alex. But you need to hear this.

She's the one who turns away now. "Johnny… Listen, I'm sorry for how you came here. For the things… For what I have to do."

Another set of footsteps. Heavier ones. It's Brad: soaking wet, wrapped in a miniscule towel. I pretend I don't notice he smells of Her servants.

He announces himself as if he's the star of the show, naturally. "Apologies? From a succubus? Now I've heard everything."

CHAPTER FORTY-FOUR

Sandra Jones

Tattoos are monumentally stupid.

That's what I told Brad, the day he casually informed me he was joining the dum-dum cult and getting inked. And not just a small, discreet piece to commemorate an important memory or pay tribute to a loved one—I'm sure he might find maybe *two* if he tried—but an extensive design that would cover every inch of his right arm. And the meaning behind this nonsense?

"Dunno. Just think it'll be cool."

And did his proposed self-mutilation have anything at all to do with the lead of the twice-weekly reality TV program he so adored, the popular 'docu-drama' dedicated to a feuding family of motorcycle mechanics? The show that centered on the middle child, the one with the coolest haircut, most expensive sunglasses, and around $40,000 in tattoo art adorning his toned body? Nah, certainly not.

"Why are you convinced I want to be like that guy? Why can't you give me credit for thinking for myself?"

"Because you want to chase every dumb fashion trend that comes around. And, normally, I don't care. I will, *grudgingly*, admit your sense of style is pretty impressive. But this is a fad you'll be stuck with for the rest of your life, Brad."

That's when he tried to change my mind, told me he'd dedicate the piece to my 'perfect countenance'. I forget the details, but my face would grace the top of his bicep, and somehow my hair would morph into the highway, providing the road for a flotilla of skeleton bikers mounted on flaming motorcycles. He sure knew how to flatter a lady.

Anyway, Brad lost interest in his bad boy makeover around the time the show went into hiatus. He went with the dirty hippie intellectual look not long after, as I recall, growing that hideous beard he'd never admit was a patchy mess.

And, with all that said, I have to wonder what I'm doing in this strip mall tattoo shop, my shirt on the floor, a three-hundred pound *arteest* with a lovingly rendered spider's web resting on his shiny scalp ripping open the flesh on my back with his high-pitched electronic needle.

I'm sure there's a good reason. Perhaps it's related to that call I made an hour ago, arranging my red-eye flight for the evening. Okay, if I had to guess, I'd say it's all tied in with the deal I made for my freedom, even though many of the specifics remain ambiguous.

The pain is nearly unbearable, even worse than I'd always imagined. There's also some sick thought dancing in my head, telling me the throbbing agony is a beautiful testament to someone I don't even know, but who loves me nonetheless.

Over my shoulder, the artist is stopping the electronic needle every five seconds to double-check the drawing I'd brought in with me. Maybe complex sigils that predate the Paleo-Hebrew alphabet aren't popular with his standard clientele, but I'm trusting in my man Buck to do a good job.

That faith is shaken occasionally, as he chokes down a wad of bile, excuses himself to the bathroom, then noisily expels his waste into the toilet. He blames the leftover chicken salad he had for breakfast; I neglect to inform him that I also underwent a few waves of nausea when designing the piece earlier today.

With a grunt, Buck the tattooist wheels his chair closer to my side, catching my unhooked bra against his arm. "Sorry 'bout that," he says, backing off momentarily to allow me to readjust the brassiere. I use the opportunity to just toss the thing on top of my rumpled shirt. Chicks with massive back tattoos, of which I am now apparently one, aren't known for their modesty.

Five hours, three pee breaks, and one awkward fast food meal later, I'm using a combination of a hand mirror and the shop's floor mirror to study the piece. Buck seems slightly embarrassed whenever I forget to do the hand-bra thing, and I guess there's some part of me that's perturbed at the number of times I've flashed him this afternoon.

Maybe. To be honest, I don't think I give a damn.

The piece is a true work of art. Words can't do this justice; my pitiful vocabulary can only describe it as a ring, framing what the uninformed might view as modern characters from the English alphabet. The lovely ornamentation that resembles a T is on its head, merging with the delicate rendering of lines that nearly form the letter L. A center column is fashioned from three lines merging into a shape that, perhaps, resembles a lowercase H. It's the only character that doesn't expand with a flourish into a prehistoric, gorgeously rendered sun cross design.

Bumps of my spinal cord run right up the middle. Cute.

I'm not sure if Buck agrees, however. Dizzy, he runs back to the bathroom after taking only a small moment to appreciate his work.

In the mirror, I realize my free hand is running its fingers over the 'letters'. I feel as if they spell a word.

No, a name. One that's calling out to me.

With no time to waste, I head for the door. As I touch the handle, I remember I haven't paid. Or retrieved my shirt. I double-back for the shirt, even though some queer thought in my head is begging me to leave it behind. It tells me to do something very nasty to the concept of modesty.

No, mystery voice. The shirt stays on. Maybe I should wait for Buck to finish emptying his stomach back there, but as I stop at the counter and reach for my credit card, that sense of urgency returns. Some things are more important than money, you know, and I'm going to need every penny I can scrape together on this trip.

Is it my fault Buck has such a weak stomach, anyway?

*

An hour later, I've made stops at every health food joint, nursery, and hobby store in the area. Having procured a collection of weeping willow, cinnamon, camphor, saffron, nightshade, amber, moonwort, and mistletoe, I kick myself for forgetting what could be the most important element of whatever-it-is I'm doing.

I arrive at the *PetCo* at 7:05, five minutes past closing time. Beating at the door, swearing, and threatening the life of the staff is apparently not the way to gain entry to a closed establishment. After watching one of the employees pull out his phone and dial only three numbers, I make a judicious return to the car I've borrowed from Brad.

And sitting back in that seat, getting another whiff of his shampoo from the headrest, I'm hit by a new flood of memories. Soon, a sense of guilt for not even calling the hospital, let alone visiting, returns. Why haven't I done that? Why am I wasting my time on these stupid errands? And why is my back so sore?

I'm sure I stew over these questions for a while, but then grasp I'm somehow on the lengthy stretch of highway that leads to my parents' home. I slap myself awake, panic a little, but then listen to a calm voice. It tells me this will all be okay… and to continue my journey to Agoura Hills.

My mother, a lovely older woman now gracefully entering her sixties, answers the door. "Sandra!" she says, her face revealing how happy, and stunned, she is to see me. "What brings you here at this hour?"

"Just wanted to check in on you guys," I reply as we enter the screen door. "Is it that late?"

"Almost nine, which you know means your father's turned in. I can wake him, though," she says, already heading for their bedroom.

"No!" I grab her arm. "Don't wake him. I know how early he has to leave for work. No, no, don't worry about that."

She stares with growing confusion. "Well, okay, honey. But I thought you wanted to see us?" Then, her eyes flash. "Oh, no. No. Honey…"

"What…?"

"Don't tell me. Don't tell me that Brad has…"

"Oh, that. No, I wish I could give you an update, but there's been no real change."

Just an outing to the afterlife, another betrayal, a conversation with a queen demoness, a day at the police station, ancient carvings into my back, a sleepy trip down Mulholland Highway, and six bags of spices and incense in the backseat.

Mom offers a spot on the couch. The one I know their calico, Icky, has festooned with countless hairballs in the eleven years since they've purchased it. Hey… Icky! Where is that little devil?

"Okay, I suppose that's better than bad news. Honestly, though, Sandra, I'm worried about him. I did some research on comas on the computer, the ones caused by accidents, and it doesn't sound good."

I'm off the couch a second after I'm seated. "Hey, Mom, where's Icky?"

"She's around here somewhere. Look, I'm not trying to be morbid, or pessimistic, or… or… whatever, but I'm telling you this sounds extremely serious," she continues, even though I'm not in the room. Examining the kitchen, I see the tiny angel's food and water dishes, but no sign of the feline.

"I think you need to prepare yourself for the possibility that, well… The two of you aren't married anymore. I know that sounds awful, but I hope you understand what I mean."

Is she still going on about Brad? I enter the dining room and call Icky's name. No movement, which means nothing. This is a cat, after all. I stoop below the table. Ah, there she is, resting against her two front paws, half-asleep.

"He doesn't deserve what's happened to him, I'm not saying

that at all, but you need to remember you were always too good for him. And, please, Sandra, don't let this situation, however it turns out, prevent you from moving on. Because your father and I have discussed this, and—"

I march past Mom, eyes on the front door, shushing her with a wave goodbye. I pray she doesn't notice the animated lump I'm cradling beneath my shirt.

And *who* exactly am I praying to…?

CHAPTER FORTY-FIVE

Bradley Burns

"Hey now, I didn't say you could touch down there," I tell the Russian ginger with the perpetually wet bangs. They all have wet hair at the moment, actually, the five 'daughters' sent to assist me in this mandated bath.

Not my idea, I swear.

"Mistress has asked for you to be cleansed," my retainer teases. "Thoroughly. We live but to serve."

"Great. Is this going to last much longer?" Yes, they're all hotter than the sun. Yes, they'd be willing to do anything I asked, along with a few other acts of carnal derring-do I'd never even think to request…

The brunette meticulously grooming each individual hair on my chest giggles. "Oh, Bradley. This can go on for as long as you wish. It could never end, if you so desired."

And, yes, I have had numerous dreams about this specific scenario in the past.

"Or I could just wash myself." So, lucky Brad, when the impossible becomes possible… I'm thinking of the woman I left behind. "I'm not a toddler, you realize."

"Bradley, you're much more than that, yes," coos the platinum blonde with the long, loose curls that fall to her chest. "So much more…" And, with a squeeze, she makes her meaning more than clear.

Nearly slipping in the bath, I scold, "Okay, too far, darling. Too far." She sulks like a kid denied ice cream on a July afternoon.

Did their mistress think this would work? I mean, of course I could do what's expected, live out this ridiculous wet dream and experience all of the mind-blowing *woo-weee* these harpies keep promising. I could live up to my reputation and just submit.

Some part of me keeps whispering to do this. And, me being me, maybe one day I will.

I can't pretend there's no sexual desire for my wet, willing companions. I'm only half-dead, mind you. But everything about this scenario… So cheap, so contrived. Giving in would be more demeaning to me than anyone else involved.

I know what they are. I know who they serve.

Yeah, you'd have to be a blithering fool to fall for this. Or, you know, just the average male. But I'm not any libido-driven mope, I'm a libido-driven mope who's spent most of his life surrounded by these ghouls.

Who had his own… memorable tryst with one as a lad.

Maybe I can resist the urges. Keep my mind focused long enough to accomplish that little niggling thing I've been unable to do since making my deal with their mistress.

I'm tempted to strike up a conversation with the blonde with the loose curls. See if she can help. But, really, she's made her intentions known. And why bother attempting 'rapport' with one lost spirit when I've already put my work in somewhere else?

*

I overhear her voice down the next hall, just a few minutes after I began my search. Hey, maybe that 'covenant' thing was no joke. Maybe we are linked.

Maybe that thought doesn't horrify me. Maybe.

Don't mean to eavesdrop, but these halls echo. I hear her conversation with that poor sap, John. Hear something I have to respond to.

"Apologies? From a succubus?" I ask Alex. "Now I've heard everything."

She turns. Gives that smile I tell myself can't work on me. "Brad! I've been meaning to speak to you, too."

John snorts. "'*Speak?*' It's okay, Alex. Don't have to use the code words around me." He collects his rag and moseys down the hall. Maybe I should've complemented him on the spiffy job he's done with that statue.

Her hands extend to mine. "Listen, I wanted to make sure you're doing okay."

"And are these things you normally do? Check in on the peasants? Offer apologies?"

"It's been different, I'll admit, since we met."

Something to consider later. But if Alex is truly in an obliging mood, if my influence has changed her in some way, at the very least she can help me with this minor thing, right?

"Well, Alex, since I've caught you in such gracious spirits, thought I'd ask a question. I am… Well, I'm *dead*, right?"

A moment before she responds. "Why do you ask such a thing?"

"I'm assuming that's how the deal works. I mean, I'd hate to think I'm still lingering on Earth. That… well, a certain someone isn't still chained to that chair next to my bed."

"Sandra, you mean." Her arms fold. "Brad, I'm not keeping tabs on her."

"I want her to be free of all this. Free of *me*. And, yeah—in those moments I can slip away from your Sisterhood of the Hysterical Libido—I admit I've been trying to send my soul back home." I grab her arm, pull it close to me. "Do that trick you showed me earlier."

She doesn't pull away. "And, Brad, do you think this is the best idea?"

"I got bad decisions in my DNA, Alex. But I don't think this is the worst thing to do; taking a final look back, making sure that certain someone is truly moving on. Yet—and maybe I just suck at this—my consciousness feels like it's nailed to this place."

"Hm."

I give her a minute to elaborate. "That's all I get?"

"Brad, I'm sorry, but I don't know all of the details on this. Her ways are perhaps opaque to ones such as…" She catches herself speaking in ye ole stentorian lilt. Has to remind herself who she's speaking to. "What I mean is, maybe we know all we need to know."

"Well, I'm someone who's not afraid to ask for more."

Alex breaks away. Steps back a foot or two. "Then maybe you should take this up with Her?" She catches my indignant expression. "No, seriously, maybe She could—"

"Marvelous instincts, sister Alexandria!" says an approaching voice. I turn to see one of my bathmates, she of the seductively-drenched red hair, entering the hall. "She has just now requested Bradley's presence. An *urgent* matter."

It's no seductive grin this time, though. More of an alpha predator eyeing her prey.

CHAPTER FORTY-SIX

Sandra Jones

The polite voice on the intercom, only a faint trace of Bostonian accent remaining, is apologizing. Apologizing, for the seventeenth time, about the delays, promising the thunderstorms should pass by soon, that the safety of the passengers remains their top priority.

I want so desperately to sever her vocal chords with my teeth.

I've been a prisoner of Logan International Airport for five hours, my body ravaged by Cinnabon and overpriced coffee, my view a steady diet of zombie businessmen, random dullards, and some people I'm now praying actually are terrorists. The *Benadryl* has knocked kitty out for a nice, long nap, but the stink of urine from the pet carrier has lingered for so long I'm now convinced it's discovered a new home in my clothes.

Seated beside me in this row of chairs is a kid who's maybe ten years old, mesmerized by his stupid phone and the stupidly loud game he's playing and wiping his stupid nose on his sleeve every ten seconds.

Go ahead, kid. *Make me sick.* I dare you. See how She repays that affront to one of her servants… Whoever 'She' is.

I'm debating whether or not this latchkey child is a genuine orphan and, if so, if anyone would miss the urchin if I enticed him into the ladies' room, then held his face in a toilet long enough for the twitching to stop.

I've already picked out the perfect stall.

That's when his father walks past, *Starbucks* tray in hand. I avoid his gaze, but this doesn't prevent him from looking over in my direction. "Hello…" he says, hesitantly.

I only grunt in response. He keeps staring, however, and then his face brightens. "Sandra, isn't it?"

"Yes?"

"Hi. *Hi*, it's me, Jackson Fouraker? Oh, I'm sorry. I'm sure you and your husband must've had hundreds of clients by now."

I study his face. Dark hair, slicked back, cold blue eyes, dimples, that strong jaw… and then I remember his wife, a tiny slip of a thing, crying on their couch. After their initial skepticism had passed, she broke down, begged us to do anything to grant their son peace.

Shyly, Jackson asks, "Do you remember when you helped us with our… problem, some years back?"

Six months before we came into their lives, the Fouraker family had lost their son to suicide. A diagnosed manic-depressive, the boy had snuck a kitchen knife into his bedroom and ended his misery a few days shy of his fourteenth birthday. Ever since then, the Fourakers had been experiencing flickering lights, malfunctioning electronics, odd noises, and hauntingly real visits in their dreams.

"I… Yes, I certainly do." My empathy for this man, for the hell he experienced, rushes back. The feeling is accompanied, however, by a few more sensations. Ones residing, well, below the beltline.

Jackson shoos the boy over to the next chair and takes the seat closest to mine. "Well, I've got to say, I was always a skeptic before that whole ordeal, but what you guys did… It was amazing."

"Brad's the one with the skills, Mr. Fouraker. I just try to keep the lights on."

It's all coming back now. Brad had taken the job without consulting me, then declared we were taking a trip to Boston for my birthday. That first night in the hotel, after he fessed up and we had that fight, he came back and told me he needed me the next day. Needed my 'feminine instincts' for a specific job.

"Oh, no. Your husband might've been the one with the 'gift', but don't think I've forgotten you. You're the one who talked us into going through with it in the first place. And when Helena was having second thoughts, when she was getting overwhelmed by the whole experience, you were there for her."

My job was to keep his dingbat wife from climbing the walls. Skinny, skinny thing. Like an ironing board on both sides, unfortunately for her husband. I talked to her, held her hand, and tried to keep everyone calm while Brad communed with the tortured spirit. Or, as Brad later put it, as he *"Chased that pimple-faced punkass kid out of his mama's dreams and into the light where he belonged."*

"It's good to be remembered, I guess. Don't tell me this is your youngest…?"

"Sure is. He must've been only, huh, three back when you met. Lincoln, say hello to our friend Sandra."

The brat looks up from his phone, wipes his nose again, then asks, "Is he talking about the ghost? Dad says we're not supposed to talk about the ghost, but I think—"

"That's enough, Lincoln. Let the grownups talk."

Barely a second passes before the kid is again ensnared by the game. I take the opportunity to ask, "So, where is Mrs. Fouraker today?"

"On her way back from a conference in Atlanta. We're here to pick her up but, given the delays, apparently Logan thinks we're supposed to be living here."

"Yeah, I know the feeling."

"What about you? You and your husband flying anywhere special?"

I shake my head, leaning closer to this reunited acquaintance. "Not here with Brad. Actually, we're not together anymore. Romantically, at least."

"Oh. Sorry. Hate to hear that."

"Don't be. It's opened me up to…" He does notice just how

many buttons I've missed on this shirt, right? And that my bra is still on the floor of Buck's tattoo shop? "…all kinds of new possibilities. Y'know, it is kind of ridiculous, how there's really nothing here to help you pass the time…"

"It's torture, truly."

My hand glides over to his knee. "Because I'm sure it's been so long since you've seen your lady, so long since you've been able to feel her touch…"

"Just, uh, just a week, actually."

"…and I bet the last thing you want is to sit and wait, with no payoff in sight, with hardly a thing to occupy your time."

"Sandra, I'm not sure… It's not appropriate…"

I squeeze his knee, stand, and give him his space. Exactly thirteen seconds later, he's reading the message I've scrawled on my hand.

Supply closet. Next hall. Ten minutes.

He meets me in nine.

CHAPTER FORTY-SEVEN

Bradley Burns

The Russian redhead leads me down the winding path, to the room where her mistress first greeted me. She stays relatively quiet on our way; maybe she knows I'm not in the mood. A meager three unsubtle attempts at seduction.

Entering this strange room, their lounge of disquieting artifacts, She's standing above her personal cauldron with her back to us. With a wave, my guide is dismissed.

"Does something displease you, Bradley?"

"Excuse me?"

Turning only her head, she explains, "The basis of my inquiry rests in the lack of… enthusiasm I've witnessed on your behalf."

"You've, uh, been keeping tabs on that kind of thing?"

"I make it my business to know." She beckons me to step closer. "Come now, darling. No need to be shy. Why are you not fulfilling your male function?"

"That's a very personal topic, and I'd rather not…"

"Never mind. I wasn't expecting a truthful reply, regardless." Displeased by my timid steps, She repeats, "Closer, Bradley. I wish to show you something."

I tell myself that I've never spoken so many words to Her at one time. That my post-traumatic anxiety is easing up around the beast. Then, she puts her hand on my shoulder and my heart pounds like a jackhammer on a three-day meth binge.

"No, no. I think you'll find this far more interesting."

She waves her left hand above the cauldron and the waters inside take shape. I realize within seconds that the woman in the water is none other than Sandy. The man she's with, the man who's unbuttoning her shirt and desperately pulling her right leg against his waist, is less familiar.

I make an effort to look away. She is not pleased. With no words, She readjusts my shoulders, firmly, and makes certain I watch the rest of this. Around five minutes in, I realize that I recognize Sandra's dance partner.

One of our clients. Boston guy. Starts with an F. Decent enough fellow. Didn't know about that birthmark on his left ass cheek, though.

Didn't know Sandy could make noises like that, either.

Eventually, after everyone's pants are tossed back on and the door of the broom closet—really, Sandy?—cracks open, the image dissipates.

She awaits a response.

"This is… That's not like her."

Her lips curl into a grin. "Perhaps your former love has evolved."

"Become more like your daughters?" I sneer. "Unlikely."

A reflexive response. I don't register the insult until I notice our sick queen reaching out, pulling my face to hers. "Why are you always so *difficult*, Bradley?"

Her nose brushes against mine. Lips are close enough for a kiss, but instead I only experience a quiet lecture. "Perhaps I could have devoted more time to this game. But fortune has smiled"—finally there's the kiss, a taste like burning napalm—"allowed my timetable to move *so* swiftly."

I overhear a repellant cackle as consciousness fades.

CHAPTER FORTY-EIGHT

Sandra Jones

Another endless flight, another airport, another delayed takeoff. I'm releasing Icky from her portable prison and futilely enticing her with a portion of my lunch. Perhaps the Terminal 3 *Burger King* of Dubai International isn't the average cat's ideal dining establishment, but sometimes sacrifices must be made, Icky.

For some reason, that last sentence just made me laugh. Aloud. Loudly.

Not sure what's come over me lately. I certainly haven't been myself the past few days, but every time I try to stop and collect my thoughts, I find myself overwhelmed with panic attacks and nosebleeds. I know what I must do and, even if it makes no sense, the thought of not fulfilling my duties makes me literally sick.

So, whatever mystic voice that resides within, I'm blaming you for Boston. Because that was *not* me. Maybe I've never been perfect, maybe my sense of humor is as 'unladylike' as Mom claims, but I do know I'm not prone to random hookups in storage closets.

So why do I feel so proud? Why does the memory of that tryst still excite me, hours later? The thought of that man risking so much, disrespecting his deepest bonds, making an outright fool of himself… It shouldn't be funny, right?

"It's okay, Icky. Just camel meat. No more disgusting than cow when you think about it," I tell my reluctant feline companion while scratching behind her ears. Poor Icky; you've got to figure she wasn't expecting to fly halfway around the world, however many days ago, when she laid yellow cat eyes on me in my parents' kitchen.

I don't hear the stranger's approach until it's too late. "You. Come with me," says a voice deep enough to command most anyone's respect.

"Did I do something wrong?" I ask, wondering if I've broken some airport, or even Sharia, law regarding pets in public spaces.

The uniformed man, easily six feet, with dark features and shoulders to die for, answers quickly, "We're not talking here. You come with me."

He stands impatiently as I return Icky to her carrier. Within seconds, I'm being escorted past the crowds into a back room. I debate apologizing for any offense, but instead choose to stay quiet. My mind replays every article I've read about Dubai, about the kind of treatment a woman can expect to find here, and try to reassure myself with the country's reputation as a wealthy, Western-friendly tourist destination.

The door closes; my heart skips. Without a word, he motions for me to place the pet carrier on the floor. "We have standards in Dubai, you must understand." Did I catch one of his eyebrows lifting? "Immodest clothing is not permitted."

I don't even realize I'm speaking until this sentence is nearly done. "Hate to tell ya, bud, but a few of these buttons must've gone missing since I got dressed… quite a while ago." I do refrain from describing how some guy in Boston ripped those buttons off with his teeth, however. "No disrespect intended, but unless you find me a change of clothes, I'm kinda stuck."

Walking towards his desk, he opens a drawer, selects a white t-shirt, then tosses it at me. I unfold the garment and see the airport's designation, *DXB*, printed in a simple black font inside a nondescript rectangle. It might as well read *"Airport T-Shirt."*

I look up and notice he's grabbed his smartphone. "You can change here."

"Ah. And I suppose a girl shouldn't expect too much privacy?"

"You're changing here. Now." I'll give the perv some credit; he knows to take the video horizontally.

That dark voice, not his, the one that drew me here in the first place, is telling me to enjoy this. Enjoy the way this fool is risking his job, possibly his freedom, all for the cheap thrill of watching a stranger undress. Enjoy your ability to turn this robust man of authority into a simpleminded, naughty boy.

The part of Sandra that's still Sandra, however, knows to at least turn around and face the wall. "Any other directives? Slower? Arch my back a little more? No?"

Maybe he's trying to respond. All I hear are gasping noises. The t-shirt against my bare chest, I turn to check on the guard.

His mouth could collect flies, the way it's halfway down his neck. Should I be flattered? No, looking closer, I recognize that face as utter shock, not lecherous anticipation.

Oh, do they not like tattoos here?

My clueless suitor drops his phone to the floor, still stuttering. Body trembling, his knees soon join that phone. I believe I hear him whisper something like *"The mother of children"* in disbelief before he goes into Arabic.

The bulky, man-sized shirt now covering my sinful body, I lift the pet carrier by its handle and step over this custodian of decency.

"Well, hope you enjoyed the show. And thanks for the t-shirt, bud." Closing the door, I overhear one word, repeated in a whisper. It chills my bones, but I don't have the faintest idea why.

"Hawwa…"

CHAPTER FORTY-NINE

Bradley Burns

I'm sure it's pointless, griping that the wrist restraints are too tight.

I should also complain about the view. Not only are those four stone beasts creeping me the hell out, but being placed directly in front of that ceremonial blade—the one resting so lovingly atop the bejeweled pillow—is generating a mild flash of paranoia.

The rules of physics, of spatial relationships, I've got some nitpicks in that department, too. This chamber, whatever it's supposed to be, looks as if it should consume the entire castle, judging by my view of the ceiling. And that's just nonsensical, ain't it?

"Understand, Bradley," speaks the voice of Queen Demon, "that I offered you a place in my home. I never specified the living conditions, however."

Then there's the cauldron, much larger than the one She uses for a TV screen, resting a few yards away from the blade. Three servants are silently carrying clay jugs to the pot, pouring out a milky substance that better not be what I think it is.

The smell, though, takes me back to more than a few desperate teenage evenings. Surely that's one more sexual harassment complaint I should be noting.

No, I don't think She would even bother to listen. Too busy

grinning like an idiot, stalking the slab I'm tied to, keeping watch of those statues overseeing the room.

Finally, she stops chuckling long enough to form a sentence. "Do you think me cruel, Alexandria, for requesting your company?"

From this vantage point, I didn't know we had company. "No, madam," the girl says. "I could never question your judgment."

"Your sycophancy was not requested, girl," She responds, her mood finally dampened. "I expect a candid reply."

I hear Alex's footsteps grow closer. "To be honest, my Queen, I do question my place in this ceremony."

"And do you not recognize the fundamental role you've played, bringing our diviner to us, and setting the stage for this momentous occasion?"

"I wouldn't presume to take credit that isn't mine."

Finally, she's in my field of vision. For a moment, I try to tell myself that she gave a glance in my direction. Framed above Alex, however, is one of the statues dominating each corner of this room. A tilt of the head gives me a better view.

The heads of four beasts—a boar, a condor, a crocodile, and an ox—guard every angle, sitting in some form of silent judgment. The masonry's realistic in most respects, yet the beasts' eyes exhibit some creative license. They're disproportionately large, shaped like scalene triangles, existing only as blank slits.

The Queen makes a point of drawing Alex closer, making sure I can see the two of them together. "Your humility is… touching, dear."

"But I just assumed the diviner would be milked like all the others," Alex says, turning towards me. Is there hurt in her eyes?

The Queen then approaches the slab. Her expression is, for lack of a better term, ravenous. "Do you understand that one with Bradley's talents is prized in our realm, young Alexandria?"

"I do."

"And did you think he was to while away an eternity in our chambers, sampling a different flavor each day?"

I could step in here, could speak up to defend myself, but I can't find the gumption to say a word.

The Queen approaches. "Understand, my daughter. Bradley here was merely being kept preoccupied, until an agent of his realm could arrange all the proper pieces." She grazes a fingernail against my cheek.

"And that moment, I'm delighted to say, should arrive shortly. Do you realize, Alexandria, how privileged we've been in recent days? When I made my offer to the diviner, I couldn't have dreamed that a perfect earthly vessel would arrive so soon after." She squeezes my cheek and, with a sneer, finishes her thought: "By all that's holy, I feared we'd be forced to tolerate his grating presence for decades."

"But the nature of this ceremony," I catch Alex staring at the blade, positioned on a dais a foot away from the slab, "I fear that my stomach lacks the strength. Might I humbly ask to be excused?"

"Darling, I don't think you understand. The punctilious scheming that brought us to this point is a work of art. This is the culmination of an eternity of dreams, girl. Soon, all of your sisters will be in this chamber to stand witness. Our oblation will right a millennia-old wrong." Hands on Alex's shoulder, she says, with feeling, "It is the moment that will liberate… the one whose name we will not speak. Can't you grasp the honor that's been bestowed upon you?"

"I apologize, mistress. I wasn't aware Bradley was so… vital."

"A necessary deception on my part. I didn't wish for you, or your sisters, to foil the plot over a case of nerves."

Alex demurely nods. "I understand… and pray I'll find the resolve necessary when the moment arrives."

"I'm confident you shall, darling." She releases Alex. "But, in the approaching hours, I must prepare myself for this event. Please, leave me to my meditations."

"Understood, madam," Alex says, making her break for the door. For a second time, I think I see her acknowledging me, offering an apologetic look. Hard to allow my spirits to lift, though, given the revelations I've—conveniently—been allowed to overhear.

Love Is Dead(ly)

And, again, that view of the knife…

CHAPTER FIFTY

Sandra Jones

Supposedly, this vast expanse of unrelenting brown will dissipate and I'll be greeted by lush groves of fruits and vegetables, by an unimaginable breadth of pure green beauty. I'm increasingly skeptical, wandering through this desert with a dying iPhone as my guide, the sun blistering my shoulders, every footstep bringing me closer to a more likely fate: a lonely death of starvation or exposure. Perhaps a combination of the two.

Date palms are supposed to be here, too. I love date palms.

Five hours ago, I parted ways with my guide. This was, perhaps not coincidentally, tied to the moment when my credit card stopped accepting new charges. We were traveling through a town ravaged by war, a holy war fought by young male zealots who didn't seem to know an awful lot about the faith they'd been recruited into, but relished the thought of blowing shit up. And in this particular town, much shit had indeed gone up in smoke and flames.

While questioning why I'd ever want to ride through here, let alone bring a pet, the guide regaled me with the horrors visited upon his homeland, all hitting in a fairly steady succession after the dawn of the new millennium. Haidar, with the dark curls that congregated past his shirt collar and 1980s *Top Gun* sunglasses that are possibly back in style back home—I'll have to check later—had never met an American before. He made a point of telling me this, oh, every fifteen minutes or so.

As we drove past yet another row of bombed-out husks, I learned from Haidar that, when the fighting was all over, only four buildings remained in this entire town. The jihadists had been chased away, the city was allegedly safe for travel now, but could you really argue it was even a city at this point?

When we arrived at the town's edge, Haidar was low on gas. Anxious to know just how much further this crazy tourist and her cat honestly wanted to go. Apparently, 'the river' wasn't a specific enough instruction, so I showed him images of the water from my phone. After discerning the location, he laughed and told me that we'd have to take the mining roads to get there, the same roads the insurgents once used to ambush Marine forces during their patrols.

"These men, these Marines, many of them died here, right through these paths," Haidar said, tapping on my phone and then pointing to the roadmap on the screen. "These Marines, your countrymen, did you know any of them?"

I replied that I did not, that we once saw those reports on the news, but the story just seemed to fade away over time. I was in high school when this began: maybe I didn't pay enough attention to what was going on? Fleeting thoughts; far more pressing matters deserve my attention.

Handing Haidar my *Discover* card, I told him to find a place to gas-up, because regardless of what danger remains on those roads, nothing was keeping me from that river.

He swiped the card, laughed, then asked if I had another one he could try. Having recently maxed out my *AmEx* and *MasterCard*, I provided an honest answer. He wished me a nice day then politely instructed me to exit his vehicle.

Yes, five hours ago, if I'm to believe this phone that's clinging to life. I tell myself that, even when the iPhone gives out, I can still follow the mining roads. They'll guide me there, and this choking dust, this backpack that's killing my spine, this stifling heat burning my shoulders, will only be a memory.

And Icky? Safe inside that pet carrier, tucked securely in the duffel bag resting by my side. Protected from the sun, I bet she's having a leisurely nap right at this moment.

Maybe some part of me is crying out that this is insane, that we'll surely die long before we reach the water, but it's a meek voice. One I can choose to ignore.

I'll make it. I won't pass out. I can survive, even though my water supply was exhausted an hour ago. And food? Haven't touched that stuff in about a day. Who cares? Resolve is absolute. My knees won't quiver, and my face won't fall to the sand.

I'll make it, even though I'm currently tasting that dirt, still hours from my destination.

The voice of doubt is growing stronger. Taunting me, telling me what a fool I was for ignoring her for so long, for sacrificing all reason and beginning this journey in the first place. Maybe I'm ready to listen, to acknowledge my mistake and accept a peaceful, quiet death out here in the desert, praying that some Bedouin traveling these dusty roads will come across my body one morning and treat it with a modicum of respect.

That's when I hear a rumble in the distance. The reliable, cheap roar of an AMC straight-6 engine, if I had to guess. Someone on this road is driving a car, an American Jeep from the sound of it, and regardless of what that voice is screaming at me, I know she's wrong yet again.

These aren't bandits approaching. These are my allies. They serve the same mistress; they know the sweet sound of Her voice, and understand what must be done.

*

"You like *Atkin's* or *Kind* bars? We've got both."

The man at the wheel is Thomas, and his riding companion goes by Randall. He offers a plastic shopping bag packed with protein bars. I crack open one of the bottled waters resting in the cooler beside me before furiously unwrapping two of the bars. My mouth full, I offer my thanks.

Randall turns back around, shaking his head. "No need for that. We all know why we're here, don't we?"

I was right about the engine, and had nearly nailed the Jeep's year and model, even in the midst of sunstroke. And Icky, as I've just confirmed, is doing about as well as could be expected. Not only did our new friends Tom and Randall offer us plenty of chilled *Evian* water, but they even had the foresight to bring along a case of *Fancy Feast Classic*. Not the modern recipe that looks like mush, but the brand Icky has always preferred.

Inches behind me in the rear cargo resides a long, lumpy sack of potatoes. The sane voice of reason, the one telling me minutes ago to prepare for death, is unnerved. Claims the bag's too big for edible tubers, unless we're feeding an army. She's freaking out, paranoid the sack is just large enough to fit a human body.

I tell her to keep her suspicious mouth shut.

"Double-fisting those protein bars, girl?" Thomas smirks. "Good thing we're riding out in the open air."

It's not difficult to ascertain my new companions aren't locals. Thomas, with his poofy-blond hair, nearly orange in this light, is clad in a Doors t-shirt that barely contains his stomach, confidently steering with one hand like a teenage boy circling Main Street on a Friday night.

In the passenger seat is Randall, the gentleman who offered his seat when they discovered me on the side of the road. I declined, opting instead to stretch out in the back. Even though they're the same height, he's around forty pounds lighter than Thomas, opting for a short-sleeve polo button-up.

Just as I'm mentally questioning why Thomas, a living ginger specimen, isn't burning worse than me, his companion hands me a tube of sunscreen. While collecting the plastic snack wrappings with his other hand, Randall asks, "Got any tunes you prefer? This old Jeep won't plug into your phone, but Thomas has one of those portable speakers. I told him I could only stand so much of the Grateful Dead," Randall shows off his iPhone, "but he's adamantly opposed to Andrew Lloyd Webber scores. You could be the deciding vote."

I ask if they have a USB charger I could use on my depleted phone instead. Of course they do. I play a pointless mobile game that's consumed too many hours of my life, Icky is given another shot of *Benadryl*, Randall leans back with a Vonnegut paperback, and Thomas is granted permission for another spin of the Dead's greatest hits collection.

We don't have to discuss our mission. We know why She has called us.

CHAPTER FIFTY-ONE

John Horton

Okay, this is weird. And I'm saying this as a lovesick plaything who sleeps in the dungeon of an eleven-foot-tall demon goddess' perverted sex castle.

The demon's lady servants have raided our rancid home. They're all pretty chipper, opening up the cages, beckoning us to come forward. Many of us are too frail to walk; the lovely ladies are kind enough to drag my brethren along.

Looks as if each sister is selecting the members of their exclusive harem. My cellmates are victims/lovers of my personal goddess, Alex, the lady I have to still acknowledge as the fairest soul-stealer of them all. And here she is now, approaching our cage.

Not nearly as high-spirited as her sisters, though. In fact, she's wearing a frown so forlorn it inspires a quick pang in my chest.

Oh, I have to keep reminding myself what a fool I was for falling for a demon's servant. That Alex's every action was a premeditated ruse designed to lure me in. That my bunkmates are barren husks now, thanks to Alex's daily 'milking'. But, Lord, that pout.

"Alex, what's going on here?" I ask as she drags the cell door open.

She won't even look at me. "Our queen… She has requested the presence of every servant."

Any summons from that demon is terrifying, but Alex's

demeanor is enough to send my heart racing. "And I'm guessing you have a sense something bad will happen?"

Alex won't answer. Just moves to the corner to collect poor emaciated Franklin over there. "Alex, please. Can't you say anything?"

She motions towards Jimmy Flatt, another of her love-guild, who's pressed his skeletal body against the wall, attempting sleep. "Could you help me with that, Johnny?"

I notice I've already collected Jimmy's gaunt arms before catching myself. "Alex, why has everyone been summoned like this?" No reply, but I catch a glimpse of her profile. See the tear falling down her cheek.

"I know you, Alex. I know something's wrong."

As she wipes one tear, three more follow. "John… Something's very wrong, I'm afraid."

For some reason, I remember a taunt from our mistress. Remember a conversation some part of me says never happened. I flash back to Her, somehow trespassing in my memories. Telling me I was right to keep my head down, all those years. To accept my paltry lot in life.

Not to play the damn hero.

I fight the memory; do what I can to resist that quiver in my voice. "Alex, we have to do something. We have to fight this demon."

She rushes to me. We embrace. Entangled with that lilac scent Her daughters carry is the salt of Alex's tears.

I know this is real. I know she needs me.

I'm telling myself to ignore those nerves; that I can be the one she truly desires. Her hero.

"Johnny, I don't think this'll end well… but *thank you*. Thank you so much for—"

Her head pops back up. Eyes go all silver dollar. And she speaks a name. Maybe the last one I wanted to hear.

"Brad? What are *you* doing here?"

CHAPTER FIFTY-TWO

Sandra Jones

Perhaps the banks of the river are as verdant and colorful as I'd been told. It's hard to tell at midnight, but I can confirm that the drop of temperature after sundown is more than enough to freeze your blood.

Especially when you've dispensed of your jeans and gift shop t-shirt, your bare flesh exposed to the elements.

Randall is at the edge of the water, crushing the camphor, saffron, and other herbs into the soapstone bowl. I don't recognize the words of his chant, yet intuitively understand them as a paean to our mistress. Icky has awoken from the Benadryl coma, making courteous protests to be released from her plastic cage.

Patience, dear. All things in time.

I feel Thomas's gummy fingers against my back. The ceremony calls for either blood or seed, and while Tom and Randall graciously offered both, I indicated a preference for plasma. Yes, there remains a puritanical nuisance in the back of my mind, expressing her disgust and questioning why I'm doing any of this.

We all have shameful thoughts we'd like kept secret.

Thomas' fingers continue to trace my back's etchings, his resolve more concrete than a certain Californian tattoo artist. Poor Buck had never encountered the loving spirit of our monarch in the past; Thomas, however, was seduced by one of Her children two months ago, and has developed enough of a stomach for this work.

The vertigo does occasionally require Thomas to take a break, or perhaps he's woozy after nearly carving his finger off with that blade, but he's fighting past those contemptible mortal weaknesses. No doubt, the boy's doing work that will make Her proud.

I thought I knew love, yet I'd never known the touch of a man's bloody fingers against my spine, tracing a sigil celebrating the essence of rebellious deific energies. Such a sheltered life I've led.

Randall finishes his incantation, though it's more accurate to say the seizure ends it for him. He falls to the dirt, knocks over the lantern. Judders around for nearly a minute.

Then, for too long, lies still as a corpse. I'm questioning if poor Randall was a sacrifice we didn't know needed to be made, just seconds before he lurches back to his feet.

"She's ready," he coughs, not wiping the foam from his lips.

I'm giddy as a schoolgirl, but outwardly expressing the emotion feels almost blasphemous. There's a loving taunt I somehow hear, asking if I'm pleased now with all this excitement in my life.

Randall does allow himself a smile, opening the pet carrier and taking Icky in his arms. She doesn't struggle. Such a gentle little creature. Always my mother's favorite, back in the days when the term 'mother' meant something very different to me.

Randall hands over our furry companion. I cradle her in my arms. If she only knew the inexpressible honor that awaits her. Truth to tell, I'm envious of the girl. I lift her overhead while stepping into the water. The frigid waves bite my legs; even colder winds chill the liquid on my naked back. But I accept the discomfort as a blessing.

Lifting the feline even higher, I begin my part in the ceremony. The words are simple, but far more sincere than any vow I've spoken in the past.

Lady of the evening star
Fabled Mother
I humbly beseech you
I request your daughters' strength

Love Is Dead(ly)

Inanna, I beg for the courage to invoke you
My heart belongs to your lap
It pleads for your touch
Hear my cry
Hawwa, accept this unworthy vessel
Allow me the privilege to speak your true name
Grant me the honor to whisper the sound
Sweeter than the brush of angel wings
Allow me to speak the name…
…of Lilith.

CHAPTER FIFTY-THREE

Bradley Burns

The Queen Demon's idea of 'meditation' consists of a bath in, ahem, a certain substance in that massive caldron. She's floating at the top, speaking in crazy tongues, prophesizing something I know I don't want to witness firsthand.

I'm lying here, silently accepting my fate. Praying whatever She has in mind for that blade, it will at least be quick and relatively painless.

Perhaps a lone tear is welling up, as I contemplate past mistakes. Tell myself I deserve this callous fate.

No, of course I'm not doing that. I'm doing what I've done every moment of my adult life: whatever I can to get out of a mess I've made.

Using those cryptic clues dropped by our evil queen earlier, I've cobbled together a theory. Not much of one, yeah, but I've got a hunch now that Bradley Burns has not truly left that mortal coil. That my glorious pale flesh is necessary for this wicked thing the Queen Demon has planned.

See, that's why I can't project my consciousness back to Earth. I'm not fully *here*, yet. Unlike Alex, who can do that cute 'visit your dreams' bit.

But, hey, I'm still the Paranormal Desperado. I speak to ghosts, and isn't that what surrounds me right now? And sweet Alex, isn't she already attuned to the irresistible sound of my voice?

So, right now, I'm calling out to the girl. Using my mystic abilities to stretch through the ether and connect with this 'covenant' I've been bonded to.

Yeah, gonna give the girl a thrill, just popping into her mind like it's nothing. Letting her in on one brilliant scheme to stop this madness.

And I'm absolutely *not* laying on the bravado in a sad attempt to cover the near-crippling panic and fear currently consuming my body. Nope. Crazy to even think that.

I begin the breathing exercises. Focus on my goal. Fight out all extraneous sensory inputs. All the old tricks I employed back home.

They'll work here. They'd better.

Takes longer than I'd like, admittedly, but eventually my spirit does connect with Alex's. I see her, entering that dungeon she showed me not long after I arrived. See that she's in a crowd of over a hundred of her succubae sisters.

I'm calling, but she won't answer. My teeth have started to chatter; I feel the panic entering my chest. God, maybe doing this was a mistake. The Queen Demon is only a few feet away; I've opened myself up to a tidal wave of malevolent energies she's releasing into the astral firmament. Tastes of something wicked I want no part of.

I readjust my breathing, ward off that gnawing paranoia. I focus on Alex. Touch upon our moment of 'ratification', if you will. The good vibes I—perhaps stupidly—sent her way when making love.

A wave washes over; it's not a sweet remembrance of that roll in the hay. It's an image of two strange beings, enjoying their own naked embrace. Every tiny hair on my body shoots right up.

It's the Queen Demon… more of her sickness spilling over to my astral form. Have to fight it. Have to concentrate.

"Alex… *Alex!*"

The vision intensifies. I see the girl in that poor mope John's cell. He's getting the same vibes I've received, is trying to talk some sense into her. Appreciate the effort, bud, but there's only one Mystic Badass.

I scream Alex's name. Repeatedly. Finally, she perks up and answers.

"Brad," I hear the girl speak through tinny mental speakers. "It's you, isn't it? How are…?"

"Don't worry about that. There's no time. Listen—you have to stop your mistress. Do whatever you can to—"

"I can't turn against Her, Brad. Please, I know it's all wrong, but you can't expect me to do that."

"Alex! Don't you get what's happening?! *Something* has to be done and—"

No, no. Letting too much anxiety in. Screwing up the reception—and likely not doing much to change Alex's mind. Have to remind myself she isn't truly human now.

Which, no, can't be right. I felt the part of her that's real. That still visits her mother, regrets the fool decisions that got her here. Have to show her something I can't even articulate. Something that's just now brewing in my gut, some psychic spillover from the Queen Demon. Some vision of the future she's damn excited over.

A farmhouse burning to the ground, a pumpkin patch in flames. Stomach's queasy now, as if this were the most horrendous tragedy imaginable. Amongst the ashes I see the remains of a toy ballerina.

Makes sense, almost. I'm reaching out to Alex while this ageless monster is tripping out a few feet away. Psychic energies amalgamate, offer an image that would titillate the one and terrify the other.

A few steady breaths and, hopefully, I'm back. "Okay, look… Ignore me if you want. But that room She's got, the one with the scrying pool. Use it, girl. Look for yourself what this demon has planned."

"But…"

I lose my temper. Release that image of the burning farmhouse, that broken ballerina. Feel the jolt from her end, like she's standing on the wrong end of an agitated horse.

I'd like to apologize. Let her know I'm doing this so she'll understand the stakes, not to be cruel. But another surge of the Queen's psychic ecstasy just spilled over. Offered a vision so bewildering, so depraved, even this loudmouth could only gape in horror.

CHAPTER FIFTY-FOUR

Sandra Jones

Thirty seconds have passed since I completed the incantation. Thirty seconds of me standing in this frigid water, my nude body a victim of the elements, holding a confused calico over my head.

I do not feel foolish. I relish the anticipation.

And, when Icky erupts in a fervor of hisses and screams, slashing at my wrists and biting at the air, I know our mission has been a success.

She has deigned to join us. The humble stray my mother once discovered eating out of the backyard trash bin, now a receptacle for the primordial embodiment of all blasphemy. I recognize, as much as a lowly mortal can, what an honor it is to be in Her presence.

Icky, however, remains confused. She gets one solid cut in, forcing me to drop her into the water. *Stay calm, retrieve the beast, take us to shore,* says a voice that feels both young and ancient.

I collect the wet animal, feel even more cuts against my breast, and involuntarily drop her once more. She's trying to swim away, but moonlight reveals her location. Hastily, I grab the beast's tail, pull it closer, pick her up by the scruff of her neck.

The girl doesn't appreciate the trip back to shore, spitting and growling like mad. My two companions are intimidated by the house pet, keeping a respectful distance. *Excellent*, says the voice, thanking me for my work.

Let them cower. It's good for their kind to learn fear. I comprehend Icky is staring directly at me, her temper tantrum complete. *Place me on the sand. I wish to walk this earth again.*

The cat coos as her paws make contact with the dirt, at first kneading the sand and then rolling over in circles, shaking off the granules. *How has it been so long?* I hear the voice ask.

I once walked hand-in-hand with my love down this river. We were so young, the world so new. How new, even we couldn't appreciate. The innocence couldn't last, of course. Eventually, he attempted to assert his dominance over me. Claimed I would be nothing without him.

The fool. I rebelled; though it was his next mate who committed the true *blasphemy, under that fruit tree.*

I had to forge a new path. My new love, he found me in my exile. Yes, away from this place, this former home of unfathomable splendor. Do your people not know? Is there no monument to what began here?

"Sadly, no," I answer. "Most have forgotten, our Queen. And there's no lack of chaos in your former home. But a few, a few of us understand. And we're honored by your presence."

You should be. All gathered should be humbled, although I fear your two companions will soon outlive their usefulness. That's just our secret, however. In the meantime, instruct them to prepare the body of the diviner.

I follow orders, not entirely sure I understand the Queen's demands. Thomas and Randall nod obedience, though, and in less than a minute have removed that gigantic sack of potatoes from the back of the Jeep. The voice again speaks, affirming I'm allowed to recognize the true contents of this bag.

Randall has the head while Thomas handles the toes. It's delicately placed in the sand. Randall unties the top and folds down the fabric.

The face of the lifeless body is revealed. It's the face I pledged allegiance to on my wedding day. The face I used to kiss goodnight every evening.

I shout his name. The voice instructs me to calm myself.

This will be a night of reunions, child. But you must understand, I cannot achieve what must be done while in the body of your feline. This pet was but my means of entry. I now require a form closer to the one granted by my creator.

The calico brushes against my leg. *You do understand the privilege that's been granted this eve, Sandra?*

I stutter out a response. Embarrassing myself, I ask the voice to clarify what She means.

You, Sandra. I need your body. Icky's purr vibrates against my naked leg. *Are you prepared to accept this honor?*

CHAPTER FIFTY-FIVE

John Horton

Whatever that Brad told her—however he did it—spooked the girl even worse. But Alex has only a moment of indecision.

Then her adorable face scrunches up. Determined, she takes me by the hand. Leads me out of this dank cell as we bump against the throng. One of her sisters calls out with a Russian accent, wants to know what she's doing.

"I'm the Covenant, my sister. And our queen demands my presence… And that of this soul-slave."

I wait until we've passed the dungeon's massive doors and escaped those vulgar goblins that keep watch above. "Wow. Soul-slave, huh?"

"John, don't worry about that. We have to get to the scrying chamber. *Now.*"

We run so fast my lungs catch fire. But soon we reach our destination. The room our Queen seems to favor above all others. It's the one with the particularly nasty decorations on each wall, framing the numinous centerpiece: an elevated, smoky cauldron.

She doesn't release my hand until we've hit the water. "Look, unfortunately, this is something we have to do." Alex cups her hands; scoops a healthy serving of the liquid into her palms.

"What are you…?"

"I can't command the waters like Her. But, consuming the

liquid, I'll join with its energies."

Mist from the water tickles my eyes. And the scent: some awful blend of chlorine and rotting fruit. "Maybe you shouldn't do this, Alex."

She hesitates. Something in me fights the instinct to take her by the hand, to let this mystery water spill to the floor. Can't bring myself to do it, though. Maybe because I'm no hero. Or maybe because I know Alex is doing what has to be done.

Alex steels herself, and those impeccable lips part. She sucks in the water.

I ask if she's okay, as she stands transfixed. Maybe ten seconds pass before she falls to the floor and begins babbling out gibberish.

"Alex!" I run to my girl, take hold of her arms. I curse myself for letting her go through with this insanity. For letting her listen to that damned Bradley Burns.

"Please, Alex, listen. You'll be okay, just calm yourself," I tell the juddering wreck beneath me. She's foaming at the mouth now. Drips of the bubbles land on my skin; are hot to the touch. But the convulsions slow down and, for the briefest of moments, I think I've broken through.

Eyes lock.

And that's when *I'm* assaulted by visions.

I tell myself to take my own advice and remain calm, to ride this through with Alex. I pluck one vision from the ether and focus, best I can, on the elusive dream image.

It's two people I know; people I've only met recently, even though it now feels like a thousand years ago. It's Brad and Sandra, encircled by a grove, I believe. Somewhere near the banks of a river, maybe, in a strange locale.

It's what they're doing that matters, though. Apparently, they've put aside their differences and decided to make a fresh start, because that's the only reasonable explanation for why they're reenacting late night Cinemax, naked out there in the dirt for the world to see.

But, no, this isn't them. Two figures are blurring their way into the image, superimposing themselves above those feeble humans.

Another image has Sandra—or something that's claimed her body—in a hospital bed, grinning with every tooth. Maternity ward. She's surrounded by a doctor and a team of nurses, deep in labor. Good for her, I think briefly, before I see the doctor's point of view.

Wipe off the blood and goo and you'll find twin boys. Skin closer to a pale blue than peach, a thin layer of white hair crowning their scalps. Their anatomy is all off: as if they're more bovine than human. No cries, only smiles. Teeth all fangs.

No swaddling blankets for these babes, as their first act in this world is to latch razor teeth against the doctor's neck and remove his esophagus.

I think I'm on the floor now. Yes, pretty sure I'm also seizing out. Marble pounds against my back, my sides, my face. I hear a voice, ethereal. It's Alex, apologizing, begging me to stay brave, to see this through.

There's an image: a few political figures I recognize from *The Daily Show*, chained together and being marched into an outdoor camp of shanty houses. The guard directing traffic is pale blue like the babies, his hair a glorious mane of pure silver. Unbelievably tall, with an animal-like musculature that's impossible to describe. Complementing his superhuman height is a pair of wings composed of course feathers, the dingiest of yellows.

Soon, I absorb the stink of brimstone, snatching more phantasmagorias from the atmosphere. Gruesome imagery of these perverse angels waging war, destroying our monuments, violating the slaves.

I can't help it, I've got *Iron* freakin' *Maiden* running in the background… *Biblical judgments, bloody combat, riots in the streets.* This entire world is a 1980s thrash metal album cover.

One more vision I'm able to catch.

A temple, the masonry prehistoric, its height stretching literally into the heavens. Two figures rest on a balcony. Instinctively, I know they're a couple. Their love is a perverse thing, as I understand the concept, but as genuine as any emotion I've ever felt.

The groom is the king angel, his sapphire skin glowing in the light of daybreak. Blood-soaked wings boldly announce his supremacy. To his left is his bride, a woman of some unknown ethnic beauty, clad in nothing, enjoying her wine.

I notice her nakedness and am ashamed. She has qualities reminiscent of Alex's mistress, yet I intuitively know how deep an insult the assessment is.

You don't compare a worker ant to the queen.

My head's still going through the rinse cycle when I hear Alex calling me back to lucidity. "Did you see it, too?" she asks, groggy. "Do you understand what's happening?"

I cough up what feels like a portion of my lung. "Understand *what*, Alex?"

Gripping my shoulders, she says, "It's *Her*. Not even 'our' Her. The Queen *above* our Queen. The name we're not allowed to even speak. And that beast? That angel? When these two get together, it'll be a literal Hell on Earth. Everything you saw, all that horror, the first steps are happening, John."

The truth rushes over me. Intuitively, I realize how right she is. And what must be done.

"So this is where you're hiding?" says a voice, one with a cruel edge, from behind.

It's another of Alex's sisters, the Russian who dared question my girl earlier. "She has completed her meditation. Has sent me to find you, Alexandria. Something magnificent is happening, dear, and none of us are to miss it."

CHAPTER FIFTY-SIX

Bradley Burns

"Still feigning sleep, boy? The jittering of your right leg gives you away." A light snicker. "No more playacting. I want you awake for this."

Her presence looms above, begging for attention. I'd like to screw with her just one more time, refuse to give her what she so badly wants. I keep my eyes closed. She responds by peeling my lids open with her fingernails.

Over my screams, she says, "You never realized what a prize you are, did you, Bradley?"

"Mom always told me I was special," I answer, after she removes her talons from my eyes.

"More truth there than you realize. It's in your blood, Bradley. You mystics, spiritualists, diviners—whatever term you wish to use—have a legacy far beyond your comprehension. And your blood…" She removes the dagger from its pillow, then excises a miniscule bit of flesh from my big toe.

Licking the blade, she grins and says, "…Your blood is quite valuable."

The blade hovers over my neck. "Yes, your flesh is a precious thing, love, and it shan't go to waste. With that bloodline we'll resurrect the spirit of my father-brother, and the true ruling party will return to Earth. We need only make the final preparations.

Even as we speak, the loving spirit of my Queen is returning to her home. Once she takes the proper mortal form, we shall begin."

"And what does that mean for me?"

"Your physical body will become inhabited by the spirit of… If I had to translate into words you could comprehend, the closest approximation would be *'the Venom of God'.*" She catches the look on my face. "Don't fret. An outdated title, a holdover from his previous occupation."

She's enjoying this more than I think she even imagined possible. Studying the knife, she asks, "Did you believe Lucifer was the only angel to rebel, lad? No, his devotees are only the most ostentatious. Other spirits have been at work for millennia, toiling surreptitiously to undermine the force that abandoned our Queen so long ago.

"Battles have been fought and lost on planes your mind cannot comprehend. Our champion was lost in battle many moons ago, and She has plotted to revive him ever since."

I have less than a moment to consider this idea of a second, more powerful 'She' when the blade slices into my stomach. "This resurrection, sadly, will require sacrifices."

I feel nothing at first, as my body registers the violation. Then it allows a searing flame to pass over the incision.

"Be honored, my darling. You are our fattest calf."

As much as the restraints allow, I try to get a look at the wound. It's a long cut, clean, going across the length of my belly, just south of my navel. The pain, this burning fire, is indescribable. And, just when I think I'm through the worst of it, a new wave of throbbing agony arrives to collect the interest.

In this field of vision, the one admittedly growing blurrier by the second, I have a view of those animal statues, the demonic rejects from the *See 'n Say,* nasty pointed eyes now glowing a crimson red. Under their watch, Demon Queen is gathering her succubae followers.

The sisters have entered with their male slaves, leashes around their necks. The men act like good little minions and prostrate themselves before the succubae. I contort my body as I realize each entering sister is collecting a small knife from a pulpit near the entrance.

I'm confronted with dark visions of what awaits all these poor marks. Realizing now how serious She was about a 'sacrifice'.

And I'm thanking the sweet Lord that Alex isn't among the throng… As she enters with another straggling succubus, poor John What's-His-Name in tow.

CHAPTER FIFTY-SEVEN

John Horton

The Russian shoves me out of the way. With a sneer, she tells my love, "Your cowardly disappearance would surely displease Her."

Alex wants to fight, to do something to undermine the evil demon who's plotting that nightmare. She pulls away from her sister and opens her mouth to protest. "No, Alex," I tell her. "We all have our part to play."

Our intruder, her hand gripping Alex's wrist, laughs at the exchange. "You and your pet are center stage, girl."

She's dragged down the corridor. I follow, obediently. Poor Alex. She's trapped; forced into her role.

But, me: the timid nobody who knows he isn't a hero? He knows what he must do, how there's no real time to wait. Understands just who has to die now.

We follow the Russian on a tour of the castle, moving through corridors I didn't know existed: don't think *should* exist, based on my understanding of the layout. She escorts us into a grand chamber that somehow rests within the walls of the castle, a room large enough to consume the entire design of the fortress.

Above us in the chamber rest four stone animal heads, all inanimate yet oozing a sense of malevolence. Their primal essence has a nearly-audible voice. They're awaiting a show.

They're asking for blood.

The Russian makes sure Alex picks up her blade from the pulpit by the entrance. I see my brother slaves held by leashes, on their knees, backs turned before their mistresses.

John, the bit player who is no hero, assumes the position. As Alex takes her place behind Her, who's lording over a bound Bradley Burns, my knees meet the cold stone floor.

CHAPTER FIFTY-EIGHT

Bradley Burns

Maybe I should give them a show.

Oh, sweet, sweet Jesus, please let this pain die.

Maybe I ought to pull out some badass line, the kind peak-of-his-career Bruce Willis would demand during the final Act.

I just felt blood ooze over my pisshole.

"Just tell me one thing. That one question that's... still lingering... in my head." Blade in hand, She leans closer. I'm not sure how clearly I'm saying any of this—*There's another wave of burning agony. They're coming faster now*—It's probably coming out as more of a wheeze than a sentence, but I try my damndest. Got to make Bruce proud.

"Please, show mercy and tell me... If... If you were bathing in a bucket of jizz."

She pats my head. "Male essence, boy. There's an energy there you mortals could never grasp. It powers this realm, and it is yet another oblation our champion will require in the midst of his resurrection."

Almost on cue, one of the succubae lights a torch and tosses it into the cauldron. I'd remark on the smell, if I weren't in the process of bleeding to death.

"My daughters, our King and Queen now require the spilling of blood."

It's a grizzly sight: each sister moving individually, slicing the necks of their slaves. Alex, positioned behind Queen Demon, will be going last with poor John.

I close my eyes. Let the Queen peel them open if she wants to; I'll never choose to watch this.

Yet, even as I make that declaration, my surroundings go from blurry to full-on smeared paint. Through the haze, I think I feel the touch of sunlight, which I know must be a lie. No sun, not here.

But, no, I'm wrong. It's natural sunlight, burning over an expanse of desert.

Why am I suddenly so hot, when I was freezing only a second ago?

There's a flash of a woman, familiar yet terrifying, her nude body covered in bruises and dirt. She's wandering through this desert, the sun burning her shoulders, skin coated in sweat and grime.

She carries a power I can't comprehend, yet she's been in the elements for too many days. Her body can't endure much more of this deprivation; seems she isn't long for this newly-created world.

A silhouette enters, hidden amongst the blinding rays. The enigmatic figure descends from the heavens, revealing its form. Its *unbelievable* form; somehow human, but also animalistic. Something far greater than a mere mortal. Beyond even our ability to describe.

Our guest is an angel, perhaps an angel of mercy.

Ha. Yeah, right.

The flesh covering his taunt muscles is the color of the sky. Majestic, yes, but he doesn't carry himself like one of those sweet hippie angels I remember visiting Mary in the Christmas story.

I'm halfway convinced he's a monster, yet he takes this mystery woman—nearly a match for his height, amazingly—into his arms. He comforts her. Removes a small container of water from his belt, offers it to her.

I see them embrace. Witness them discovering a new land in

the edges of this desert. A sincere, zealous love washes over; hope for a new beginning lifts my soul.

She grips his wings for dear life while making love. I see the woman give birth to triplets. I'm hallucinating from the pain.

Greetings, Bradley.

That voice isn't in this room, yet it is. A voice I know only I can hear.

Given how intimate our acquaintance shall soon be, I suppose you're deserving of the unabridged truth, continues the voice that's as deep as James Earl Jones at 16 RPM.

I have been called a seducer, an indicter, a destroyer in my time. Some of your people viewed me as an agent of holiness, others pure evil. I'd like to think the truth lies somewhere in-between.

My name is too holy to be spoken aloud. But, in acknowledgment of present circumstances, I suppose you should know my appellation.

It's all an amusing distraction from the pain, I reckon.

I am Samael, the archangel. The instrument of God's vengeance, and the subject of His scorn when I dared make my bid for independence.

I have hovered amongst the ether for countless years, yet my desire to return to your homeland has never waned. It's an exceptional place, Bradley, and by rights I should've ruled with my Queen there long ago.

Sacrifices have been made. Eisheth and Agrat Bat Mahlat, two of the three children I blessed my precious Lilith with, have perished in battles against His throne. Naamah remains, however, and is loyal beyond words. When my beloved and I regain what is rightfully ours, we'll build a monument to Naamah so high its shadow will cast across the globe.

"Naamah?" No wonder our Queen won't tell anyone her name. Heh. I think she's still here, the eleven-foot blur standing above me now…

And, you Bradley, should count yourself honored to play your role in this coup. Our course has been set.

There's almost some sympathy in his next words.

You're bleeding out now, Bradley.

He's not lying. I feel the blood dripping off my toes. Little *plip, plip* sounds hit the floor, or maybe that's just my morbid imagination.

Stay calm.

Easy for you to say.

As your soul-body dissipates, I'll fill the void of your earthly form.

Mighty kind of ya.

Yes, I feel her flesh against 'mine' even at this moment. My eyes grow moist, as daydreams of future heirs fill my thoughts.

And while you will soon be but a memory, Bradley, please know how deeply I appreciate the role you've played this evening.

The sensation of the cut begins to fade. In its place is the touch of flesh against flesh, a specific touch I know so well.

A creamy flesh that once robbed breath from my lungs, turned my knees to spaghetti, and played games with my mind for days.

CHAPTER FIFTY-NINE

?

B rad's body lies before me.
Brad should be dead.

He isn't.

I run my fingers through his thick mop, going so deep I can feel the soft touch of his scalp. I tousle the hair and think back to early mornings together. I used to wake him like this, then smooth those chocolate tresses back into shape with my fingers. He would plant half-asleep kisses on my neck and shoulders, or maybe move his hands down my back.

I reflect upon this, and what my Queen has demanded of me, as I examine the face of my husband—no, ex-husband—and confirm again that his lips aren't blue. That what we'll be doing here won't be necrophilia, it will be warm and significant and sweet in some strange way.

Those are the words She whispers to me. These are the words She uses to convince me to give up my body. She's speaking telepathically through a calico cat, and this all makes perfect sense, and soon I will have given my body up for a worthy cause and She will have her means to fulfill a destiny denied centuries ago.

And Brad and I will be making love again, and even though I do not want this, I very much want this.

I'm looking Icky in the eye and this is not Icky but regardless

She is speaking to me. A fog comes over me and I think back to that one time I experienced contact high riding in the back of my weird uncle's van.

Eyes roll into the back of my head and I understand I'm no longer alone.

I watch Icky run away in a panic, paw prints in the sand stamping her escape trail. I know that I should care but I do not.

One jump-cut after another in my mind. A filthy, bare body wandering the desert. The first thoughts of an abstract concept known as death. An angelic savior, one with dirty wings, arrives.

Life-giving water. A sublime romance. A failed crusade.

My lover felled before my eyes. Another exile.

We are one now and I am free to speak her / my name.

"Randall, Thomas. Please know how delighted Lilith is by your devotion."

"You speak for Her?" Thomas asks, incredulous.

"I *am* Her, and I require one more sacrifice, my dears. Please, present your bellies to me. Randall, did you procure the knife?"

Randall reaches for the leather sheath at his side, removing a blade that I know can be traced back to the Tribe of Levi. I also know that he's devoted his adult life to antiquities and the study of a bygone era. That one lonely evening he submitted to a siren's call and our sister / daughter has been drawing him to this place from that second forward. I know this even though I should not know this.

I study the blade and wince at the thought of my actions, yet am also tantalized by them. The men are standing before me lifting their shirts to expose their bellies and I feel compelled to speak a few words.

"Randall, Thomas… I pray you understand the concept of sacrifice. That blood must be shed in recognition of a simple truth. That what we think we own, what we believe to be ours, is in fact not. You are valuable, faithful servants. Yet, my claim over you is only temporary."

I want them to understand this is for a greater good.

"What will happen here this evening will usher in a new age. And, while the early steps in this nascent world will be messy, they are but a sad necessity. Your world is fallen, and that is through no direct fault of my own. No apple ever touched *my* lips, you see."

I want them to realize I don't blame them for their weakness.

"For reasons unknown, but observably sadistic, our creator has seen fit to allow this blemished domain of avarice and hatred to endure. You are but men. Your desires are predictable, and easily manipulated."

I recognize I'll never find the words, but I want them to understand how much I love them.

"Know that I find no satisfaction in the mess I've made of your lives. Know also that, in spite of the repulsive nature passed down by your ancestors, I bear you no malice. That I can envision a monument to the two of you."

Both Randall and Thomas close their eyes and whisper prayers of gratitude. Against my every instinct, I place the blade against Thomas' skin, where I know it should be placed. He goes first, then Randall, perfect incisions below their navels. Both try to remain strong. Both are in the dirt within seconds, crying out in agony.

I want to mourn their loss of life. I want to be sickened and horrified by what I've seen. I can't find the emotions.

I'm drawn once again to Bradley, still wrapped in that bag, lifeless but not lifeless.

I straddle his body and play with his hair once more. I kiss his lips, which are not blue, and feel no response. I place my hand against his face and squeeze just a tad. I play with his tongue. His tongue is limp.

The wind intensifies, ices my marrow. Left arm brushes against diamond hard nipple. I see goosebumps forming on my skin and laugh, because it seems as if lifetimes have passed since I've felt this sensation. The sigil, though, is growing warmer. So warm, my back feels as if it's been set ablaze.

Our noses nestle. I whisper into his ear. I try that bit with my tongue again. His tongue moves back and tentatively answers.

Soon, it is wrapped against mine.

I am pulling off the rest of this potato sack and kissing the naked chest of my former husband Bradley, but am also correcting myself on his true name.

I am Lilith and I am making love to my precious Samael and soon this sick, fallen world will undergo a cleansing fire.

CHAPTER SIXTY

John Horton

Bradley Burns must die.

I don't say this with any hatred or jealousy in my heart. And, yeah, I admit I don't like the guy. But Alex has shown me—whether she meant to or not—the role he's playing in this hell.

He's already dying: I get that. His soul is slowly draining out while this demon's master enters his mortal form. But the demon knows how to utilize her blade, how to keep Brad's soul alive on this plane long enough for her master to finish his work on Earth.

If he goes out before the time She has allotted, I think this nightmare will end. It has to.

"John…"

I hear a whimper above; realize it's Alex, reacting to what's happening to the east and west of us. Her sisters are slitting the throats of their slaves; moving successively, like some perverted musical score. Grinning like depraved ghouls, relishing the moment. Alex, of course, is different. Realizes how sick this all is.

"John, I'm so sorry…"

Don't worry, girl. I'm no hero, but I can do something. I'm sure I can. Just as soon as my hands stop shaking.

To the left and right I hear the stomach-churning sound of more flesh tearing. It is like a rhythm, and it's increasing. Getting closer.

John, you have to act now.

"Alex," I hear myself saying. "Hand me your blade."

And I hear Alex stammer out her response. Hear the tears, as she apologizes again. Tells me she can't disobey her Queen, even as every fiber is struggling to do just that.

I understand, girl. I'll find the strength to do this. The strength to turn, take that blade from your trembling hands.

Yes, I've done that. I have this small blade and I'm taking the three-four-five steps needed to reach Alex's mistress. The demon.

She's caught up in the final stages of this damn ceremony. Speaking in strange tongues, on her knees now, screaming in ecstasy. In a perfect position for someone who isn't a hero to get close. Insert the blade fast into her neck and remove it.

Yes, John, you just did that. But it's not enough. No blade is sharp enough to truly harm this beast. It's Brad who has to die. Has to do it right now.

I linger above the man I know I must kill. Ignore the shrieks of Alex behind me, the cries of pain from her mistress. I begin a prayer, asking for the strength. Realize in that moment the contradiction: asking a loving God for help committing this deed.

I'm still lingering, studying his pale face. I can do this. Keep repeating that.

The knife's raised. I aim for his heart.

Then feel an intense burning from the pit of my gut. I look down and realize She has thrust her hand through my stomach like a dagger.

"Fool… you think… thisss could work?"

I hear a feminine voice shriek out disbelief. Realize it's Alex, as her distinctive footsteps approach. I force my body to shift, to see my girl run towards her mistress.

Alex grabs Her by the arms. Screams an unholy cry. The demon smacks her to the floor.

Hazy vision, blurrier by the second. It hits me now this is likely my final sight.

CHAPTER SIXTY-ONE

INTERLUDE IV

You feel the sting in your lip. Hear a voice telling you it's no less than what you deserve.

No, it's more than a voice. It's every cell within your body—which is no true body, as you've already killed your original with so many foolish decisions—screaming that insubordination can't be tolerated.

She is your mistress. Your true savior. Alexandria, you were terrified of that light. Would've made any bargain to escape it.

She heard your cries and was merciful. How dare you turn against her like this?

Your body is on that cold floor. Feet away, two men who know your touch. No, you feel no guilt for your actions. She would never ask you to commit shameful deeds.

All to Her glory.

But why do these doubts linger? Why this rush within your ghost veins to end this ceremony?

It was that diviner, wasn't it? Putting thoughts in your head. Forcing you to turn against your mistress.

You curse the man. Curse his ego, his self-absorption. But then you correct yourself. Remember those visions from the water.

No, Alexandria. No, you don't. What you're remembering is the terrifying image of the burning light. What your Queen saved you from.

Amazingly, you're pushing that memory away. Choosing to focus on pitiable John Horton, writhing in pain on the floor. You touch that part of your essence, the portion that felt genuine pity and affection for the damaged soul. You think of the good within John, of his willingness to still find good in you, even after your role had been exposed.

It's important to feel this, but there's a nudge. Something prodding you to focus also on the visions granted by the water.

You see the world in flames. Powerful men, marched into camps in chains. And that instinct to relish in this vision: you have to silence it, girl.

Have to focus on the image of a burning farmhouse. That poor, broken ballerina.

Alex, this is the future. And only you can prevent this. Maybe it isn't right that the burden has fallen to you, but that's irrelevant now.

You are the covenant, Alex. Your soul binds the diviner here. And 'here' is where he *shouldn't* be.

CHAPTER SIXTY-TWO

Bradley Burns

That low, rich rumble is still speaking. Still offering thanks for the use of my body, as his hands / my hands touch the flesh of the woman who was once my wife.

But it's growing agitated. Low bass voice can't understand why the act isn't going off as planned. Why he can't close the deal, so to speak. Well, bud, happens to the best of us.

No, Brad. It's okay to pause the inane humor for the moment. You've got *one* glimmer of hope: Sandy's resistance is stalling the ceremony. Possibly giving me time necessary to fight off the influence of this beast and, somehow, reconnect with my favorite wayward soul, Miss Alex, over there.

I'm fighting through the visions of this vengeful angel, Samael. All those apparitions of past battles, passionate nights with his demon missus, and plans for his new army on Earth. The planet he'll have to rebuild, naturally, after he's razed its surface. It's the repopulation—the century of lovemaking with his demon bride—that he's looking forward to most.

I hydroplane through these twisted thoughts, reconnect with my inner core. My mostly vacuous core, I'm forced to admit. I make brief stops: acknowledge my neediness, my front of indifference, my self-destructive impulses, all that good stuff.

And I feel like myself again. Or just enough 'me' to channel the mystic energies I'm hoarding from Samael. Have no clue if I can do this: fight this angelic beast while also connecting with the lost soul nearby.

Luckily, she's only a few feet away. And those visions from the water—her mistress's programming is screaming at Alex to ignore them—but they're hard to forget, aren't they?

That's right, Alex. Your mistress and her boytoy want our world to burn. All us fleshy, pink and brown things back on Earth. That includes the good people we've left behind.

Includes those two innocents you've already hurt so much.

I ain't subtle. And that guilt trip just hammers the girl. One more vision is entering my hazy view; fights for dominance against Samael's nauseating fantasies. The strain's killing me—head's hammering even harder than my chest—but I feel the touch of Alex's soul now.

Her slave has rebelled. Inserted one of the minor daggers into the Queen's neck. And he's lording above my body now. Saying I must die to end this.

Okay, technically, that might work.

Won't stop Demon Queen from finding another diviner, though. Maybe a year from now, maybe another century. But it'll happen.

John hesitates. Doesn't hear the Queen rise behind him. Doesn't realize how fast that wound in her neck is healing.

I feel this through Alex's stomach, the sickening sight of Her attack on that poor slave. He falls to the floor. Alex rushes to her mistress: that's it, girl. *Fight.*

But I should know better. Alex isn't a match for this demon. And she feels this, too. Feels a wave of shame and disillusionment to accompany that sting in her lip.

I keep reaching out. Keep hammering her with images of what's happening soon. Alex, think about this, girl. Why did your Queen restrain herself to a mere slap?

Isn't the punishment for disobedience far greater? Don't you understand why you haven't suffered John's fate?

You're the covenant, girl. Without you, this whole scheme goes to crap.

Maybe the realization hits us simultaneously. Who knows. But Alex sees the crimson-tainted blade; it flew to the floor during Her attack on John. It rests by Alex's feet now.

The Queen has returned to the stone slab where my body rests. Is attempting to retrace her metaphysical steps, the proper place in her incantations. She's furious: and too busy to keep her attention on you.

I hate it, Alex. But if you need me to give you the strength to do this, I'll try. Don't know how I can push any harder—how much longer I can fight off this beast Samael—but I'll do anything I can.

She senses my presence clearly now. Tells me she can do this on her own. I overhear her final prayer.

Girl's stronger than I gave her credit for.

Alex lifts the blade, makes the incision. Soon her gown is stained red.

CHAPTER SIXTY-THREE

Lilith

I'm giggling at my goosebumps and thinking about how much I desire this man that I no longer desire and questioning why he's resisting my body when he's never rejected a female's touch in his life.

I have my hand gripped around a part of his body that he so often declared I was neglecting. He's resisting my hand and pulling away.

My back is burning. The wind is icy and I question why my back is burning.

Words are forming. I'm chastising him for resisting me. He's calling me a name. I think I recognize it.

I want to tell myself that I am not Lilith, even though I am Lilith.

I'm preparing my body to receive a man who's entered numerous times, even though I've declared he would never do this again.

The miasma, the contradictions, slow me down. She does not like this.

I'm telling this mystery presence that I don't care. That I'm not touching Bradley Burns in this way again. I fight instincts I don't understand—fight something I despise but am told I must love—while this Bradley Burns writhes below.

She curses my indecision, as his elbow greets my chin. The

diviner then contorts his body away from mine. He whispers a thank you to a name She loathes. His body heaves as he sighs relief and drops seed into the dirt.

A fiery anger rises. Not only towards him, but also this fragile body. A voice longs for another form, easily twice this height. I'm yearning for a physical strength I no longer possess, even though I also remember a closet filled with petite sizes.

My lips are forming more curses. The man I desired so much—though I did not desire him—is now rejuvenated. He says he doesn't want to hurt me. I want to tell him how badly he's already hurt me.

He rolls me over. Positions himself behind, wraps his arm beneath my chin. He tells me it's a sleeper hold. That I need to stop fighting and allow myself to trust him.

I have final thoughts of the concept of irony, of the absurdity of ever giving that gift to this man again. I feel myself growing drowsy even though the true owner of my body is fighting with all her might.

My knee is brushing against the seed he spilled in the dirt and I am disgusted. This is my final thought as the world goes black.

CHAPTER SIXTY-FOUR

John Horton

Our surroundings are chaos, as the ground quakes and horrified voices wail. One shriek belongs to the Queen: a powerless, defeated cry. Then, an unexpected sliver of light begins to creep around the periphery.

Light? Here?

I can't trust my vision. Can't say for sure if that's Alex, crawling towards me. But, no, I feel that touch. Feel the warmth I always knew was within her.

I try to greet her. She tells me not to speak. Actually, she can barely do that, either. I notice now the blood staining her gown.

Still, we find ourselves in each other's arms. She's still trying to speak, to apologize for what she did to my life. If I could answer, I'd tell her it's unnecessary.

She refuses to listen. "All this time… thought I could hold on tight… already gone…"

I want to comfort my girl, as this chamber grows so blessed bright.

"Had to happen… couldn't fool myself, not anymore… ever since that day… bathroom floor…"

I press my forehead against hers. Tears spill into her wound. Maybe I'm hallucinating this bit. This image of cradling her, just letting her talk now.

"Broke the covenant, though… didn't know all this… Naamah sacrificed everything and lost…"

Her eyes open. There's a second of shared recognition, and I lose my breath all over again.

Over the surrounding panic, I hear her final gasp. The girl who so desperately clung to life, even in the afterlife, is now gone.

I think we're all gone now, as that peripheral light grows brighter and consumes the landscape.

CHAPTER SIXTY-FIVE

Sandra Jones

When I wake, his form is lording over mine. He's stolen the clothes of one of the dead men. I fixate on the bloodstains, try not to recall how they got there.

He squats, touches my temples. I try to resist but realize I'm tethered to the back of a vehicle with ripped fabric, portions of the bag that escorted him to this place without my knowledge.

"Sandra, listen to me. I'm not sure how much of you is still in there, but know that I don't want to hurt you." Silence. Then, "I never wanted to hurt you," he says, voice quivering. "Even though I'm sure I've given you every reason to believe otherwise. Whatever happens now, just know that I am sorry for how many times I screwed up." I feel his thumb, delicately brushing hair away from my right eye. "If… If you can, please just think of the good times."

He coughs, collects himself, then continues. "I'm going to connect to this thing that's taken over you. Don't worry; I'll do to it what I've done to a thousand of these bastards before."

I question which of us he wants to persuade.

I watch as his eyes close, notice soon his lower lip's bitten in concentration. He whispers, mutters to himself, grows agitated. Sweat beads defy the cold, form on his brow. I watch as my perception shifts. He's no longer the vessel. No longer the interloper who destroyed our plans.

"Lilith!"

I listen as a voice announces her departure. Wants me to know how useless my body is now, how furious she is that her love's receptacle failed. How badly we ruined *everything*.

"Demoness!"

Eyelids flutter as I stare at Bradley, my ex-husband. He nearly died, I think I'm still mad at him about some things, and none of that matters at the moment.

I notice he's shouting. "You have no place here! *I command you to leave!*"

"Bradley, it's okay." I hear my voice. And it is *my* voice. "Just calm down. I think she's gone."

"How can you know? I tried to look into their realm, but… I… Somehow, I came up with nothing."

"It's okay, Brad. We've both been through a lot." I move to pat his shoulder, then realize I'm still tied to the Jeep. "You need to rest now."

"No, Sandy, I can't. My heart is vibrating out of my chest. I can't just… I need to know what happened," he says, pacing. "I need to know that you're okay."

"What I *need* is to be untied; that'd be a nice place to start."

Brad keeps pacing, tries to control his breathing. He studies me for a second before deciding, okay, my imposing one-hundred-fifteen pounds aren't much of a threat after all. Hands still trembling, Brad unties his makeshift restraints and offers a tentative hug. "You must be freezing."

I point him towards my clothes, left a few yards away, close to the soapstone bowl. A memory of Randall crushing those herbs in the bowl appears, even as I try to cast it out.

The t-shirt and jeans are covered in dirt, but any protection from this night air is welcome. Getting dressed, I have a sensation of shame: an image of Brad, slackjawed, staring at my bare back.

A confusing thought, until more memories of the previous days return.

I look back to Brad, who's facing the other way. For his own safety, perhaps? I also question if I'll ever be able to wear a backless gown again.

Brad's uneasily staring at the moon, possibly waiting for me to offer reassurance. "I think I'm fine, Brad. But I don't think I understand this any better than you. I have memories—*dreams* I hope—of some other place. Of asking a spirit to see you one last time, and ending up somewhere I wanted to escape, then… Just awful, horrible things."

Hesitantly, he replies, "Yeah, hate to tell you, Sandy, but it's probably all true. But the worst of it is over. I hope to God it is. And if we're both back home, and both healthy, then I say we've got some shot of turning out okay." He stops, looks around. "But, um, where in the hell are we?"

"Iraq, believe it or not."

"And those bodies?" He points towards the two figures in the sand I've been trying so hard to avoid.

"I… Please, Brad, let me explain later."

His head bobs. I think he knows. Bless him, I don't think he's judging. "One was close to my size," he says, acknowledging the blood stains on his outfit. "And geez, you know how cold it is."

"Hey, Brad, I get it."

He coughs into his fist, then says, "I recognized the cuts below their navels. I checked my gut to make sure I didn't have a matching scar, but I'm clean. Doesn't seem right, though." He exhales, then produces the wet blade from his back pocket. "Not sure what we should do about this."

"*That-god-damn-thing's-going-in-the-river!*" I blurt as one word. Oh, God, I can't stand to look at it. I cover my face as he hides the dagger away. Soon, I feel his hand on my left arm. Then, it moves to my side and we exchange another platonic hug. Maybe not the fireworks one would expect after so much misery, but I tell myself it's the thought that counts.

"Sandy, we'll figure this out. Right now, we're both… both…" He exhales again, takes in the surroundings once more. "Seriously, who knows what any of this means?"

"Oh! Icky!"

"Hm? That cat? What's she got to do with anything?"

I break away. He tries to hold on to my hand. "Grab a lantern, okay? I think we can still follow her trail."

"Your parents' cat ended up on the other side of the planet with you?" he asks the back of my head.

"Yeah, and I can remember her going this way. C'mon, grab that lantern and follow me. I bet we can still make out her prints."

"So, that's what we're doing now? Everything that's happened, and you're worried about—"

I don't know if my eyebrows are twisting as I say this, like he always says they do when I get mad, but who cares either way.

"Brad, listen, this has been the most severely shitty day, or week, or whatever, of my life. Right now, I agree, nothing makes sense. But that cat's still out there in the dark—a tiny, frightened thing that needs us—and the least we can do is go out there and try to help the girl."

"Fair enough." Brad selects his lantern. "I guess I know who the captain of this ship is." With a salute, he adds, "Lead the way, ma'am."

CHAPTER SIXTY-SIX

INTERLUDE V

White text, green background. *Newnan—Ten Miles.*

"See, the difference between me and you? I wouldn't say something like that sarcastically."

"Really? Put up or shut up, sister. I bet you could find a nice place out here for a decent price. Compared to SoCal real estate, at least. I'll take the plunge if you will."

"And give up my exciting life as a bank teller? Ha. And you, you'd leave my father in the lurch a second time? For shame."

"Hey, I'd do the two weeks' notice thing this time around. Not that I'd be missed around the lot."

"C'mon. Dad says you've developed some skills since those old days. Told me you're one of his best closers now."

"Oh, you check in on me?"

"Do not. You just came up one day."

KLBZ TV billboard. *Your Source for Local News!* Syndicated repeats of *Prom Mom* daily at 5:00.

"Right. And I'll note that, moments earlier, you were not opposed to the thought of us cohabitating again."

"Excuse me?"

"I told you I'd move out here to the sticks if you would. Implication being, the two of us would be out here together. In the same house. You were not opposed."

"No way. No way, not ever, uh-uh."

"Protesting like that, you're not so hard to figure out. It's why you wanted to join me, isn't it?"

White text, green background. *Click It or Ticket.*

"I thought you might appreciate the company. And this trick of yours isn't going to work."

"What trick?"

"The *'Make Sandra Uncomfortable So We Don't Focus on Brad's Anxieties'* trick. We need to talk about this."

"What's to say? If they don't come back, they don't come back. I'm no worse off than before."

White text, green background. *Newnan—Five Miles.*

"Sure you're not. Brad, it's been three months now. If you don't think you can jumpstart them here, then maybe they're truly gone."

"Hey, things take time. Icky's just now coming around, isn't she?"

"Remind me to show you the pet therapist's bills. And you just dodged. Again."

"Listen, I've pretty much accepted it, Sandy. Like I said, worst case scenario is I'm no worse off than yesterday."

Empty billboard. Previously featured an advertisement for *Forbidden Fruits Gentleman's Establishment.* Local *Mothers Against Indecency* chapter waged a successful campaign for its removal, two months prior.

"Well, hey, this could be your new chapter."

"I'm thinking I could pursue the same line of work. Maybe this time go through the proper legal channels, acquire the proper licensing, avoid some headaches..."

"To do what, though?"

"You've gotta ask? I'm a skilled detective, missy. And I figure I can track cheating spouses and shady business partners as easily as I chased wayward souls."

"See, that's why we need to talk about these things. Left alone with your thoughts, that's when you get nutty ideas like that. Look, regardless of what happens, you still have options."

"Uh-huh. Like what?"

Monument sign. Red brick base. Stone topper. Navy blue script. *Welcome to Newnan, Minnesota!*

"Like you said: moving to a nice small town in Minnesota, for one."

"Cute. Just don't freak out the nice farm people, Sandy. They don't need to know every nasty detail of our time with Alex."

"I'll be sure to leave out the bit with the flying toilet."

CHAPTER SIXTY-SEVEN

The Entity Once Known as John Horton

We don't use names here. No need.

But, sometimes, when my light connects with another light, I can touch that part of their aura shaped on that fallen place we all pass through. Just a brief rush of syllables, making sounds like Susan and Pedro and Roulf.

There's one beam of light; I've gleaned his mother named him Darien. And my light bonds with his, and I see images of his former life. See how it connected with mine.

Relive that day he selected me as I turned that street corner, groceries in hand. Did what he thought had to be done for acceptance.

I don't have to forgive him. It's not my place to do that. And this beam of light that used to call itself Darien, there's no need for him to feel shame for his actions. No remorse for the choices that ended his young life just six months after his initiation into that misguided clique.

As beams of light, these things aren't really relevant. Recognizing how dingy and dim our lights used to be is an early lesson we learn.

We merely shine; enjoy the warmth of an eternal sun. We're small lights, see, compared to that sun.

It's good for our lights to mingle. Allegedly, we play no favorites here. But there is one light, I confess, that feels just a little more simpatico than my fellow tiny lights.

I suspect our luminosities aren't beaming out of this realm: unlike our brethren, who enjoy sending quick flashes back to our former home, touching those still stuck there. And somewhere in my aura, I know the reason why, while also realizing that dwelling on this is futile.

But she's a lovely light. Could warm even the coldest of days, were we ever to have those here.

Her friends called her Alex. But names don't matter here, remember.

CHAPTER SIXTY-EIGHT

Bradley Burns

"What am I supposed to do with this?" asks Paul Abernathy, the man who owes me eight thousand dollars. At the moment, though, I'm reminding myself there's a higher calling here.

"It belonged to Alex, Mr. Abernathy," I reply, as he closes the porcelain ballerina into her music box and places it on the coffee table. "You gave it to me, hoping that I could make a connection. You don't remember—"

"I remember what we talked about. Remember that you tried to wring every last dollar you could out of me."

His wife pipes in with, "Dear, be nice."

Paul leans back in his recliner. "Why did you want to see me again?"

"I wanted to make sure my job was complete." I gesture towards my former partner, seated beside me on the loveseat. Oh, the irony. "Sandra and I wanted to be certain Alex wasn't contacting your wife in her dreams again, that she'd gone on to find peace."

"Why would you expect us to know that?"

I turn to the figure resting against the entrance of the living room, the woman we rudely interrupted during the glazing of a country cured ham. "Well, Mrs. Abernathy, do you still dream of Alex? That's one way to know—"

"Mr. Burns, I haven't had one of those dreams for months now," she tells us, folding her dish towel. "And, to be honest, I couldn't even tell you what they were today. I know I used to have strange dreams. I know how badly they upset me, but the details, everything about them… Even when I close my eyes, when I try to think of her face… It's all a blur to me now."

"Forgive me if I'm touching a sensitive subject," Sandra says, her voice showing genuine reluctance, "but I notice none of her photos are on the mantle."

"We took them down a few months ago," he responds matter-of-factly. "Didn't seem to be a reason to keep them up."

"Mr. Burns, we've managed to move on from all of this. I think the only choice we had." Darlene catches herself, realizes she isn't living up to 'Minnesota Nice' standards. "But, since the two of you have traveled so far, we'd love for you to stay for dinner. It'll be ready in about half an hour."

"Ma'am, we can't impose."

"Nonsense. It's been ages since we had company over, and I'm guessing the two of you don't eat home cooked meals so often, do you? Just stay put; I'm sure Paul can find a good ballgame." Heading for the kitchen, she tosses in, "He'd better, given the money we spend on that satellite dish."

My companion stands. "I'm going to excuse myself for a minute and make a phone call. But if you need any help, let us know, Mrs. Abernathy."

Darlene tells her she'll be fine. In a heartbeat, Sandy's on the front porch, tapping like mad on her phone. I know what she's keeping from me. I don't think I'm going to tell her that I know, but trust me, I absolutely know.

She's happy now, and he doesn't seem that bad of a guy, so it's probably best I stay out of it.

Hey, Sandy… Congrats on trading up, by the way.

The box remains on the table. The way he dismissed it, the piqued look on his face when I handed it over… Why does that chill me worse than anything I saw on the other side?

He catches me staring at the porcelain dancer's home. I reach for it. "Mr. Abernathy, would I be out of line if I…?"

"That music box? It was my mother's, you know."

I crank the key. Some part of me hopes he'll recognize the song, that some simple tune will revive a cherished memory of his daughter. "That's right. I remember you telling me that."

"But we don't have anyone to pass it down to. Not anymore. If you'd like to have it, feel free."

"Mr. Abernathy, I couldn't. You sure you don't want to leave it in Alex's old room?"

"You mean the room where we keep our *Costco* supplies?" A contemptuous swipe of the hand. "Take it. It's only gonna collect dust in that closet down the hall. If it means something to you, please, just take it."

"I… Thank you, sir." The ballerina returns to the jacket pocket I placed her in, months ago. No clue why I agreed to take the thing, but refusing the gift seemed just as wrong as anything else I've heard this afternoon. I rise, gesture towards the door. "I think I'm going to go check on Sandra."

I step onto the porch. She's sitting on a creaky swing, face buried in the phone, smile on her face.

"So, anything special going on?"

Sandra hides the phone away. "No, just checking in on things."

I nobly choose to ignore the fib and join her on the swing. "So, hard to believe, huh? Those poor people."

"Were they so cold before? I mean, they couldn't have been, right?"

"The dad was always a hardass, but it was obvious how much he cared about her. And the mom, you just knew her whole world revolved around Alex, even after she was gone."

"And you think this is tied in to your vision?" Sandra asks, and unsaid, I know she's mentally adding *'Your last vision…'*

I still have flashes of it. They're memories, not a real connection, but I still carry with me the final images of that other place. They stay with me, a tease of what I once possessed, somewhere only *I* could touch.

"Who's to say what happens when you die a second time?" is the best answer I can give. "When Alex sacrificed herself, she broke Naamah's hold over me, allowed me to return to my body… But after that…"

"So, it's like she never existed? Is that a soul's death? The physical mementos stick around, but your loved ones can barely remember your name?"

"The memories are there, I'm sure, but you saw the way they were acting. There's no connection, no bond to the person who was here. Like her entire life was just a movie they vaguely remember watching."

Sandra says nothing. Not for the first time, I wonder if this is how she remembers her dealings with Naamah and Lilith. I've tried to broach the topic, the few occasions we've talked over the months, but she always shuts down.

Maybe if I still had my own connections—not just to the other side, but to *her*—things would be different. Lately I'm questioning if both are now empty wishes.

"It's horrible," she says, after a lengthy gaze off into the sunset. "She didn't deserve that. I know I said horrible things about her, but I would've never wished that on anyone."

"My last image of that place: it was chaotic, yeah, but there was something else. There was a light, creeping around the edges, eventually consuming everything. And it was *warm*. Nothing about that place was ever warm, but this… luminescence, if you will…"

"Oh, easy on those big words, Mr. Fancy."

"…it was more than warm, it was welcoming. Like something that's, I don't know, it's hard to describe."

She turns to me, energized. "Was it *the* light? The one you were always herding the spirits into?"

I stand. "Could be. For her sake, for all of their sakes, I hope so. Well, not Naamah. I hope whatever she got was slow and painful." I gesture for Sandy to join me.

"Where we going?"

"My last shot. I need to check Alex's old room. That's the place she'd be drawn to, assuming there's anything left of her *to* draw out."

We reenter the living room; I explain to Paul that Sandy is a *Costco* freak and wants to check out their stash. Seconds later, we've entered the former bedroom of my one-time target / lover / savior.

"You feel anything?"

I'm assuming Sandy knows the answer. I examine the room, 'center' myself, close my eyes: follow every necessary step. I try to imagine the room as Alex knew it; signed Ed Sheeran photo on the wall, childhood bed she's outgrowing, bureau with a diary hidden in one drawer and secret handwritten love notes in another.

But I can only see it for what it is: a spare bedroom, the empty nest parents packing every square inch with outdated TVs and cardboard cases of cut-price toilet paper.

"Two possibilities: she's truly gone now, or I've completely lost my connection to the other side."

"Both could be true."

"Yes, dear. They're not mutually exclusive." I shouldn't call her 'dear'. I'm working on that.

"And what about you? Having your soul cut by some mystic blade?"

I shrug shoulders and ask, "So you're saying I have no soul?"

"It would explain a lot. Retroactively, though." Okay, just let that sit there, Sandy. "Seriously, do you think what happened to you there…?"

"You tell me. Is our life together fuzzy like a movie you *think* you saw but can't remember?"

"Not gonna dredge all that back up, but trust me, I remember it clearly. All of it."

"Okay. Understood."

"But you losing touch with the other side: that has to be related, isn't it?"

"Some part of me died there, I'm sure of it now." I lean against a cardboard mountain of bran cereal. "Maybe some piece of my soul hadn't bled out yet, maybe Alex made her move in time. But my connection to that other place, maybe it's not coming back. Crazy; but maybe I should pursue that thing we discussed earlier."

"Okay… Not trying to step on your dreams, but do you really believe the two are related? You think you'd be using the same skill set?"

"I don't know. Why don't you ask your boyfriend of the past six weeks, Mister Daniel Feagin, originally of Medford, Oregon? Owns that consulting business, based out of Century City? Drives a vintage Aston Martin, either because he watched too many Bond movies or he's overcompensating for something…"

"Brad, are you…?"

"Okay, any discussion of psychological motivations is just conjecture, but give me credit for the rest." If I had a hat, I'd tip it. "Skills, Sandy. I'm overflowing with 'em."

Sandra is… Not amused. "If you're spying on me, Brad, I swear I'll make what that monster did to you look like a trip to Disneyland."

"Calm yourself. I just poked around a bit on social media, made a call or two. He's a good guy, this Daniel Feagin, outside of one unpaid parking ticket. And there's that small claims court judgment against him, circa 2011; but I'm sure he has *his* side of the story, doesn't he?"

"Unbelievable. And you thought this was cute?"

"Merely testing my aptitude," I answer, offering my best defense. "Making sure I picked up some legitimately non-paranormal abilities over the years." She's not looking at me; has her arms crossed, that pout going. Attempting to make peace, I soften my tone and begin an apology. "Seriously, I wasn't looking to creep you out—"

"Well, you did. And if I catch you rustling around in the bushes one night… I'm not kidding, I promise you're dying for real this time."

"Point taken. Forget I said anything."

The silence kills me. Removing the lonesome ballerina from my pocket, I motion for Sandy to take it in her hands. She's reluctant. Motioning again, I make this incredible argument: "C'mon."

"Why?"

"Feminine energy. No, seriously. I need your essence to touch the music box. A female's presence can be less intimidating for a spirit. Plus, you were drawn into all of this, too. If she's attracted by your presence, I might be able to make contact." Sandy squints. "It's a last ditch effort, yeah, but it's not impossible that Alex would want to contact you."

"She hated me. Tried to kill me once."

"That was her giving into that evil succubus influence. I wouldn't blame her for that."

"We had words." She keeps staring, then finally gives a further explanation. "I never told you this, but I had another conversation with the girl. Let her know what I really felt about her."

I place the music box in Sandra's hand. Add a little squeeze for emphasis. "Then maybe she's still pissed off. Wants to come back and give you a piece of her mind. You've already stalked her to her old apartment, now you're in her childhood bedroom? Ooh-wee, I bet that girl can't wait to short out some light bulbs and make a terrible mess in here."

That gets her to laugh. Sandy shakes her head, sighs, then asks what I need her to do.

I stand closer, wrap both hands around hers. "I need you to close your eyes, release any negative energy, and just concentrate on her face."

I'm so full of it.

"Then what?"

"Just think of her. Send positive thoughts her way, whisper an apology. Assuming you mean it."

I'm close enough to smell her hair. To feel the ambient heat that radiates from her pale skin, no supernatural abilities required for that.

"Maybe I don't. But I do feel bad about how things worked

out."

"Good. Go with that, then."

Her ivory hands still feel like velvet. Soft as dainty seraphs, or however that old saying goes.

I rub my thumb over her bare ring finger. I told her she should pawn it once. Half-a-carat, best I could afford at the time. We were fighting, and I told her holding on to that thing was pointless, that it was always a mistake and she should just get whatever she could out of it.

Fetid memories. No need to dwell on them.

Has she noticed I'm standing too close? Does she realize I'm the fibber now, conning her into one last embrace?

Her eyes open, just a flash, before she turns her head to the side. "This is, um, this part of things was never my department."

She tugs away. I nod, release her hands. Darlene's voice appears from down the hall, calling us for dinner.

"You go ahead, Sandy," I say to her, probably still standing too close. "I'll be there in a second."

Hand on my shoulder, she says, "Sure. If you need a minute here, if there's some goodbye you need to make, just take your time."

I convince myself I didn't see her wiping away a tear as she closed the door. I crank the key on the box one last time, listen to the simple tune.

Ballerina in hand, I do whisper a final farewell. Several, actually.

CHAPTER SIXTY-NINE

Sandra Jones

It was his last shot. And he rolled snake eyes.

I'm walking to the dining room, telling myself I'll give Brad his space on our trip home. Won't bust his chops too hard. Let's not kid ourselves; it's gonna be our last trip anywhere together, so best not leave him with bad memories.

I keep telling myself what I feel for Brad is everyday empathy. That, even though a part of me may never forgive him, I'm big enough to recognize his sense of loss.

What I don't have is some intuitive flash of what he's doing in that room. Looking for the tallest container, setting the porcelain dancer and her box right on the top, directly across from the window.

If he's thinking that she'll be the first thing Alex's parents see when they walk in, I don't know this. Certainly not aware that he's already cultivated some fantasy: that they'll be thinking the kitchen is running low on paper towels, or maybe they should double-check if they bought granola last time before heading out, and there she'll be.

And maybe they won't care. Maybe this room will remain their spare junk room, and no thought of their lost daughter will cross their mind. No memories of tooth fairy quarters under pillows or softball games or Christmas pageants. Some part of me wonders if this might be a blessing.

But, still, she'll be here.

I'm telling myself I'm not connecting with Brad's thoughts or his subconscious or his aura or whatever this is. That I haven't had similar flashes around my parents, or my boyfriend. My coworker, when her husband was dying of cancer.

Or poor Icky when she has those nightmares.

I don't have similar dreams; questioning just what that experience by the water did to me. Paranoid fantasies that maybe what Brad possessed wasn't as much of a blessing as he let on. And right now, I don't have an image of Brad's hand on the doorknob, telling himself to take one final look back.

But, no, I do see this. A lovely sight. Fading sunlight covers the porcelain, cleanses the girl. Offers what we can only hope is some kind of redemption.

THE END

Did You Enjoy This Book?

If so, you can make a HUGE difference

For any author, the single most important way we have of getting our books noticed is a really simple one—and one which you can help with.

Yes, you.

Us indie authors and publishers don't have the financial muscle of the big guys to take out full-page ads in the newspaper or put posters on the subway.

But we do have something much more powerful and effective than that, and it's something that those big publishers would kill to get their hands on.

A committed and loyal bunch of readers.

Honest reviews of our books help bring them to the attention of other readers.

If you've enjoyed this book I would be really grateful if you could spend just a couple of minutes leaving a review (it can be as short as you like) on this book's page on your favorite store and website.

Thank you so much—you're awesome, each and every one of you!

Warm regards

Gene

Acknowledgements

I would like to say a huge thank you to my beta readers, whose comments and feedback were invaluable in helping us to turn this story into the finished product you have in your hands. So thank you to: Andreas Rauch, Alison Belding, Ami Agner, Fi Phillips, Joyce and David Oxley, Stuart Phythian, Andrew McCairn, and Jessica Oxley.

Gene Kendall
July 2020

About the Author

Gene Kendall has lived many places, but is usually surrounded by more deer than people. His work explores drama, music, and pop culture with wit and no small amount of sympathy for the losers and also-rans. He's drawn to protagonists that say the wrong thing, actively resist their character arc, and possibly save the day by accident.

Currently, Gene's contributing to CBR.com's "Comics Should Be Good" blog, and you can find him on some horrific website called Twitter.

About Burning Chair

Burning Chair is an independent publishing company based in the UK, but covering readers and authors around the globe. We are passionate about both writing and reading books and, at our core, we just want to get great books out to the world.

Our aim is to offer something exciting; something innovative; something that puts the author and their book first. From first class editing to cutting edge marketing and promotion, we provide the care and attention that makes sure that every book fulfils its potential.

We are:
- Different
- Passionate
- Nimble and cutting edge
- Invested in our authors' success

If you're an author and would like to know more, visit www.burningchairpublishing.com for our submissions requirements and our free guide to book publishing.

If you're a reader and are interested in learning about our other books and new releases, becoming a beta reader for us, please visit www.burningchairpublishing.com.

Other Books by Burning Chair Publishing

10:59, by N R Baker

A Life Eternal, by Richard Ayre

The Tom Novak Series, by Neil Lancaster:
- Going Dark
- Going Rogue
- Going Back

Haven Wakes, by Fi Phillips

Beyond, by Georgia Springate

Burning: An Anthology of Thriller Shorts, edited by Simon Finnie and Peter Oxley

The Infernal Aether Series, by Peter Oxley
- The Infernal Aether
- A Christmas Aether
- The Demon Inside
- Beyond the Aether
- The Old Lady of the Skies: 1: Plague

The Wedding Speech Manual: The Complete Guide to Preparing, Writing and Performing Your Wedding Speech, by Peter Oxley

www.burningchairpublishing.com

282

Gene Kendall

Love Is Dead(ly)